MAN EATING F**S: THE LEGACY

David Owain Hughes

A HellBound Books Publishing LLC Book
Houston TX

David Owain Hughes

**A HellBound Books LLC
Publication**
Copyright © 2019 by HellBound Books Publishing LLC
All Rights Reserved

Cover and art design
By Kevin Enhart
For HellBound Books Publishing LLC

www.hellboundbookspublishing.com

Other David Owain Hughes Titles
<u>Novels, Novellas and Short Story Collections:</u>
All-Wound Up
Wind-Up Toy
Wind-Up Toy: Broken Plaything
Wind-Up Toy: Chaos Rising
White Walls and Straitjackets
Escapees and Fevered Minds
Choice Cuts
Walled In
Man-Eating Fucks
Man-Eating Fuckers
The Rack & Cue
Collision Course
Granville
Home Improvements
Psychological Breakdown
Brain Damaged
Puckered
Cold Cocked
<u>Anthologies:</u>
Shadows and Teeth Vol.3
Trapped Within
Hell of a Guy
Unleashing the Voices
Rejected for Content Vol. 4, 5 & 6
Crossroads in the Dark Vol.1 & 2
Fifty Shades of Slay
How to Cook a Baby
Madame Movora's Tales of Terror
Big Book of Bootleg Horror Vol. 1, 2 & 3
Shopping List
Depraved Desires
Easter Eggs and Bunny Boilers
Bah! Humbug!
Slashing Through the Snow
VS Vol. 1 & 2
Black Candy
Into the Abyss
<u>Compiled & Edited Anthologies:</u>
What Goes Around
Man Behind the Mask
Fuck the Rules

David Owain Hughes

MAN EATING F**S: THE LEGACY

David Owain Hughes

Chapter 1
Then

I want this journal to act as a record, a bible, to me and my family, for the stories of my clan and clan members from yesteryear must be carried throughout the generations to come. I owe it to Skull. Eight-Ball, too.

I don't know everything, but I know a lot, and I plan to scribble it down and pass this book to my daughter when the time is right, so let me start by giving my name: I was Paula Harris, but she's dead. I now go by Hydra.

I'm mother to Skull's baby girl, Cerberus, and Eight-Ball's twin boys, Typhoon and Tempest. I'm also the new tribe leader and solo adult cannibal. I'm the woman who will start the cycle again and give life to a new age of tribe and lead them into a bright, lasting future. A future where they won't have to fret about hiding in the woods or being hunted down and killed like wild animals, for I have plans in place.

Plans that involve vengeance, blood, and murder.

Plans that will wash a town away in a river of gore.

But before I get ahead of myself, let me first go back . . .

* * *

After rushing off into the woods with the babies and stumbling along a new home, Paula had tried to make things as comfortable as possible, and as quick as she could, because the cold months were ahead of them.

As the children were infants, she was able to go out at nights for short amounts of time and scavenge what she could whilst they slept. Her plan was to stockpile as much food as she could, setting them up for the winter so they could, in essence, hibernate in their newfound cave.

But things didn't go to plan, and Paula often found herself returning to camp with little or no food at all. Being the time of year it was, wildlife was slim pickings, and not many campers or travellers passed by. When they did, they turned up in large numbers, scaring Paula from trying to kill them even though she was more than capable.

It started to look like Paula and her small clan would die in the bitter months, but Paula didn't give up. Every night she went out, she inched farther and farther into the woods in the hope of hitting gold. And hit gold she did, when she ran across a family camping.

At first, she didn't know the number of people in the single tent, but, going off its size, she figured there couldn't be more than two adults, three at a push. Unless they were teenagers, which meant there could be more.

"It's a risk I'm going to have to take this time," she said, eyeing the bright canvas. Her hands went to the knives at her hips, one of which had belonged to Skull, the other homemade. "I'll sit and watch for a bit. Someone is bound to answer the call of nature."

Minutes ticked into hours.

When the sky lit with the infancy of dawn, Paula was ready to give up and skulk home. But she couldn't. Times were beyond desperate. Her babies, including the unborn one, needed nourishment. *She* needed sustenance if she was to continue hunting. She grew weaker by the day, which wasn't down to lack of nutrition alone, but pregnancy and continuous failure as well.

Thinking all hope was lost, Paula crept towards the tent. She drew Skull's knife when she got within touching distance of the multi-coloured fabric. Her heart rate increased, sweat broke across her brow and she thought she was going to piss herself.

Someone inside the tent yawned.

A trickle of urine zigzagged down her left leg. Paula didn't flinch; instead, she ducked and parted the branches in front of her, moving the leaves that were hampering her view.

"Don't be long, babe," a man said. "My cock ain't going to stay hard without you around to stroke it."

"Give me two, Jake, will you? You've been hounding me for pussy all weekend," a female answered, yawning. "I'll be right back."

"Yeah, well, don't make me send a search party for you."

"*Shh*! You'll wake Paul and Jasmine, and that *will* be the end to your planned fun and games."

"We could always ask them to join us... Tick it off your bucket list."

"*Ew*! Not with Paul. Jasmine, maybe."

"Yeah, she has cracking tits—*argh*! I was joking, babe. Nobody has a better set of knockers than you. Honest."

"Humph."

The next thing Paula heard was the tent's zipper.

Four of them inside . . . Maybe I can lure ol' Jakey-boy out by killing his bitch? I'm sure he'll come looking.

Paula's smile wavered. She was starting to worry about Typhoon and Tempest—they'd been on their own for hours, asleep. However, she had no cause for concern. They slept deeply and would be out for another couple of hours yet.

"Don't worry, beauties. Mummy's coming home with a hearty breakfast."

Skull's knife cleared leather as Paula's gaze fell on a young blonde emerging from the tent. She couldn't have been more than seventeen or eighteen and wore only her birthday suit. As she skipped off into the woods, snapping twigs and crunching leaves, Paula followed at a safe distance.

When the teen ducked behind a tree, Paula waited.

Within seconds, the familiar sound of tinkling assaulted Paula's ears. With stealth and accuracy, she rushed to the tree and jammed the blade into the girl's eyeball, causing it to pop and jettison blood and other gooey fluids, which splashed up Paula's arm and into her mouth.

"*Mmm*," Paula groaned, rubbing the blood into her skin and tasting it on her palate. Her nipples stiffened as the body before her bucked and twitched. To make sure the girl was dead, Paula rolled her over and drove her steel into the teen's throat.

Paula ripped the knife out and placed her mouth to the wound, drinking from it as though it were a water fountain.

It didn't take the horny boyfriend long to come searching, and when he did, Paula almost burst out laughing from where she hid.

"Trix? Where the fuck are you?" he asked from the tent, his head and hard-on poking out of the flap. "Trix? *Fuck*! Don't make me come out there and play your stupid games."

His dick started to lose its firmness as he stepped outside.

"Tri—"

"Come and get me, big boy!" Paula called. "I'm wet and waiting. What's the matter? Don't you want to fuck me in the open?"

And then she *did* giggle.

"You racy bitch." Jake started to stroke his shaft. "Not worried the others will catch us?"

Paula remained silent as the youngster walked closer to the tree she was hidden behind. *Looks like a surfer.* "You're getting warmer . . ."

"Where?"

When he got within striking distance, Paula jumped from her place, catching him off-kilter, and slashed the serrated steel across his throat. Jake didn't so much as gasp as he buckled to his knees and crashed to his face. Like Trix's body had, his bucked and squirmed as his life drained away.

Before he died, she turned him over and cut his cock off, ramming it into her mouth as if she hadn't eaten in months. Paula then fed on his testicles and drank as much of his blood from off the ground and around his body as possible.

Sated, Paula decided to finish the job, and so gathered herself from off the floor and staggered towards the tent in a blood-dazed state.

After sneaking inside, Paula found the other couple sleeping in a second compartment (from where she'd been standing upon discovering the tent, she hadn't seen the way in which it extended to the left). Paul was asleep on his back, snoring. He was a burly chap with as much hair on his body as a gorilla's. Jasmine, who had her back to Paul, also made rhythmic breathing sounds.

Wasting no time, Paula stabbed the knife into Paul's mouth with so much force that it punched through the back of his neck and thwacked into the ground.

He was pinned, gasping and choking.

"*Argh!*" Jasmine turned to jump up.

Paula snarled, lashing out with a hand, but was too slow—the girl was off and running, tits bouncing, long brunette hair swaying. By the time Paula was on her feet and giving chase, her target was beyond the tent's opening and making her way towards where Trix and Jake lay dead.

"*Help!*" she said, flailing her arms.

Fat girl won't get far, Paula thought, giving chase. She drew her second knife, not wanting to lose Skull's, and threw it. It sailed through the air, hilt flipping over tip. The homemade blade missed Jasmine by inches, taking hair with it as it thudded into a tree.

The teen didn't seem to notice.

"Help *meee!*"

"You sound like a stupid fat pig, girl." Paula laughed—her heart thundered against her ribcage. It had been a long time since she'd chased prey. "Going to cut your cunt off and eat that first, fatty. You can bet on that." More maniacal laughter. *If I wasn't already crazy, I'd be scaring myself.* Her smile grew to lip-splitting proportions. "That mass of yours will keep us going *all* winter, Jasmine."

Paula hurdled logs and the bodies of Jake and Trix as she picked up speed. She was now close enough to hear the girl's rapid panting and hitching breaths.

"Crying isn't going to help you." Paula reached out, her fingertips brushing the teen's shoulder.

She yelped and looked back at Paula—a mistake.

Paula stopped running and stood still. *This should be fun.*

When Jasmine faced front again, it was too late: her nose made a sickening crunching, splitting sound as she crashed into a huge oak. Her forehead rebounded off it, her neck snapping back. She was unconscious before her hefty frame hit the dirt.

"Got ya."

Paula walked over to the spread-eagled girl and cut her throat open with Skull's blade.

With the bodies stacked in the tent, Paula stripped some flesh off Jake and went back to check on her babies. Whilst there, she packed a few supplies and, with Typhoon and Tempest still having their nap, headed back to the dead teens.

It took Paula most of the day to get the carcasses to her cave, having to stay with the babies now and then to soothe or feed them.

When Typhoon and Tempest went down for the night, Paula went back to her killing ground and packed up the teens' tent, camping equipment and everything else she could find.

By firelight outside of her cave, Paula rifled through everything, finding hatchets, knives, a hunting rifle and ammunition, sleeping bags and pillows, heaters, cooking implements, bottles of water, food, clothes and personal effects. She discarded what she didn't need and stored the rest within her home.

The next day, before moving her family deeper into the cave ahead of winter, Paula stripped the bodies of their flesh. Eight-Ball had shown her how to cure meat, to make it last. Paula then jointed them the best she could and put their organs in jars and containers she had accumulated over the last couple of months.

She even drained as much blood into flasks as possible, hoping it would keep inside the freezing cave. It didn't matter if it didn't: there was enough meat to last her and the children through winter and into spring. By that time, the woods would be ripe with wildlife, campers and the like.

It was now a matter of bunking down and waiting for the baby to arrive, which Paula had prepared for by making herself comfortable. The extra clothes and blankets she'd found in the camping equipment helped build her nest and keep the little ones warm.

Paula found the remaining weeks of pregnancy testing, but felt things were getting easier, especially with the new supplies taking the unwanted pressure off her.

I think we're going to be just fine, she thought, looking at her sleeping babies. *I think Daddy's looking down on us, my loves, keeping us safe and guiding me.*

Two months later, the baby arrived. Unlike her brothers, she was free from disfigurement.

At first, Paula had been stuck for a name, wanting to give the child a strong, fierce one, and so she chose one from Greek mythology, a subject she'd had a keen interest in whilst studying English at university. Paula's favourite fables were that of Heracles and his Labours—she was fascinated with Cerberus and his sister, Hydra, the name she adopted after naming her child.

"Yes, Cerberus: the mighty Hound of Hades."

Now that she'd given birth and found enough food and supplies for them to last until at least springtime, the self-dubbed Hydra thought things would be simpler. But they weren't, because she had a weak body due to childbirth and providing for three babies.

However, after three months of resting as much as possible whilst fending for her family and teaching the boys to talk, crawl and then walk, Hydra felt the strains ease.

As time pressed forward, more food and supplies came into the home, which helped Hydra relax further into her role of mother and tribe leader. When the boys were three years old and able to communicate, Hydra gave them responsibilities: when she took one out hunting, the other would stay behind and care for Cerberus, and vice-versa.

And that's how things progressed until Hydra had enough confidence in her boys that she could leave them to look after their sister and home whilst she scavenged. At times, she'd be gone for days, returning to find her sons had kept things ticking over in her absence.

At the age of five, Typhoon and Tempest, who were huge for their age, had become competent hunters, with good speaking, literacy and numerical skills. Hydra had educated them to the best standard she could, even teaching them etiquettes, all the while instilling in the boys what they were and where they'd come from.

Hydra drilled into them that the outside world and the people in it were their enemy, and that they'd killed their daddy, family and ancestors.

"We'll be taking revenge for your father, boys," she told them one evening.

"When?" Typhoon asked.

"Soon. The next couple of days."

"What, or who, are we going after?" Tempest asked.

They look like Skull, she thought, staring at their disfigured faces by aid of firelight. "A little bitch by the name of Storm and her family. She killed your father, boys, and she won't be expecting a fucking thing." Hydra ripped flesh from a bone as she spoke. "We'll be pissing on her bones before the week's through."

The boys smiled.

"You know where she is, Mum?" Tempest asked.

Hydra nodded. "I've been venturing into the outside world to find out about that day your dad was murdered. I've got all the details I need."

"How?" Typhoon asked.

"I cleaned myself up, put on *their* clothes and acted like one of *them*. It wasn't hard to pass them by and get the knowledge I needed— I knew where to look, how to access information, and when the time's right, I'll teach you."

Again, the boys smiled.

"Mum has plans, boys."

* * *

Three nights later, with Cerberus strapped to her chest and the boys in tow, Hydra led them out of the woods and into the world in search of Storm.

Chapter 2
Then

Storm lay on her bed. She couldn't sleep, not on the fifth anniversary of her dad's death.

She looked at the framed photo sitting atop her night table, the glow from her lamp illuminating it. It depicted father and daughter standing outside the gates to the fairground at Porthcawl. A happier time. They had teeth-exposing grins on their faces. Storm was laughing, as she'd stuffed her whippy ice cream into her dad's nose.

"I miss you so, so much, Daddy."

Storm clasped the frame in her hand and hugged it to her chest.

* * *

After the funeral, Storm had fallen apart. She stayed in all the time, cutting herself off from the world. No Internet or phone. She became a recluse, and found it hard to interact with her mother, who tried to get her to continue counselling.

"Maybe we should move?" Skye had suggested.

"Not a chance, Mam. Dad died here."

"Exactly, baby. What good is that doing you?"

"Plenty. His soul is here with us, Mam."

Skye stood in silence for a moment. "Okay, baby. As you wish. But talk to me, yeah? I'm worried I'm losing you."

"No need to worry about me."

Over the course of time, Storm's intake of weed and alcohol hit dangerous levels, but there was nothing Skye could do to reel her in, not even when she told Storm that she should be thinking of Stevie.

"She's inhaling that, baby. Try and keep it to a minimum."

But all talk fell on deaf ears.

She ate little, slept less.

Storm lost her curvy shape, becoming skeletal, her face gaunt and her ribs showing through her skin. Most of her hair fell out due to stress and depression, leaving her with bald patches. But it didn't coax her into seeing a doctor or therapist.

"It'll grow back, and my body'll fill out, too, Mam. It's all cool. I just need time to grieve."

"I just think if you talk—"

"To a professional? Look what the last *professional* did, Mother."

"I—"

"The fucker brought a convicted killer here so he could—" Skye's head dropped, her chin touching her chest. "I'll be fine. I need to work through it in my own time. Please."

"I feel useless."

"You're looking after Stevie, and you're here for me, should I need it. That's a lot."

For close to six months, the press had pitched camp outside her house, hoping to get a few lines from Storm. But they'd been disappointed, as the curtains and doors remained closed. Skye, the only person to venture outdoors, had nothing to say to them either, and would often leave home under the cover of darkness.

"Can't you do something about them, for Christ's *sake*?" Storm heard her mother yell into the phone to the police one day. "I think my daughter's been through enough, don't you?"

The authorities tried with half-hearted attempts to keep the papers away after Skye played the 'Huw was one of *yours*' card, but it did little. As soon as they were cleared away, they'd come back time and again until the police gave up.

"We'll make sure to sweep the woods for any more of them, Storm," had been the words of one of Huw's superior officers. "We won't sleep until we know they're gone for good."

They hadn't cared, Storm had believed, regardless of all their crap and bravado at her dad's funeral.

After a couple of weeks, the search parties were called off. A press conference was held with DI Watson.

"We're confident the savages who dwelled in the woods have been killed off—"

"What about the woman who was snatched?" a reporter pressed.

"There have been no traces of Paula Harris, leading us to believe she was killed and . . . *consumed* by them. Her family has been notified."

When the reporters finally gave up, things started to settle down in the small valley town: mothers let their children play outdoors, people were no longer afraid to walk the streets after dark, and the seven-p.m. curfew was lifted.

Every so often, stories about the attacks would appear in the mid-to-end pages of newspapers.

After a year, nobody mentioned it. The town tried to forget, and the authority buried it like a dirty secret.

* * *

Storm lifted the photo off her chest and looked at it.

How old was I when this was taken? Six? Seven? She couldn't recall the moment from memory, and had it not been captured, she doubted she would have ever recalled it. *What does it matter? He's gone...*

She replaced the picture, her eye catching the clock on the wall. "Two minutes to midnight," she mouthed, the simple words bringing fresh tears to her eyes.

"The best damn Maiden song *ever*!" her dad had once confessed.

"The Trooper, surely," had been her giggly response.

That conversation had taken place a few days before their 'big night out'.

I can't believe how many years have passed. Storm pressed her thumb and forefinger to the corners of her eyes and tried to stem the tears, but they still came. *So many gone: Scuzz, SS, Tev, Z, Pitman, Mr. Gibson, Daddy . . .*

"I'll *never* forget you, Dad, or the great moments we—"

A board creaked outside her door.

Storm turned her head.

"Mam?"

Silence.

Storm braced herself up in bed on emaciated arms, letting the duvet fall and gather at her waist. The nightshirt she wore hung from her body, exposing her gaunt chest, her bones protruding through her skin.

"Mam, are you out there?" Storm threw her quilt aside and moved her undernourished legs out of bed, placing her sock-covered feet to the floor. "Please answer me . . ."

She made her way over to the light switch and turned it on, even though her lamp was burning. Ever since the attack in the house, Storm hadn't been able to sleep without a glow of some sort in her room. Complete darkness gave her panic attacks, setting off her waking nightmares.

Storm screamed until her lungs burned when someone tapped on her bedroom door.

"*Jesus!*"

"It's only me, baby," Skye said. "Are you okay?"

The door opened to ajar.

"I was calling you, Mam. Didn't you hear me?"

Skye poked her head into the room. "No, sorry. You should be getting some sleep."

"You know I'm not able to."

"Try, honey. Please."

"Where are you going?"

"Off to get a glass of water. Do you need anything?"

Storm shook her head. "Mam?"

"Yes?"

"Do you think Paula Harris would want to harm me? Us?"

"Oh, baby, is that what's troubling you? After all this time?"

Fresh tears slid down Storm's cheeks. "Why can't they leave us alone? They've taken *everything* from me."

"Paula Harris is dead. The rest of them, too. And, even if she *was* alive, why would she want to hurt you?"

"I killed him. Skull."

"Paula was taken and killed by them, baby."

"But—"

"Look, why don't we talk about this in the morning? Maybe you're finally ready to start opening up? This is a good thing."

"I'd like that, Mam. Maybe we can take Stevie to the park? It's about time I got some fresh air and some sun on my bones."

Skye smiled. "That's my girl. Now, off to sleep. We'll start sorting through things in the morning."

When Storm returned to bed, Skye helped her in and tucked the blankets around her.

"Thanks for sticking around after Dad died. I know we haven't had the best relationship—"

"Shh, Storm. None of that matters now, and as soon as we get over this, we can work on our thing." Skye kissed her daughter on the forehead and got up to leave. "Night."

"Night, Mam."

Storm lay there, eyes wide open, and listened to her mother descend the stairs. Seconds later, she heard water running and a cupboard door opening and closing.

Maybe moving would be for the best? Get away, once and for all. If only we'd done that the first time . . . Dad would still—

The sound of breaking glass pulled her out of her thoughts in time to hear a muffled cry.

"What the fuck?"

Storm sat bolt upright and thought against shouting to her mother.

Maybe someone has broken in?

More sounds: a chair scraped and toppled, thuds, whimpers. Someone was coming upstairs.

"M—M—Mam?" Storm looked at her baseball bat, which was propped against her chest of drawers. It was out of reach. She trembled and clutched the duvet tight. "Please. Answer me."

More sounds from downstairs, as though there was a struggle underway.

Her door inched open.

Storm pressed her legs together. "Who—"

A small, dirty, disfigured face appeared around the wood. A second face poked in, as grimy and flawed as the first. They were boys, and they were grinning at her.

A scream lodged in Storm's throat. Her hand shot out and landed on her phone. She pulled it out of the cradle and placed it to her ear.

No dial tone.

She pressed the pip down several times, to no avail.

"We cut the wires, Storm," one of the boys said, startling her.

"You can speak?" she whispered. "You're not who I—"

"You killed our daddy, bitch," the second boy said.

She groaned.

"Now we're going to kill *you*!"

When they entered the room, she could see they were naked, their bodies caked in mud, leaves and twigs.

It's a waking nightmare. Close your eyes and count.

"One . . . Two . . ."

"Three, four," the second boy mocked.

The other lad joined in. "Five, six."

"Nice bat, whore."

"Don't let Mum hear you using such language, Tempest."

"Mum won't find out unless you tell, Typhoon."

"Nine . . . Ten . . ." Storm continued, opening her eyes. "You're here. You're *really* here!" She tried to get out of bed and make a dash for the bat, but the large, brutish boy named Typhoon pushed her down.

The other, Tempest, picked up her bat and slammed it against the side of her head. Storm blacked out.

* * *

Storm woke up tied to a dining room chair. The boys stood in front of her grinning. The one with the bat clubbed his open hand.

"Can we *do* things to her, Mum?" Tempest asked.

"*No!*" came a woman's voice from the kitchen.

Storm turned her head and saw a feral woman clutching her mother to her chest. Like the boys, she too was caked in grime, but Storm recognized her face. "*Paula*?!"

"The one and only."

Skye's face was cut and bloody, her eyes bulging. She moaned. Paula had a hand over her mouth.

"There's no need for this . . ."

"Save it," was all Paula said, drawing a butcher's knife across Skye's throat. Blood sprayed, covering the table, floor and cabinets.

Storm screamed as her mother crashed to the floor, her body twitching. Skye pressed her hands against her wound. Within seconds, a pool of blood spread beneath her, and she stopped moving.

"If you're wondering where your precious daughter is," Paula said, "the boys dispatched her whilst she slept."

"*Nooo!*" Storm tried kicking her legs as she bucked in the seat the best she could. "You're going to fucking die! All of you."

"I don't think so. Before my boys club you to death, I'm going to make you watch me skin your child and eat it."

More screams.

Fresh tears.

"I'll kill you! Kill—*you!*" Storm's breath hitched between sobs.

"Tempest, Typhoon: get the child and bring her here."

"Yes, Mother," the boys said in unison.

Paula stepped out of the kitchen, licking the blood from her fingers, and walked towards Storm. "I've waited a long time for this, bitch." She pressed the tip of her blade underneath Storm's chin. Blood snaked down the steel handle and onto the floor.

The smell wafting off Paula was overpowering.

Storm lunged forward, snapping her teeth, trying to latch onto Paula's lip or nose, but the woman stepped back.

"Nice try." Paula smiled and then laughed, all the while tapping the knife against her mouth.

"Here she is, Mum."

Storm turned to find Typhoon carrying her six-year-old daughter into the living room. She eyed Stevie's blonde hair. Blood slipped off her golden tips and splashed against the carpet.

She was limp.

Lifeless.

"What have you done? You fucking murdering, monstrous fucking freaks! *Cunts!* Let her go!"

"My pleasure." Typhoon dropped the child. When she hit the deck, blood squirted into the air. Her trousers were missing; her knickers too.

When Storm looked again, she could see Stevie had been tampered with: blood drizzled from between her legs and plastered her inner thighs.

"Oh, God! No! No! Not—"

Paula slapped her. "Shut up, whore. You shouldn't have fucking meddled with my family in the first place."

Storm spat in the woman's face and would have clawed her eyes out had her hands been free. She bucked and wriggled until the fight drained away, her chin dropping to her chest. Saliva clung to her drooping lower lip. "Just kill me."

"In good time. Look at this," Paula said, taking her blade and slicing strips of flesh off Stevie's leg and devouring it. She licked her fingers clean and smiled when she saw Storm's mouth hang open.

"Fucking bitch-cunt-whore-*fuck*—I'll kill you. Rip your tongue out—"

Paula nodded at Tempest, who brought the bat down on Storm's head.

Blood spurted out of her mouth. "*Ugh!*" she cried.

A second, third and fourth blow rocked her.

"I want to help, Mother," Typhoon said, picking up the poker from the fireplace.

"Be my guest."

* * *

Typhoon joined his brother in bludgeoning Storm whilst Hydra stripped more flesh from Stevie and ate, all the while smiling and rubbing Storm's squirting blood into her mud-caked skin.

The sound of snapping bones dampened her pussy and stiffened her nipples.

Hydra's eyes descended to her sons' penises, thinking she could see them grow a little. *Soon they will need to learn how to use them,* she thought.

She sat at the table with a pad, dipped her finger into the infant's skull (which had been cracked open like an egg) and started to write the events down in Stevie's blood.

* * *

I had thought about sparing Storm, or her daughter at least, so that the boys could mate with them. But I don't think it would have gone to plan. They would have tried escaping. No, it would have been too much work. Besides, they had to pay in full. All of them. It's what Skull would have wanted.

* * *

Hydra stopped writing and glanced at the bloody and battered Storm. Her sons stood either side of the busted girl, wheezing and panting for air.

"You can stop hitting her now, boys. Go and tend to your sister in the kitchen whilst I finish up in here."

Tempest and Typhoon nodded and grunted.

When they smiled, Hydra could see Storm's blood coating their teeth.

She returned to her writing.

* * *

Now that I've exacted my revenge, I'll be putting the second part of my plan into place over the next couple of weeks, which will help ensure my family will grow in a safe environment. Once that's been completed, I'll try my best to sack this town and cause as much fear and panic as possible.

They think they can shit on my family and get away with it?

Not a fucking chance.

I won't go into the second phase of my arrangement whilst I'm here as it may take too long to explain, but soon I'll reveal all. For now, I need to get my children home, back to safety.

* * *

When Hydra was done, she closed the book and licked the blood from her finger. She took one last look at Storm before joining her children in the kitchen, strapping Cerberus to her chest and aiding the boys in setting a fire.

Once they were finished—a blaze erupting—they left via the back entrance and disappeared down the alley and into the night.

* * *

Hydra, thinking they'd pulled it off without a hitch, failed to notice one of Storm's neighbours watching from a window. They called the police as soon as they saw smoke rising from the home.

Chapter 3
Then

I'm home.

Not the cave in the hills—my actual home. The one I once lived in with my husband and children before I was captured in the woods by Skull and Eight-Ball.

Not much has changed, apart from my husband and his girlfriend—my sister—don't live here any longer. However, I'll get to that later. First, I want to explain what happened to me after my boys and I killed Storm, and the years in between.

I'm not sure how, but as soon as we left the house, I heard police cars approaching. They filled the streets and roads, cutting off escape routes back to the woods.

We were trapped, but I knew if we could make it onto our turf, the police wouldn't stand a chance . . .

* * *

"I think I see movement ahead," Hydra heard someone call from beyond the shadows in the lane they were hiding in.

"Tempest," she addressed her son, removing Cerberus from her chest and handing her over. "Take your sister and run."

"Yes, Mama." The boy didn't waste time shouldering his sister.

"Go home. Stop for nothing. If we are not back by sunup, we're either dead or captured. Don't come looking. Raise your sister."

Tempest nodded. "Okay."

"Now, go!"

He didn't need telling twice and was soon out of eyesight.

"What are we going to do, Mother?" Typhoon asked.

"Our job is to get home, but to keep *them*," Hydra said, hooking a thumb over her shoulder, "off Tempest's back."

Typhoon drew his knife and smiled.

"But not here. There are too many following. We need to pick a better killing ground. Come on, boy."

Mother and son raced down the alley, shot out of it, and ran into another. Overhead, they heard a helicopter circling.

"There—look!" She pointed out a gap in a fence that encircled a large building. "Let's see if we can get inside."

"They're over here!" someone screamed from behind.

Dogs barked and growled.

Through the fence, Hydra ran towards a pair of docking bays that lorries used to unload goods.

"Must be some sort of factory," she muttered. "There's a window over to the left, son. Break it and get inside. Quick." Hydra looked over her shoulder. Men and canines spilled through the hole in the fence.

"Freeze!" a man called.

"Hold it right there," another said.

"Release the hounds," a third chirped.

Sounds of shattering, sprinkling glass drew her attention back to Typhoon, who was making his way through the broken window.

Hydra followed.

Inside, they found the place to be in total darkness.

"Right," she began, but was stopped when a dog sprang against the window, teeth snapping. Saliva plastered Hydra.

"Back, Mother." Typhoon stepped forward and punched his knife into the German shepherd's belly. He pulled the blade up the dog's body and yanked it out once he'd slashed the mutt's throat.

Blood and guts splashed the floor and Typhoon's body.

The carcass hit the deck, and another German shepherd slammed against the window for Typhoon to dispatch.

"Bastards are killing the dogs. Go around front, men," a voice called outside.

"Come, Typhoon. We need to go!" Hydra pulled on her son's arm.

"You go, Mama. I'll stay here."

"No—"

"Please. I'll catch up. Go. I know what I'm doing."

The mob of police officers outside grew closer.

"Careful at that window, lads."

"The fuckers can have one of *these*, sir."

A second later, an object flew through the window and landed on the floor. Gas escaped it.

Another smoke grenade came spinning in, landing close to the first.

"Come," Hydra said, grabbing her son's bicep. "We'll make a stand elsewhere."

Typhoon sheathed his knife and went with his mother.

As they moved between the machines inside the factory, Hydra turned them on to help cover their tracks. They kept the lights off.

"They have us trapped in here, Mama."

"We'll pick them off from the shadows."

"Should we split up?"

"No. Stay close. Over here, quick." Hydra led her son into a darkened corner and hunkered down.

Flashlights lit up. Voices reverberated off the walls, but they were barely audible over the drone of the factory machines.

"Will someone cut the power?" a man yelled. "And get some lights on in here."

It didn't take long for someone to wander close to Hydra and Typhoon, and so Typhoon, skilled at making animal sounds, made one of a whining dog.

"Hammer?" The man turned, sweeping his light into their corner. He wore a tactical vest with POLICE written across it in stark white lettering.

"Is that you, boy? What have those fucks done to you?"

Typhoon leapt from the darkness and slashed his blade across the big man's throat. He dropped his torch and gun, his hands going to his wound. When he collapsed to his knees, Hydra stepped forward and helped drag the dying officer into the shadows.

Mother and son finished the man off by repeatedly stabbing him in the face, jugular and chest.

Blood spewed.

Flesh ripped.

Typhoon placed his mouth over the copper's ruptured oesophagus and drank. He also used his teeth to tear away and devour chunks of skin.

"John?" another police office said, sounding close. His torch beam skirted around the dark corner concealing mother and son.

When he turned his back, Typhoon stabbed him, covered his mouth with his hand and dragged him into the darkness where Hydra waited to slit his throat and spill his guts.

A radio crackled nearby. "Do you see them?"

No response.

"Come back. Do you see them?" The walkie-talkie spat static, its sound growing distant.

"Come on, son. We need to get moving."

Typhoon nodded with a grunt. Strips of flesh hung from his mouth, and blood covered his forehead and cheeks.

Hydra crept from the shadows and led them back to the window they'd broken. The police were deep inside the building. Nevertheless, a guard had been left behind.

"She looks pretty, Mama. Can we keep her?" Typhoon asked, spying the young, short blonde-headed PC.

"No, boy. She would prove too difficult."

"Aw, okay." He hung his head, then snapped back to attention. "Can I?"

Hydra nodded.

Typhoon got closer to the woman, who swept the surrounding area with her torch and kept her radio to her ear and threw his knife. It flipped hilt over tip until the point slammed into the woman's forehead. She was propelled backwards, out the window.

"Let's go, son." Hydra broke cover and grabbed Typhoon's hand.

When they were outside, Typhoon retrieved his blade and ran after his mother.

Exiting the alley, Hydra thought they were in the clear, but a spotlight fell on them from above.

The helicopter swooped in for a closer inspection, its rotating blades kicking up debris.

"*Stop*! Hold it right there," a voice boomed over a megaphone.

Sirens wailed in the near distance, along with dogs and the sound of people shouting and rushing.

"We have to run faster. Quick," she demanded.

The helicopter pursued as Hydra and Typhoon weaved in and out of streets, hid behind cars and ducked into alleys, never losing sight of the whirlybird.

"It's guiding the others to us," Typhoon pointed out when they stopped behind a couple of large industrial bins to catch their breath.

"Doesn't matter. We're close to the woods."

"Once we're in there, they won't find us. *Ever*."

Hydra shook her head and smiled. "No. I just hope we can get that—"

The chopper came around the bin and illuminated them. "Over here!" the voice boomed.

Dogs barked.

"Stay right where you are!" A man holding an object that looked like a gun appeared out the helicopter's side.

"Get down, Mama," Typhoon said, pushing his mother aside and grabbing a large stone off the floor. The youth hurled the brick with all his might. It smashed through the whirlybird's windscreen and connected with the pilot's face.

The chopper pulled up violently, tail-spinning.

"Well done, Typhoon. Now's our chance." Hydra caught her son's hand and led him into the darkness.

Somewhere behind them, an explosion rocked the night.

They didn't stop to gawk.

By the time they got to the woods, dawn was breaking.

The police were still hot on their tail but nowhere near close enough to capture them.

"Come on, we need to keep going. In an hour or two, there's going to be teams of them out here searching the forest and surrounding areas, lad."

"I hope Tempest and Cerberus are safe."

"They'll be fine. Keep up, now."

They walked for what seemed like days, the rising sun at their backs along with the distant sounds of chasing men and women.

Now and then, they stopped for a few minutes to catch their breath and to check if anyone was closer than they thought. When they were deep in the woods, their pursuers gave up.

"We're almost home, Typhoon."

A few minutes later, Tempest, Cerberus and their cave came into sight.

"Did you have any trouble, brother?" Typhoon asked.

"No."

"Nobody saw or followed you?"

"No, Mother. I made sure I was careful."

"I've taught you both well. How is Cerberus?"

"Sleeping. I fed her when we returned."

"Good, son. Good. Now, inside, all of you—we could have trouble this way soon."

Trouble came a few hours later: more dogs, three helicopters and a massive team of police officers who searched the woods in roving packs.

When Hydra spotted the first wave of them inching toward her cave dressed in high-visibility jackets and wielding sticks to thrash the green, she retreated inside and made sure her boys and daughter were nowhere in sight. She also checked that all their stuff had been moved deeper into the cave should someone make it inside, though she doubted they would. After hustling the kids into their dwelling, Hydra had spent some time covering the mouth of the home with branches and foliage, camouflaging it the best she could.

Worst comes to the worst, she thought, *we can always go farther into the cave and exit elsewhere.*

Hydra was uncertain of how many routes there were in the tunnel but knew there was at least one other mouth to the dwelling. When she'd first settled here, she'd travelled the cave for miles, eventually finding a rear exit.

There were also multiple paths to the dark, dank cave, and she didn't know where they led or how far they stretched.

After discovering the back exit, Hydra had made sure to leave tell-tale signs of the route.

I should have told the boys to head that way. Then again, the boys are smart—they'll know.

"Tempest? Typhoon?"

No answer. Standing still, holding her breath, she listened. All she could hear was the faint sound of running, dripping water. "Boys?" she said, raising her voice.

Nothing.

Good. They've gone far enough.

"Is there much point in going deeper?"

Hydra froze when she heard the voice outside. She leaned into the branches that hid her from sight and parted them as quickly as she could, making little noise.

There were two of them.

No dogs.

The speaker was rather rotund, and he was puffing for air and sweating. "That was one hell of a steep climb. Damn near killed me," he stated.

"The heat isn't helping," his friend added.

"Looks like we've been cut off from the others."

"I saw Christopher lead his team through here, Shane. We've fallen behind, that's all."

"Can't we take five?" Chunky whined. "They're probably miles—"

"They killed my dog last night, Shane."

"I know. And I'm sure we'll come across them sooner or later, but who's to say they've even stayed in the woods, Charlie?"

"You haven't heard the rumours?"

Shane smiled. "That the cannibals are back in these hills?"

Charlie nodded.

"Ha-ha! You don't believe all that crap, do you?"

"It made the papers! Why would respected detectives lie?"

"They were probably chasing crackheads out here, Charlie."

"Don't let the top brass hear you say such things. Now, come on—we need to catch up with Chris—"

"*Shh!*"

"What is it?"

"Didn't you hear that, Charlie?"

Both men stood still for a few seconds until Charlie shook his head. "No, what was it?"

"There's someone in those trees." Shane raised a meaty hand and pointed. "Come on."

Hydra pulled back from the branches and slipped into the darkness. When she was hunkered down out of sight, she drew her knife and hoped they'd go away.

If I kill them, then they'll be presumed dead or missing in the woods. I can't have that, she thought. *They'll send more, and they won't stop coming until they've torn these woods apart.*

"It's a goddamn cave, Charlie!"

"We need to call—"

"Hey, wait. Don't radio it just yet."

"What? Why not? Are you crazy?"

"Come on, we're rookies—if we go home with the bad guys, we'll be up for promotion. Think about it."

"Okay, but the first sign of trouble and we call for back-up, okay?"

"You got it, Charlie."

Hydra heard the men enter her home, followed by the sound of clicking. Lights brightened the dwelling.

"Smells like someone's taken a massive shit in here, Shane."

"*Fuck*! That's pretty rank."

"How far back do you think this thing goes?"

"No idea, but I don't think we should venture too far. Let's poke around and see what we find. We can still be the heroes by finding evidence."

"Come on, let's go a little—*argh!*" Shane gargled and choked as he tried holding his slashed throat together.

"Shane? Shane? What—where are you?" The second beam of light swept the cave in a frantic motion. "I can't see you!"

Hydra made sure to catch as much of the hot, squirting, spraying blood in her mouth as possible before Shane collapsed to the floor. She then turned her attention to the now whimpering Charlie, who was making his way back to the entrance.

Before he could part the greenery in front of him, Hydra stabbed her knife into the small of his back and dragged him to ground.

"I wasn't going to kill you bastards," she told him, leaning close to Charlie's face. "But then I thought, what the fuck, right? Nothing wrong in keeping the home stocked with meat—you pair'll last us months, especially tubby guts over there."

She stuck her knife in his eye, bursting it like a water balloon.

His screaming hit its zenith.

"Now the other—"

The sound of distant voices stopped her.

"Help!" Charlie screamed.

Hydra rammed her blade into his mouth, forcing it down his throat and killing him outright.

"Did you hear something?" she heard someone say.

"Can't say I did."

Hydra sneaked to the cave's entrance and peeked between the branches in time to see two hikers walk by.

"Nobody will be coming for you pair," she whispered, returning to Charlie to retrieve her knife. "Not that there'll be anything left of you to save . . ."

Over the course of the days and weeks that followed, the police continued their search of the woods, never coming close to Hydra's cave.

After a few months, they gave up—the search, which had turned into a rescue, was called off. Not that it mattered: Hydra had moved her family and the fresh bodies to the back end of the cave and concealed the entrance.

* * *

In fact, the new location worked out better for us. I was sorry I hadn't explored the caves further when I first found them. You see, our new patch opens onto an enclosed lake, providing us with drinking and bathing water. Even though I want the boys to remember what and who they are, I still wish to raise them clean and healthy.

Cerberus will be taught the same, along with the other children.

I want the tribe to flourish.

Anyway, enough of that for now—I'll come back to it later.

After killing Storm, escaping the police and making things safe at the cave once more, I hatched a new plan, one I hoped would keep me and my family from harm's way once and for all.

I decided I was going to visit Tony, and he was either going to join rank or die a horrible death . . .

Chapter 4
Now

Elizabeth, who was named after her great-great-grandmother, had been the sole manager and proprietor of the Lamb and Flag pub for the past nine years. When she'd first acquired the establishment fifteen years ago, she'd been the joint owner, along with her brother. He died six years into running the place, forcing Elizabeth, who preferred to go by Liz, to take on full responsibility.

Paul, Liz's brother, had taken ill unexpectedly.

"I'm sorry for your loss, Elizabeth. It seems Paul had a rare, and certainly unusual, blood disease that we've not seen or treated in this hospital," had been the doctor's cold, unforgiving words. "We'd like to keep your brother's body for a couple of weeks, run some tests and see if we can prepare for the next case we have involving the extraordinary illness."

She'd found his frankness astonishing. Had she not been emotionally drained at the time, Liz would have taken more than a few strips off him, but then he added, "It would be a good cause towards medical science . . .", swaying her judgment somewhat.

Her mind had reeled. *What if it's in me? What about Jason? The babies!*

"By all means, come in for a check-up," the doctor had said after she'd voiced her concerns.

Six weeks later, Paul's body had been retuned, and the green light to bury him had been lit.

Liz hadn't had time to mourn. She had a business to look after along with her family: her baby twin girls, four-year-old nephew and younger brother Jason, who all lived at the pub with her.

The first four years without Paul had been tough. A slog. Not just physically, but mentally, too. Had Liz not had Jason to help mind the children whilst she worked every hour God sent, then it would have been an impossibility to keep everything going no matter how good she was at spinning plates.

When Jason turned sixteen, Liz put him to work behind the bar—not that she had to do much arm-twisting. He'd been chomping at the bit to get involved ever since Paul had passed.

"It's not fair to take all the work on yourself, sis," had been his words after they'd buried their brother. "Let me at least do some bar work for you."

"No," had been her stern reply. "You can help me out by looking after the little ones—keep them entertained, warm, and their bellies full for me. That would be a massive help."

Jason coming of age had been a welcomed relief, taking away much of the strain that had been building and threatening to cave her in. When Liz realized how much of a good thing it was, she'd suddenly become scared, knowing that if her baby brother had been slightly younger, meaning there wouldn't have been aid for another year or two, then she would have gone under.

Stress would have killed her.

And if the stress hadn't, then giving up the pub would have. That act would have been like the hammer called Life slamming down on the one bullet in her revolver's chamber.

The Lamb and Flag was her life force.

Not only that, but the place had been in the family for four decades—it had been passed down from father to son, mother to daughter, brother to sister, and so forth. And, with no immediate relations around except for her nephew, brother and children, who were all too young to take the pub on, then it would have been sold to a stranger and lost to her blood forever.

No, Betty wouldn't allow that to happen. She'd think of something, Liz had thought. *However, her and her lot, especially Igor, could never come here. Not if they want to protect the family secret and keep Twin Jesters under our control, which was Hydra's wish. . .*

Besides, working the Flag gave her a sense of purpose in life. It filled her with pride and get-go whenever she thought about how hard she'd worked to build the place up—to get back a lot of the trade and punters it had lost when it had been in the hands of her parents.

Her mother had placed blame for the pub's decline and descent into near rack and ruin squarely at her father's feet. "He's become a no-good lush and womaniser," she'd said. Whereby he had drained the profits dry, she had chased off the female customers by accusing them of fucking her husband.

When it looked as though the pub was going to close down, a miracle happened: her mother died, and her father fell ill within weeks of her going. The doctors had labelled his sudden deterioration into an early grave as a 'broken heart'.

"Yeah, you see it all the time," the undertaker had told Liz and her brother. "When one dies, the other normally follows pretty rapidly. They start pining, see. A sad thing, the human heart."

He'd said it in almost a cheery way; Liz could have sworn she'd detected a wry smile on the bone collector's face.

Not that she'd cared. She was glad to see the back of them, knowing her and Paul could start their new venture together and breathe new life into the battered, bruised business.

All it's going to take is a bit of elbow grease and some honest sweat and toil, she'd thought, standing before the pub with her brother.

They'd gutted the place, all four floors, getting rid of the olde-worlde décor, fixtures and fittings that had been there since their parents had taken over the pub.

"This joint probably hasn't seen an update since it was built, sis!" Paul had commented. "Let alone a lick of paint or a splash of colour."

"You know how Mum and Dad were..."

"Frugal?"

They'd both laughed at that one.

All the booths, sofas, tables, chairs and the bar were also ripped out so they could modernise completely. They'd decided that they wanted to make the place hip and chic, so it would attract the attention of the younger crowd. They even put in stylish and expensive drinks, along with craft ale and a pool table.

When they were fully up and running, they decided to upgrade the rear of the pub and install an elegant kitchen so they could start providing meals.

"You don't go to a pub for food," their father had always argued. "The only grub that should be served is nuts and pork scratchings."

He's such a short-sighted fool, Liz had thought when her dad had responded with that after their mother suggested a chef be brought in. Even as a child, she'd had good business acumen. Her mother had clearly had it too, because she was forward-thinking: serving food to bring in a healthy profit/income in an ale house around the time was uncommon.

But with him gone (her mother too, God rest her soul), they'd been free to turn their business into a booming success—something she knew their mother would have been proud of.

Things had been going swimmingly.

The place ran like clockwork, and there was hardly ever any violence or the need for the police to be called, unlike when their parents had run it. Liz could recall many occasions when there was trouble at their door late at night, which had been scary. Still, nothing ever came of it.

Then again, I can thank Jonesy and his crew for the safety, she'd thought. *Paying them for protection is well worth it.*

Liz had used to look forward to getting up in the morning and heading downstairs to the bar to get an early start. Life was good. Great, in fact. She had her brothers, nephew, baby girls and her own business. *What more could a girl ask for?* she'd thought.

But it had all crashed down around her ears after her brother died, and it had taken all her strength to keep the place from slipping under.

"You should get some staff in to help you," a drunk, loyal punter had once suggested.

But Liz hadn't wanted that—she wasn't particularly keen on the cook being there, but knew it was necessary. So she'd struggled on until Jason was able to fully help take control. As soon as he'd become of age, she'd made him a legal partner, too. She'd showed him all the ropes, from locking up and setting the alarms to filling in orders and keeping the books.

"I want you to know all this stuff in case something ever happens to me," she'd told him.

And so she'd soldiered on with Jason, who helped her iron out all the creases that had occurred after losing Paul. It took them less than a year to get the place back on track, with the punters and money flowing in once more.

Since then, things had been peachy.

They were living the dream.

It's been a rocky road, she thought now, looking across the bar at Jason, who was serving someone a pint of beer. *But I—no, we—have managed to pull through it. And look at us now!* "And to think I almost lost my dream job . . ." she muttered, looking about her. *Betty is proud of me. Hydra would be, too.*

"Any chance of some service here, *bitch*?!"

Ugh! Liz inwardly groaned. *But sometimes, just sometimes, the arseholes on a Friday night have a knack for getting you down,* she thought, turning to the man who had so rudely interrupted her chain of thought.

"Give me a fucking beer!" the guy demanded again, belching. His eyeballs resembled marbles: they were glassed over and rolled around in his skull. Liz couldn't tell if he was looking at her or through her.

She wondered if he'd been eating tuna and had a hard time in not pinching her nose closed. He didn't so much as stand there, but swayed, as though manipulated by a breeze. Liz couldn't understand how he hadn't collapsed or fallen backwards onto a table.

His face didn't look familiar, either.

He didn't fit.

"*Sir*," she said in a calm yet firm tone, "I think you may have had enough to drink. I can't, and won't, serve you another—"

He slammed his fists down on the bar. The knuckles on both his hands were scuffed and bloody. "No fucking bitch is going to tell me when I've had enough!" he screamed, his voice breaking.

A hush fell over the crowd in the pub—only the jukebox could be heard.

Her tone took on an edge. "Don't make me have to call the police, *sir*!" Whilst he mumbled and drooled, she glanced over at Jason and saw he had his hand on the phone. All it would take was a nod off her, and Jason would speed-dial the police, or Jonesy and his crew—and they'd be here in minutes.

She shook her head and turned back to face the drunk.

"Call the fucking army or the prime minister, *whore*! See if I care!" He slammed his hands on the bar like a spoiled brat.

Whore? How dare he! She saw red, walked around the bar and grabbed the man by his ear. She twisted it and escorted him to the front door. He tried to protest and wrestle free, but he was no match for her sober superiority. "And stay out! You're barred."

She went to the window. The man hung around outside, and then slipped down the alley connected to the pub. Inside, after a few people commended Liz on how she'd handled the situation, the place became raucous once more.

* * *

He eyed her from a barstool located at the counter. He was lost among the drunken barflies who sat all around him; his face was invisible, his person unknown and nameless. He knew her but she didn't know him, and that's the way he intended to keep it, right up until the point when he killed her.

Then he would tell her who he was.

He wanted to hear her scream his name; to see her cry, bleed and plea for her life.

He picked up his glass, put it to his lips and sipped at the whiskey. All the while he kept his eyes on her from over the rim of his tumbler. The scotch was sour and fiery, just the way he liked it and his women. It caused him to pull his lips, exposing his well-polished teeth and healthy gums.

"That's a damn good drink," he muttered, nobody hearing him due to the thumping music and the hubbub of laughter and chatter.

His stare remained on her.

He watched her every move, like he had done for the last six years. He'd stalked her, crept in her shadows; he knew when she ate, slept, shit and drank—all there was to know about her.

Or so he thought.

Liz. The name sounded poisonous. *That's because it* is *fucking poison. Her whole fucking family is toxic.*

As he continued to glare, he rolled the glass between his palms. He enjoyed playing this game of cat and mouse. *Soon it will be cat eat mouse,* he thought. *Liz thinks she's so clever—thinks nobody knows about her and her lot. Well, I know. I made it my business to know.*

Most people around town didn't pay much attention to the killings and the missing people, but he had. Especially after his son had been murdered, his body dumped and discovered in woods roughly ten miles away.

The police had called it an accident. They had said the lad, who turned eighteen on the night he went missing, had stumbled through the woods drunk and fallen. His head had been caved in. The authorities had also reported that the wildlife had picked the body clean—foxes and other wood-dwelling animals had ravaged his face and shredded his carcass.

There hadn't been much of his lad on the slab to identify. Had it not been for the tattoo on his left shoulder blade, he wouldn't have been able to ID his own flesh and blood.

The man sitting on the stool burning a hole through Liz as he nursed his whiskey went by the name of Tokyo. He didn't even want the drunks knowing his real name.

If someone should come asking questions, he thought, *it wouldn't take the cops much to put two and two together.*

Up to now, he'd been fairly confident his tracks had been well and truly covered—nobody had suspected a thing. Nobody had come knocking. And, since he'd killed three members of her family over two decades, he was certain he was safe.

She has no idea that I've been slowly tearing her family apart. He laughed into his whiskey as he raised the glass to take another few sips.

At first, he'd been happy with the police report. Like a man, he'd accepted it, and reminded himself that life can sometimes throw you a curveball, and that the senseless accident that had happened to his son occurred the world through on a daily basis.

Life, sadly, is fragile.

Not only that, the youngster had been drinking copious amounts. After all, it had been his eighteenth birthday.

But then word reached him that two of his son's friends had also disappeared that night—their bodies were never discovered. And, when he'd looked further into the matter, he found that a series of people had been going missing around the same time, and were still doing so here, near the town of Twin Jesters and throughout Bridgend and its surrounding areas.

Soon, his son's case, the missing friends, and scores of others hooked him. Consumed him. It took over his life, forcing him to give up his job as he played private dick. In the process, he lost his home and wife as well—his life came away at the seams.

You've cost me more than you will ever know, you fucking cunt! he thought, glaring at the pub owner. If he could have killed her there and then, along with her other brother, he would have. *Going to keep biding my time. Soon. I just need to see the rest of her family before I make my final move. Then again, killing babies won't fucking bother me. They've all got to die.*

At the start of his investigation, he'd retraced his son's footsteps on the night he'd been killed. By then, he'd been convinced his son had been murdered and his body moved to the woods. His search was narrowed down after the police divulged to him the approximate time of his son's death—this meant he was able to eliminate some of the pubs he knew his boy had called at.

The Lamb and Flag had been last on his list, and after an uneventful quest for justice up to the point of visiting this final ale house, he had started feeling despondent.

Like in all the other pubs he'd been to, he'd shown Liz's parents a photo of his son and asked a series of questions. When he'd asked about viewing their CCTV tapes from the night of the murder, they'd agreed, but something about their vibe, body language and facial expressions told him something different. They'd also bumbled their way through some of his questions.

The husband had gone off in search of the tape.

"Surely you mark your tapes?" Tokyo had said to the mother.

She'd given him a forced smile.

As he'd expected, the husband had come back empty-handed. "I appear to have misplaced *that* tape, along with a few others. Would you like to call back in a few days?"

A smile briefly flickered across Tokyo's face. "Sure, why not?" he'd said, turning to leave. As he did, he could almost feel the weight of relief and panic lifting off them. After he walked out the door, he took a sneaky look through one of the windows and saw the pair arguing.

He knew then that something was up, and that they knew more than they were letting on.

The jig's up, kiddos! he'd thought, walking away and not returning to ask about the 'missing' CCTV tape.

Instead, he'd started looking into the couple: he did background checks and asked about them around the town. Not only that, but he watched them and held stakeouts outside the pub.

This went on for months, with nothing strange occurring. Also, he'd drawn blanks on finding out about them: who they really were, where they'd come from and if they had more family in the area. It got to such a point of boredom and frustration that he thought he had the wrong place and people; that they lived a quiet, peaceful life, and didn't want trouble. At that point of breakdown, he'd thought himself a stupid old bastard—he'd thrown his life away playing detective.

But then a few things happened. Two more people went missing—they'd been reported as being last seen at the Lamb and Flag pub. When he saw photos of the teen girls, he remembered seeing them enter the pub, but not leave.

Secondly, an old friend he'd asked to dig up details on the pub owners had finally found something. The information had been relayed to him on his answer phone whilst he'd been on a stakeout.

Beep: "*Looks like your friends at the pub there are hiding a huge secret, Tokyo. I'm not sure if you're old enough to remember the incident in Bridgend some sixty or seventy years ago, when a pack of cannibals living in the woods attacked some concert that was being held there? It was massive news at the time. Anyway, I won't go into it over a robot. If you want to meet for coffee, get back to me. Also, if you check the library archives, you'll find plenty of information."* *Beep.*

Tokyo had set up a luncheon with his friend at a café around the corner from where he lived.

"Your message more than intrigued me, Sam. Tell me the rest."

"Did you go to the library?"

"I did, but I couldn't find much—a lot of information was missing from the archived documents."

"Yes, I should have told you: the authorities tried to cover it up, but they did a poor job. I know the full story, and I'll probably have the answers to all your questions."

"But?"

"It's going to cost you."

"I'll give you five hundred for everything you have," Tokyo said.

"Make it a plump thousand and I'll also give you my services. You might need my help in what you're dealing with, friend."

The revelation had startled Tokyo. What was he getting into? How deep did the river of shit go? Who exactly were the people at the Flag?

His mind had swum.

"Deal," Tokyo had said, offering his hand. "Shall we go back to mine for more privacy? I have a bottle of Hennessey with ten years worth of dust on it."

Sam unfurled an age-old story before his brandy-glazed eyes, once Tokyo had slid his lifesavings across the table and into the small, bespectacled fella's greasy mitt.

"The tribe that came out of the woods were old—hundreds of years old, Tokyo. They attacked a concert and snatched the daughter of a police officer. The father went looking, along with a few other men. They thought they'd killed all the 'Man-Eating Fucks', which is what the trashy tabloids labelled them as. But they came back a couple of years after and went for the father and his daughter once more, succeeding in doing plenty of damage."

"But the wood-dwellers were all killed off. What does this have to do with the Lamb and Flag?"

Sam was visibly shaking. "No," he whispered. "Between us, we've managed to unearth something quite extraordinary, my friend."

Tokyo had felt his patience wearing. "Right, but what does it have to do with my dilemma?"

"The tribes people were killed off the second time, yes, but what people didn't know, and still don't, is that a woman had been snatched at some point in the two years the cannibals laid low. Also, one of the cannibals that survived the first attack had babies. When the cannibals made the second attempt on the police officer, or so I can gather—the story is rather sketchy, but it's all true—the woman was left behind with the offspring. She was also pregnant with the tribe leader's child."

"Are you trying to tell me this woman stayed in the woods and raised them?"

"No, but you're not far off the money. She stayed in the woods for a number of years, allowing the babies she'd adopted to grow and mate with each other. She then moved her 'clan' out of the woods. She taught them to count, read and everything else a growing mind would need in the real world. The family grew fast, and it's suggested a third party was involved—a secret society of sorts, who brought in men, women and children to help out. However, I *think*, they succumbed. The disfigured children were kept out of sight. As the tribe grew, they were shipped out into the world to fend for themselves. I've heard that some have gone as far afield as the States, but I've yet to confirm this. Most of her children and grandchildren stayed here and continued to grow the tribe. Yes, Tokyo—they walk among us!"

"How do you know all this?"

"When I started digging, I had to go to other sources—people who are up on local legends, history and various other fields. Most of this has been dispelled, but I believe it's true, and the couple living at the Lamb are direct descendants. I also have a contact who was once close to the tribe, but I will never divulge his details."

"But . . . but they're normal!"

"To look at, yes. But they still have the urges. It's built into them; it's something their 'normal' breeding will never stamp out. Also, if it's true about the secret society, then the women brought in would have bred normal-looking children, I suppose. I have no real idea of what we're up against. There's so much history . . ."

"Jesus . . . If half of it's true, then we're dealing with *real*-life monsters."

"We are indeed, sir. And I think it's our duty to rid the world of as many as we can, starting with the nest in the Lamb."

"But some of them are children!"

"Who will grow up to kill and devour our fellow man, Tokyo."

He nodded. "I certainly want vengeance for my son."

"And you will have it. So, will you help me destroy as many as we can, starting with that lot? We might be able to get Liz to talk, to spill the beans on the location of more of her kind."

Tokyo picked his glass up, reclined, and thought about it for a couple of minutes. He eyed Sam as he took delicate sips from his tumbler. "Yes, I will."

After hatching a plan together, Sam and Tokyo had visited the Lamb and Flag—because Tokyo had already exposed himself to the owners, he'd gone in disguise.

Their idea had been simple: poison.

They'd gone equipped with a couple of vials of untraceable killers: wolfsbane and cyanide. The former of the two was slower-acting than the latter, which they'd decided to give the father.

After biding their time within the establishment, they'd taken their opportunity after seeing the couple with drinks in their hands at separate periods in the evening. Once the cyanide had been dumped into the mother's coffee, they stayed to watch her die, which wasn't the spectacle they had been hoping for: a few minutes after taking a gulp of her drink, the woman collapsed, never to move again. The husband had been paralyzed with grief.

When they knew she was dead, Sam and Tokyo had left.

Within weeks of her dying, the father was reported to have lost his life, too.

Their plan had worked but it took Tokyo a few more years to claim his next cannibalistic offspring, as Sam had gone underground several years prior and was unable to assist him any further, leaving him in disarray.

At first, Tokyo had taken Sam's disappearing act as a huge blow. Luckily, the man had told him everything he would need to know.

He never did find out if a few had made it to the States, though.

Well, they're not our concern! Tokyo had thought at the time.

After a few weeks of reflecting on Sam's leaving, he'd started to see it as a blessing. Did he really want to kill the parents' children? And, more importantly, the children's children? He didn't think he could do it.

Tokyo became dormant.

The way he saw it, he'd had his vengeance—his thirst for revenge had been slaked.

And then people started to go missing again, forcing him to take action.

Sam told me they'd kill. I should have listened to him. Had I, then lives would have been saved.

Before others were murdered, Tokyo took immediate action. He went back to the pub but didn't bother with a disguise. Along with him, he took the slow-acting poison and slipped some into the brother's drink when he wasn't looking.

The result had been perfect: he'd died within a few days of taking it, the blame falling on a rare blood disease.

With him out of the way, Tokyo had then planned to wait for the perfect moment to storm the pub after closing and kill the reminder of the family in their sleep, with hopes of getting Liz to talk before she died.

* * *

All this rushed through his mind as he watched Liz escort the drunk out of the pub and then spy on him through the curtains. He could see lines of anger pull her face this way and that.

Your next victim, cannibal? he thought, draining the last of his whiskey. "Another!" he snapped at the younger brother serving. *Jason? Yeah, that's right.* He looked at the lad and smiled. *I killed your brother, fuckhead.*

The drink was placed down on the bar, the money asked for.

When Liz pushed away from the window and walked towards the bar, Tokyo got ready to follow.

"Watch the bar a sec, Jay. I'm off to the loo," she said.

Tokyo caught her wink. When she shot by him, he got up and slopped out of the room behind her. He was careful to hang back and duck into doorways and hidey-holes when she stopped. As soon as she started walking again, he was hot on her heel.

She led him to the back of the pub and walked through a door marked Staff Only.

"Fuck that!" Tokyo said, carefully opening the door and peeking around the corner. Liz disappeared out the fire exit at the end of a corridor. He rushed after her and followed her out into the night. He scrambled behind a bin and watched from the shadows. In the poor light, he could just about see her standing guard at the entrance to the alley.

What the hell is she doing? he wondered, shifting into a more comfortable position.

Chapter 5
Now

Liz carefully peeped around the corner as the drunk pinballed his way towards her. He was mumbling something, but she couldn't quite make out what.

A fool like him won't be missed! A nice treat for me and the family—it's been a while . . .

The man crashed through bins and almost went down, but a car kept him up as he fell against it. He laughed as he pushed himself off it and lurched forward. Now he was close enough for her to hear what he was saying.

"Fucking hotshot cunt thinks she can tell me wha—*HIC*! —what to do. I'll fucking show her." He bent over to pick up a bottle that was rolling towards the gutter. As he was doubled over to retrieve it, he farted, which followed through.

The seat of his blue jeans faded to a watery brown colour. The stench floated through the air and assaulted Liz's nostrils, but she didn't bat an eyelid.

The drunk put his hand to his arse and felt the wet patch. "Fuck!" he said, sniffing his fingers. "Ah well, who cares." He burped again and walked towards the street.

He didn't stand a chance against her fierce, ferocious strength.

She pulled the man back into the alley, disarmed him and threw him up against the opposite wall. His head struck the concrete, and he slid down it, leaving behind a bloody, slug-like trail.

"Fix me, will ya?" She stood half-in, half-out of the moonlight that slanted in through the alley's opening.

"N-n-no!" he cried.

She walked up to him and kicked him hard in the balls.

He instantly threw his guts up and pissed himself as he clutched his nuts.

She picked up the dropped bottle, which hadn't smashed, and held it before her. It had once held Beaumet Cuvée Brut. Liz put the top of the container to her nose and inhaled the fumes that had been left behind. "Must have been a bloody good year."

When she looked down, she noticed the drunkard was slowly pulling himself up the lane and out of harm's way.

Liz looked out and saw the streets were dead.

Time for some fun. To let out some of that repressed family rage. Her face creased into a smile. "Where in the *fuck* do you think you're going?"

"N-n-no . . ." the guy continued to cry.

Liz stepped up behind him and grabbed his trousers with her free hand. In one violent movement, she ripped the garments from his body, exposing his shit-spattered anus and scrawny legs.

"You're fucking disgusting!" She turned the bottle around, knelt beside him, grabbed his sagging ballbag and rammed the neck of the Beaumet up his arse.

He screamed, but not as loud as she'd hoped.

His puckered arsehole has been lubed by his crap.

She crushed his bollocks in her grip until they were nothing but mush as she fucked his arse. Finished, she stood, breathing hard. When she noticed he was still alive, she got on her knees again and repeatedly smashed him about his head with the thick end of the bottle until his skull was nothing but a concaved mess.

* * *

Tokyo watched on, mortified, as Liz got her face close to the dashed-out brains and splintered bone, scooped it up and shoved it into her mouth. He put his hands to his ears to close out the awful sound of her smacking lips and sucky, chewing sounds.

Bile raced up his throat, burning it.

He crawled deeper behind the bin, fearing she would either see him or sense him with the wood-dwelling instincts that were buried within her.

Once she'd finished feeding, her face, hands and arms plastered in blood and dripping gore, the sexy, lath-like woman picked the man off the ground and threw him over her shoulder as though he were a rag dolly.

She then went back to the fire exit and slammed the door closed behind her. There was no trace to indicate anything had happened in the alley.

Sitting there, Tokyo found it hard to take control over his shivering body, but he did.

He didn't know how long he'd been there, but when a light flashed on him from somewhere above, it startled him back to reality. From where he sat in a crumpled heap, Tokyo looked up—there was a glow coming from a second-floor window.

Something splashed against the glass.

"Oh, Jesus! What *is* she doing?" Tokyo crawled across the alley and pulled himself up with the aid of the ladder attached to the wall. He started to climb it, noticing it led onto a steel veranda that was opposite but looking down on the pub window that was lit up.

Tokyo tried to make as little noise as possible as he climbed the steel rungs to the top. His heart thumped against his chest. Sweat poured down his face, forming a liquid moustache, and dripped off the end of his chin.

I'm out of shape!

He huffed when he reached the top and pulled himself onto the balcony and into a shadowy corner.

"Oh. My. God," he muttered, looking through the window opposite. He put a hand to his mouth, aghast, as Liz and her family crowded around the drunk she'd put on the dining room table.

The twin girls, who he'd thought were mere babies, were indeed grown women—teenagers, possibly—but he couldn't tell due to their hideous disfigurement: their heads were misshaped, with lumps and bumps at the back, and they had little hair.

Their mutant-like fingers dug into the drunk's ripped-apart belly and scooped out all the soft bits. They ladled blood into their greedy mouths with their huge, shovel-like hands.

"Nice, Nine-Ball?" Liz asked. "How about you, Billiard-Ball?"

The inbreds nodded.

"They're horrific," he whispered, continuing to watch on in morbid curiosity.

The man's entrails were yanked on, his tongue pulled free from his mouth. The twin who'd been referred to as Nine-Ball now had her hand up the man's back passage. Tokyo didn't know, or *want* to know, what she ripped out of him and put in her mouth.

Liz stepped out of the picture and back into it with a carving knife. "Who wants the pecker?!" she asked, smiling and flapping the man's limp penis with the blade's tip.

The girls started squabbling, Liz chuckled and then someone else entered the room: a monstrously disfigured man who had to stoop so his head wouldn't drag along the ceiling.

"That can't be the nephew?" Tokyo blurted, slapping a hand over his mouth when Liz stepped close to the window. She appeared to be looking straight at him, but he knew that was impossible.

Before she turned her back, Liz closed the curtains, blocking his view entirely.

His whole body trembled. He felt as though he was lucky to be alive.

This can't go on. I have to stop them. I was foolish to wait so long—why did I not listen to Sam and take them all when I had the chance?

The one positive to come out of this exclusive viewing of a cannibalistic feeding frenzy was that Tokyo now knew exactly what he was up against.

And I thought I'd be killing children. Fuck this. They all need to be wiped out.

He stood on shaking legs and stepped down the ladder's rungs one at a time. Once he was at the bottom, he rushed down the alley and onto the main road.

Tokyo didn't stop running until he made it to his front door, breathless, exhausted and terrified out of his mind. When he removed his key from his pocket and tried to slip it into the lock, he kept missing the snug slit due to his shaking hands.

"Come on, come on, for fuck's sake."

Unlocking the door, he rushed inside, slammed it closed and fell back against it. He wiped the beads of icy water from his forehead and puffed hard—his breathing came in ragged rips.

No time for resting, he thought, pushing himself off the door and making his way through the living room and down to the cellar.

Once there, he went to his work bench and sought out the stuff he would need.

Tokyo removed a hammer and screwdriver from off the tool rack attached to the wall, along with a flashlight and saw. From there, he went to the wall opposite and dismounted his .410 bolt-action shotgun normally used for hunting wild rabbit. On a smaller bench beneath the gun was a tin of slug cartridges. He opened it and grabbed handfuls of them and stuffed them in all available pockets.

Finished, he grabbed a heavy-duty satchel and shoved everything inside, including a half-empty bottle of whiskey he kept stashed under a floorboard marked with an *X*.

"I hope you aren't drinking down there. You'll have my broom across your backside if you are and I catch you!" his wife used to call down the cellar steps. Of course, she was only partly serious. "You know what the doctor told you, love."

Five years before his wife had left him due to his detective antics, Tokyo had suffered a mini stroke and had been told to lay off fatty foods, nicotine and booze. But when his son had gone missing, the stress of it and trying to find out what happened to him had brought it all back on—the drinking continued.

With the shotgun loaded, a slug of whiskey in his guts and a heart full of bloody murder and vengeance, Tokyo was ready to go back to the pub and finish what he and Sam had started so many years ago.

Tokyo took the cellar steps two at a time and headed out the front door. He was worried that if he stopped and thought about what he was about to do, then his nerve would fail him.

His jaw clicked as he clenched it. *Not a chance!*

The streets were deserted, which was a good thing. Before he'd exited the house, he'd slipped on his old high-visibility jacket, hardhat and duffle coat to disguise the shotgun on his back. If anyone should see him, they'd think he was on his way to work and wouldn't stop or think to question what he was up to.

Still, to be on the safe side, he took backstreets and lanes and stayed in the shadows where and when he could. In no time at all, he reached the Lamb and Flag. The pub was in complete darkness, as were the surrounding houses and businesses. There wasn't a soul on the street.

Tokyo made his way into the alley he'd been in earlier and walked up to the fire exit. Gently, he tried the bars. Locked.

He set his bag down and drew out the work tools. He wedged the screwdriver into the door jamb where the lock was and started tapping it in deeper with the hammer. When it was in far enough, he pried it. Wood splintered around the bolt in the door, and, soon enough, it popped open with minimum effort and noise.

After replacing his tools, he went inside and closed the door at his back. Darkness enveloped him and panic lodged in his throat, but it was dispelled when his flashlight kicked in. He tried to slow his heartbeat and control his rapid, ragged breathing.

Tokyo felt he needed another shot of whiskey, but knew it was a bad idea. He had to keep his mind as clear and sharp as possible. He stood still for a few moments and shifted his torch around as he listened for any movement with pricked ears.

If they've had a good feast, they'll be sleeping soundly and won't hear me coming! he thought, moving forward at a slow pace and keeping vigilant.

He soon found himself in the bar area. Tokyo took his time, making sure to avoid the tables with glasses on them and the few chairs that blocked his path. When he got behind the bar, he spotted a knife block and drew the biggest blade. He then went through a door and found a staircase. He climbed to the second floor.

Once he was on the landing, he swept the upper floor with his torch and found another door. He went through it and found he was in the kitchen—his feet crunched as he walked about. When he looked with his light, he noticed he was treading in dried blood. His nostrils suddenly filled with the smell of iron.

Tokyo gulped down the bile in his throat.

His eyes glazed over.

"Jesus," he whispered, his torch beam falling on the drunk's remains on the kitchen table. There was nothing left but a husk. The eyeballs, nose, most of his cheeks, ears and lips were missing. His chest, like his stomach, was ripped open—there was nothing inside. In fact, when Tokyo peeked in, he could see the table through the gaping hole in the torso.

Small flies buzzed.

Stepping away, he aimed his light at the sink. In it was a pile of blood-spattered plates, utensils, pots and pans—even the kitchen units were plastered red.

More odours assaulted him.

"Can I smell shit and piss? Surely not!" he blurted.

Chunks of human flesh littered the floor, along with congealed pools of blood.

Shaking his head, Tokyo started towards a third door. Opening it, he saw it led into the living room.

There's got to be another set of stairs leading to the bedrooms, he surmised.

A floorboard creaked as he walked into the sitting room, which was rather sparse of furniture: no TV, just one sofa. A few baby toys lay scattered about the floor, and a playpen stood erect in one of the corners.

There are no babies here . . .

Tokyo then found what he was looking for when he rounded a corner: stairs leading to a third floor. He went up them as fast as he could, not wanting to hang around much longer and take any chances.

He was faced with four doors at the top.

Ideally, he wanted to take out either the big fucker, who he was convinced was the nephew, or Liz, the tribe leader, first.

Upon gently opening the first door, he was greeted by Jason. The sleeping lad was lying on his back with his legs dangling over the side of his bed. His sheets were in a knotted mess.

As Tokyo got closer, he could see the blood stains on the lad's face.

None of them are innocent. Just because he's a mere child, I can't let that stop me from taking him down. He must *die.*

Swiftly, Tokyo straddled the boy and clamped his free hand over the youngster's mouth. He was worried the lad would have impressive strength like his mother, but he didn't appear to. With his weight alone, Tokyo was able to keep Jason pinned to the bed as he slowly sawed through his neck with the knife.

Jason gargled and bucked.

Blood sprayed Tokyo's face.

When he felt a warm wetness spread beneath his arse, he knew Jason had soiled himself.

Jason stopped moving, allowing Tokyo to get off the dead boy. He didn't let what he'd done dawn on him and moved back to the landing.

One down . . .

Tokyo headed back the way he'd come. He crept along the carpeted floor and gasped when he was forcefully shoved down the stairs.

He yelled as he rolled down them like tumbleweed, his legs smashing through the spindles that helped make up the banister's railing. When he hit the bottom and slid along the floor, he felt paralyzed. The pain in his back and shoulders was beyond anything he had ever experienced, but he knew he had to get up, and fast.

From above, a light came on. This was followed by someone screaming and crying.

His vision was foggy, but he managed to see the huge blurred shape moving his way.

"*Fuck!*" Tokyo scrambled backwards on his arse, using his hands to help him. "No . . ."

The massive cannibal grabbed him and threw him against the playpen, which collapsed to the floor under Tokyo's weight. "Ugh!" he cried, feeling a rib pop.

He tried to scramble away again but was picked up like a rag doll and hurled across the living room. He crash-landed near a bunch of toys: cuddly bears, rattles and plastic keys, all covered in bloody fingerprints.

Tokyo crawled towards the kitchen.

If I can make it there . . .

His foot was grabbed, and he was hauled into the kitchen—the drunkard's body was swiped off the table. Tokyo was scooped up and thrown down on it, which forced a violent coughing fit to ensue.

"*Jason*!" Tokyo heard a woman screaming, taking it for Liz.

Lazily, he opened his eyes and moved his head. The big cannibal had lumbered off towards the sink, where a wicked-looking cleaver rested.

"*Argh*," Tokyo wailed, rolling off the table and slamming against the floor.

The cannibal glanced over his shoulder but didn't stop his journey towards the meat-chopping utensil.

Tokyo tried to slip the gun free. He screamed in frustration when he couldn't quite get to it. "Come on, man."

The cannibal grabbed the cleaver, turned, raised it overhead and stalked towards Tokyo, who was still scrabbling on the floor with his shotgun. Frantically, he wrestled to get the strap over his head as the beastly man moved closer.

He heard the cleaver cut through the air, and then felt it slam into his shoulder.

Tokyo screamed, but he didn't allow it to stop him getting the gun free and into his hands. Before the cannibal could knock the gun to one side, Tokyo cocked the weapon and fired. The shell bit through his opponent's collarbone, propelling him backwards. This gave him a chance to reload and fire again.

The second cartridge drilled through the giant's chest and threw him onto the table.

Tokyo reloaded and fired once more. The slug smashed through the overgrown cannibal's forehead, killing him, before the shotgun was knocked out of Tokyo's hands. The gun slid under the fridge.

"Mother*fucker*!" Liz screamed in his face, and then slashed her knife across the bridge of his nose and cheeks.

Tokyo fell to the floor and spied the dropped cleaver. Grabbing it, he sprung to his feet and went at her. "Fuck you, cunt!" he screamed.

Before he could reach her, a set of teeth clamped down on his left shoulder, and then his right, forcing him to drop his weapon and crash to the floor.

He felt his flesh being torn away in strips; his blood guzzled.

"Enough, girls. We don't want to kill him just yet."

Tokyo rolled onto his back and looked up at the hideous faces of the girls looming over him. Strings of bloody saliva clung to their drooping lower lips and chins, bringing to mind strawberry laces. Their teeth were broken and misshapen, and their eyes were mismatched in colour. Like Liz, they were naked—their sagging tits were covered in boils and blisters, which bubbled and oozed.

"Bite fingers off," the one said, drooling.

"Chomp cock," said the other.

Both girls giggled.

"This fucking bastard killed our Jason and Bear," Liz said, looking down at her dead nephew with tears in her eyes.

"I murdered that fucking brother of yours too," Tokyo yelled, spitting blood everywhere. "Do your worst."

Liz's face changed. "Onto the table with him, ladies," she said calmly.

"*Wait!*"

"It's too late for pleading, fucker."

He was once again slammed down on the table, his clothes ripped from him. Their talons raked at his skin, face and privates. "Don't you want to know about your parents?" he yelled, feeling he had one last card to play.

"What about them?"

"Spare me and I'll tell you all."

Liz called the girls off with a wave of her hand. "Tell me how you know so much about us first."

Tokyo relayed all the information about his son and Sam, and how they had unearthed the dark secret.

"It's true—we do hail from a long line of cannibals."

"Why?" he choked out.

"Kill?"

"No. Why expose yourself by living out in the open? Some of you have genetic fail—"

"Because we've been able to survive much better this way. Long ago, your kind used to hunt my family down in the woods and kill them. Now, though, there's no stopping us." She smiled. "You were foolish to come here tonight. Even if you had killed us all, it would have still been a failure. We have family everywhere. Globally."

His mouth formed a perfect *O*. "So it's true . . ."

"What of my parents?" She put the cleaver to his face.

He licked his dry lips. "We killed them, Sam and I. Poison."

She laughed. "You did me a service. They were old, useless and in the way."

A flutter of hope swelled in his belly.

"Still, they were my blood and gave me this workplace . . . Have him, ladies."

"Oh Jesus, *no!*" he begged. "Let me go and I'll—*Argh!*" he screamed as one of the girls bit down and through his cock, ripping it and his testicles from his body.

The second girl tore his nipples off and sank her teeth into the side of his neck. Whereas the first girl's fingers had started to burrow into his arsehole, the second teen's digits worked their way into his mouth and yanked on his tongue, tearing it free.

Then there were fingers in his eyes and up his nose.

He prayed for death, but the pain continued for a few more torturous minutes before everything slanted and turned black.

The last thing he heard was Liz's laugh.

Chapter 6
Now

"That's enough, girls," Liz commanded, calling Nine-Ball and Billiard-Ball off Tokyo. There was nothing left of his face, which had been pulled apart and scoffed by the twins. "We have to take care of this mess. Others will come now."

Nine-Ball looked up at Liz, a flap of flesh dangling from her mouth. In one hand, she held one of Tokyo's testicles. "Who come?"

"More like him, sweetie. A lot more. He's more than likely told others." Liz scowled and repeatedly stamped her foot on Tokyo's face until it broke through the bone.

Billiard-Ball squealed, clapped her hands and lapped at the gore that oozed out of the split cranium. When she got frustrated at not being able to get to the soft, gooey bits, she dug her fingers inside and scooped brain and bone matter into her eager mouth.

"I said *enough*, Billiard! You'll get fat and unhealthy if you eat too much, child." Liz went to smack her daughter around the side of the head but restrained herself.

"I'm hungry, Mamma."

"Me too," Nine-Ball admitted. Blood drizzled down her chin. She held Tokyo's other bollock.

"You *can* eat, but later. We need to get this place sorted. Our position has been compromised. We have no idea who this dead sack of shit has told altogether. There might be an army at our door come morning, maybe sooner."

Billiard-Ball threw her arms around her mother's leg. "You won't let them hurt us, Mamma?"

"Don't be silly, child."

"Or let them take us?"

"No, Billiard." Liz ran her fingers through the child's hair. "I won't let anything happen."

"They hurt Jason and Bear . . ."

"They got sloppy. Now, listen to me, both of you—we're going to be fine."

"We stay with Betty?" Nine-Ball suggested.

"Going to your aunt at Twin Jesters might be our only way out of this if things go the way I expect them to. But I'm unsure—"

"Because of trouble there?" Nine-Ball asked. "Ask Jonesy for help?"

Liz shook her head. "There's no need to involve him. Not yet, anyway, and I don't know if there's any family left alive there, let alone the town itself. I've not had communication in months. Who's to say this bastard hasn't killed Betty and the others?"

"You call now," Billiard-Ball suggested. "We clean."

"Cut the bodies up and pack the meat into the freezers below, girls."

"Bear? Jason?" Nine-Ball wanted to know.

"Them, too."

"But—"

"They'd be happy in knowing they fed us, Billiard. Promise. Before you finish, I'll be back, and then we can clean between us. Now, get to it."

"Yes," the girls said in unison.

Liz walked away, stopped at the door, and turned to look at her naked, blood-covered girls.

"Grab legs," Nine-Ball told her sister, catching hold of Tokyo's arms. "Put him on table to cut up."

Billiard nodded and grunted, heaving up the dead man's legs.

Content that the girls were getting on with their task, Liz left the room, walked downstairs to the bar and entered the cellar.

Her hands were shaking, not with fright, but frustration. Annoyance.

Of course, she was saddened by the loss of Jason and Bear, but her and the girls' survival was the most important thing to deal with right now. Grieving could come later, for if she broke down now, everything she and her family had built to protect could be wiped out within days.

Hours, even.

It's probably too late anyway. The secret's out, but then again, who's going to believe it? Regardless, I need peace of mind for me and the girls, Liz thought, flicking the switch that operated the cellar's lights. *Now that Bear and Jason are dead, I have little protection around me. I need family.*

When she got to the bottom step, Liz walked through the cellar to a back room that acted as an office. Opening the door, she kicked her shoes off and stepped over the threshold onto plush carpeted flooring.

A desk sat close to the back wall with a PC, printer and telephone on it. Dotted around the sparsely decorated room were other bits and pieces that qualified as office equipment and work implements, such as a filing cabinet, racks filled with manila folders and shelves lined with books on business, taxes and pub-running 101-type manuals.

No pictures or paintings hung from the uniform white walls, which gave the box-sized room a padded cell feel.

Liz pulled the roller chair from the desk and flopped into it. Her gaze fell on the dust-covered phone. She couldn't remember the last time she'd had to use it since taking over ownership of the Lamb and Flag.

Mum was probably the last to use it when calling Betty about Dad, she thought. *When his drinking got completely out of hand, Mum was worried he'd shout his mouth off or lead trouble here.*

* * *

"We can always silence him . . ." Liz heard Betty say over the phone one evening. Mum hadn't known it, but Liz had been hiding behind the desk, fearing her mother would find her cowering there. But she didn't. "I'm sure the others would agree on such action."

"No, I don't think I could do such a thing. The children. I— "

Liz wouldn't have cared either way. Her dad was a loose cannon. A threat to the family.

"I'm here if you change your mind. In the meantime, keep me posted."

Her mother collapsed to the floor and sobbed after hanging up the phone. It was a state Liz had never seen her in. She'd wanted desperately to hold her mum at that point, but if she'd known Liz was in the room, she would have had the belt.

When her mother left, Liz continued to snoop around the office.

* * *

She shook the memory from her mind, picked up the dusty receiver from its cradle and thumbed the single key on the phone's pad four times. It rang twice before being answered.

"Liz, that you?" Betty's sharp, no-bullshit tone answered. Betty headed up the clan residing in Twin Jesters and was every bit as formidable as her voice suggested.

"Yes."

"Trouble? Because we're fucking swimming in it. The jig's up, girl. Our days are numbered."

"I think we've been found out here too, Betty. Someone came and attacked us tonight. Jason and Bear are dead. He said things . . ."

"What? *Jesus*!"

Liz bit her bottom lip. As tough as she was, she'd never wanted to get on the wrong side of Betty. "I worried you were all dead there."

"You never thought to call? What did this attacker of yours say?"

"He told me that he killed my brother, mother and father."

"On his own?"

"What do you mean?"

Betty sighed. "Did he have an accomplice? Were others involved?"

"I'm not sure—he didn't say. I'm worried, Betty."

"I would tell you to pack up and move out here tonight, but it could cause suspicion. This dead killer of yours could have been acting alone. Nobody else might know a thing."

"You want us to stay put?"

"For now, yes. You might be better off, Liz. We've lost numbers, with many wounded, and there's soldiers everywhere. I can see us having to go back into the woods again by week's end."

Liz gasped. "No . . . Our people haven't lived like that in decades, Betty. What's happened?"

"I won't go into it over the phone. Besides, the forest could be our only hope of survival."

The line went dead, but it didn't stop Liz from keeping the phone to her ear as she stared vacantly at the wall.

"Our *only* chance of survival?" she uttered. A shiver slid down her back. Liz lowered her arm slowly and replaced the receiver, cutting off the drone of dead air.

Maybe I should *take my girls and get as far away from here as possible. There are others like me—I'm sure Betty would tell me where.*

She turned to leave the room.

"Do I even want to be with them, though? We'd probably stand a better chance on our own. Less conspicuous that way."

Liz thought about this as she made her way back upstairs to check on Billiard-Ball's and Nine-Ball's progress.

The three carcasses had their limbs and heads removed, which were nowhere in sight. Neither was Billiard-Ball.

"Where's your sister?"

"Freezer, Mamma."

"You grab one torso, and I'll grab another, child."

As they were about to leave the room, Billiard-Ball appeared.

"Grab the remaining trunk, Billiard. The sooner we get this over with, the better."

Two hours later, with all body parts stored in the pub's walk-in freezer and everything cleaned of blood, brain and bone matter, Liz lay in bed, staring at the ceiling.

Sleep wouldn't come.

In the room next to hers, which was situated behind her headboard, Liz could hear her girls snoring. She envied them and their feeble minds—they were free of constant worry and having to make hard choices for all concerned.

However, she had more pressing things challenging her mind at the current moment than her daughters' sleeping habits.

How do I explain Jason's whereabouts? Will people ask? I could say he's moved away, gone to live with family. Hell, I could pass his absence away as being on holiday. And what if the police come?

Her bladder tightened.

What if someone else like Tokyo does come? Will I detect them? They could kill us all before I get the chance to defend us . . .

She turned onto her side and forced her eyes shut.

Got to get some sleep. I still have a business to run. I hope.

Liz's eyelids sprang open, her gaze falling on the clock sitting atop her bedside cabinet.

Three a.m.

Maybe a few shots of brandy would help, or Mother's Ruin?

Forget it—sleep!

Managing to empty her mind, Liz drifted, but her haunted dreams about dead family members, her parents and floods of blood kept waking her often until her alarm chimed at seven o'clock.

She threw the duvet back, got out of bed and grabbed a shower.

I can get the girls to help me set up the bar for morning trade, she thought, getting out of the shower and dressing.

After breakfast, with the pub ready for its first customers of the day, Liz set a smile on her face and reassured herself that everything would be okay.

And then *he* walked in.

Liz couldn't put her finger on it, but the man's searching, quizzical looks and the way in which he scrutinized the premises set her on edge.

He seems angry. The way his jaw's set...

She could tell his smile was synthetic when he approached the bar.

"Are you the landlady?" he asked.

The question froze her insides.

He's trouble, her mind screamed. *Definitely.*

Liz didn't let her smile falter. She nodded. "How can I help you Mr, err?"

"Oh, er . . . Hengroth, Jim Hengroth."

"And *what* can I do for you?"

"Any chance I could get a coffee first?"

Liz was uncertain about leaving him alone in the bar. His shiftiness made her uncomfortable. "Would you like to take a seat? I'll bring it over to you."

"No, I'll have it here at the bar if that's okay. I have some questions I'd like to ask."

"Very well. Give me two minutes." She smiled, exposing her teeth, and walked out to the back room to put the kettle to boil.

From where she stood, Liz could see into the bar area—he was moving around. Snooping.

Who the hell is he? And what does he want? Maybe he's with Tokyo . . . Her gaze fell on the large knife that lay on the work surface. *Kill him. Get it over and done with.*

About to poke her head into the bar and call him into the back room, she stopped herself. *Get information from him first. Size him up.*

Something's definitely off with him, I can sense it.

"Awful business about Twin Jesters," he called.

Liz almost dropped the mug she'd prepped with coffee and milk. The teaspoon clattered against the china as she placed it inside. She raised her voice over the grumbling of the kettle. "Sorry, what did you say?"

"Killings, I've been told. You've not heard?"

"No, nothing. What's happened?"

"Oh. The police and army have the place sealed off, by all accounts—a spate of murders, or something. Still, you can't believe everything you hear, right, Miss . . .?"

"Please, call me Liz." She re-entered the bar and placed his mug of coffee on the counter.

"How much?"

"Two pounds, please." Liz ran the purchase through the till.

He handed her a two-pound coin.

"You didn't come here to tell me that, I'm sure." She managed a false laugh, hoping it didn't sound forced.

He eyed her. "Of course not. I was making polite conversation."

Not your everyday, run-of-the-mill type of chit-chat, she thought, reaching a hand around her back and feeling the knife she'd tucked down the rear of her jeans. *Just in case . . .*

"Have you seen this man before? He may have called in for a drink at some point last week," Jim said, putting a photo down on the bar and sliding it across to Liz. He picked his coffee up and looked at her over the mug's rim.

Liz grabbed the frozen image of a well-groomed man and held it close to her face.

Certainly looks like someone we had for supper the other night. "No," she lied, maintaining her composure. "Who is he?"

"He was a well-respected private investigator by the name of Sam Enrich. I was told he was looking into this place."

"*Why?*"

"I'd rather not say at this point, Liz."

"Well, I can honestly say I've never seen this man in—"

"Okay." He smiled, placing his coffee down.

"I'm not sure what this is all about, or what it has to do with *me, Jim.*" Liz stepped back and folded her arms across her chest.

"This—"

"Are you with the police?"

"No, I told you—the newspaper. Like I said, your pub was mentioned in a scoop I'm working on."

"Oh? And?"

"Like I said, it doesn't matter. For now. I came here hoping you'd have something to tell me."

He was annoying her with his vagueness and silly, round-the-mulberry-bush questions. More so, she could detect he was enjoying himself. She growled inwardly, and the coolness of the knife against her skin was calling.

No, I can't. I need to know what this man's all about. Besides, the bastard's only here to needle me. To make me slip up. Be on guard.

"I honestly have nothing to tell you, sorry." She relaxed her stance and let her arms dangle at her sides. "If an unknown face such as this,

this *Sam* walked in here, then I would have remembered him."

"Even with *all* the customers you must get?"

"Yes. Most are regulars. It's a pub in a small village, Jim."

He drained his mug and set it down gently. He had a wry smile on his face. "You seem rattled, Liz. Have I said something to upset you?"

"No. I just don't like being threatened or accused."

"Excuse me? I only—"

"I think you should leave and take this with you." She slid the photo back across the bar. "Don't come here again, please."

He placed the photo in the breast pocket of his jacket. "Thanks for your time and coffee." Jim gave her a final smile and left.

* * *

On the street, he reached for the black shades in his pocket and slipped them on. He was amused.

She's definitely hiding something, Owen. You will be pleased when I tell you.

After his conversation with his star employee, Jim had decided to come here after work and do some snooping himself, to see if he too could unearth some dirt.

He walked down the street to his car, getting behind the wheel.

I may not have any evidence for Owen, but she sure the hell was rattled.

Jim started his car.

Maybe I'll come back tonight, once I've heard from Owen and know he's got off in Twin Jesters.

Yes, he liked that idea.

I think it's time to get my camera out, step from behind my desk and act as a true journo again.

He pulled his Ford away from the curb and headed back to his office.

Chapter 7
Now

Owen heard their harsh, raspy breathing and low snarls mocking him from the shadows as they gave chase. They weren't racing after him, although it felt like it. They were teasing him, much like a cat does with a mouse.

He dared not stop, not even to wipe the stinging sweat from his eyes. His only hope was to push forward and make it back beyond the border of Twin Jesters.

They may not wander that far from their town...

Owen's mind was a scrambled mess.

The sound of rushing blood pounded the inside of his ears. He coughed, stumbled and staggered over a small stone bridge with parapets lined with flowers. On the opposite side of the humpbacked structure, a warm glow spilled from a large edifice looming in the darkness. A low hubbub of chatter and laughter floated on the air.

"Goin' to rip your gutssss out, ssssnoop..." a snake-like voice said from just behind.

"Argh-*ugh*!" he cried, holding a hand out towards the pub.

Tears threatened.

Owen stumbled again but stayed upright.

His laptop carry case and camera bag slapped his back as he continued at a jog. He took a fleeting glance over his shoulder, spotting their red eyes that stood out in the darkness like burning match heads, and tripped over his feet. He didn't go down. Instead, he rushed headlong down the other side of the bridge and slammed into the pub's side wall. He bounced off it with force and flopped to the ground.

More hissing from the shadows got him moving.

He didn't see them advancing.

I thought they'd stay—

Owen got to his feet, and a rock sailed from out of nowhere, missing him by centimetres. The projectile ricocheted off the floor and rattled out of sight. He didn't have time to think about it, as a shower of stones rained down on him. He covered his face with his arms, but it was no use—the rocks struck his head, arms and shoulders. One cut his cheek, another hit him in the eye and a third split his bottom lip.

Yelling, Owen ran for the pub's main entrance. Rocks continued to pelt against the wooden tables and chairs, walls and ground as he entered.

He crashed through the door and slammed it closed, then collapsed against it.

His actions brought the roaring pub to a graveyard silence. People ceased talking and laughing; men playing pool looked up and stared, mouths open, whilst darts missed the dartboard; the landlord stopped drawing a pint.

"Jesus!" Owen managed between sharp intakes of breath. His eyes were running. *Don't—* He shook his head, unable to finish the sentence. *Keep quiet. I don't want to be carted off to a mental hospital.*

"Brandy," he told the owner. "Make it a double-double, Rodney."

"You been out there chasing 'em big, wild cats of yours again, Owen?" he asked, drawing a hearty laugh from the barflies and the men playing darts.

A laugh hitched in Owen's throat as he wiped his face clean with the sleeve of his coat. Blood mixed with snot, smearing the fabric down to the cuff. "Something . . . like that . . ." he managed, his breathing coming back under control.

Pool balls began clacking; darts thumped at their black, red, and green beds.

"You okay, matey?" a man at the bar asked, turning on his stool to look at Owen.

He nodded. "Fine, thanks. I took a tumble on my way here."

His hands shook, and it took both to grab his drink from Rodney. The ice cubes clattered against the tumbler's rim, bringing to mind ships caught in a storm. The fiery liquid was in danger of sloshing over.

"You positive you're okay, Owen?" Rodney asked.

"A little shaken," he reassured him. "I went down pretty hard, banging my knees and elbow."

He winced, making it look as convincing as possible. He even grimaced as he hobbled to a corner table, out of sight, out of mind. "A couple of hits of your finest Eight Bells and I'll be as right as rain. You'll see."

Rodney shrugged and went back to serving his punters.

The chatter and laughter hit their zenith by the time Owen sat down and got comfortable. His camera bag, laptop case and weatherproof jacket lay by his side.

Shit—my phone! He took another deep breath, realizing he must've lost it during his mad dash to safety. Not that it mattered. The damn thing wouldn't have had a signal anyway. He'd hardly got a bar while in Twin Jesters.

Before reaching for the laptop, he drained the glass of half its contents and set the brandy to one side. He gasped, sighed and wiped his mouth. On the table was a glass tube housing a candle which was burnt down to a stump. It offered little light. A faint smell of jasmine rose from it.

The wallpaper was drab and uninspiring, and in the spots where it had peeled off to reveal the bare wall, damp had taken hold. Still, the place was warm—a safe haven—and Rodney was someone Owen had known for years. If need be, he could spend the night, no questions asked.

Owen guzzled the last of the brandy and ordered another.

"Run me a tab, Rod, please."

"Sure thing, Owen."

He took his drink back to his table, hands no longer shaking, and sat down. Placing his glass on a coaster, he took his laptop case and unzipped it. He removed his mobile PC, opened it and switched it on.

The battery was full.

Good, it'll need it.

With his laptop set up, he turned to the carry case and dug out a pile of handwritten notes, files, a pad and pen. He also removed the memory card from his camera and paused when his gaze crossed the backs of his hands. The skin had been torn off both sets of knuckles. Dried blood had crusted over the cuts. Ignoring this, he slipped the small plastic card into a port at the PC's side.

I may as well send the images. I don't think this can wait. Besides, if something should happen to me after I leave here, it'll be good to know my information has been passed on to Jim and Sam.

Owen opened a fresh Word document and took a large gulp of brandy, inhaling deep and exhaling noisily.

Where, and with whom, do I start? What about Twin Jesters itself? The people have a right to know about the town, about its checkered past . . . But is the violence and bloodshed relevant? Of course—it shows how cursed the place is. In that case, I'll start with Sam Enrich.

"Sam Enrich," he said aloud, making him recall the conversation he'd had with the private eye the week prior.

* * *

"Hello, this is Owen Figs, Bridgend News Post. How can I—*Sam*?" Owen smiled into the phone.

"I need your help, Owen."

"Okay, if I can. What's on your mind? You don't sound yourself. Is everything—"

"Dandy, mate," Sam cut him off. "I'm looking for information to help me with a job I'm on."

Owen slid his legs off his desktop, sat up and huddled closer to the phone. "This wouldn't have anything to do with Twin Jesters, would it?" he whispered into the receiver.

"How—?" Sam stammered. "Doesn't matter. Yes, possibly. They've put you on it?"

"Yes, I'm looking into it. Strange, don't you think?"

"Very. Do you believe the grapevine?"

"And what would that be, Sam?"

Sam laughed. "Look, you scratch my back and I'll scratch yours. Deal?"

"Depends . . ."

"What will it take to get you up off your arse and out there with your camera?"

"You think I'm crazy enough to go there?" Owen replied; his voice pitched. "The police have the town sealed off. It's a no-go area. I'd be arrested on sight."

"Then what the hell have you been doing? You're supposed to be a ball-busting journo."

"Sure—talking to eyewitnesses, the police . . ."

"Oh, really? I suppose you know the army is planning to bomb Twin Jesters?"

"What?" Own sat bolt upright. His colleagues turned to look at him; the hubbub in the office died.

"You heard," Sam grunted. "In the next week or so, they're sending in a team of soldiers to try and eradicate the problem. If not, bombs away."

"Don't be crazy, man."

"You're talking to the best damn snoop there is, friend. I have contacts everywhere, and I paid good money for this information. Now I need some from you."

Owen's hands shook. "What?" he choked out; voice barely audible.

"I need you to get into the town and confirm the problem's existence, Owen. With photographic proof."

"Why?"

Sam hesitated a long string of moments before responding, "Because I believe the problem has spread to another town close by. Like I told you, I'm working a case, and I think it coincides with Twin Jesters. My client seems to think there's something strange going on at a pub by the name of The Lamb and Flag. I've confirmed it. If this truly does connect with Twin Jesters, then we could be sitting on something huge."

Owen chewed his lower lip in trepidation. "Okay, you've got my attention. Tell me more."

"Remember the incidents in Bridgend many years ago? The ones involving the cannibals?"

Owen almost laughed. "No!"

"Then I suggest you look it up, connect the dots."

"But—"

"We've wasted enough time talking. I've got a pub to visit. Research Bridgend's history and seek out the murderers they used to call the 'Man-Eating Fucks'. When you do, get back to me *after* you've been to Twin Jesters."

"I—"

The line cut to a dial tone. Grimacing, Owen dropped the phone back on the hook.

A day after the call with Sam, Owen had a meeting with Jim Hengroth, his boss and head editor at the Bridgend News Post. Jim was a good man and a blessing to work for, the hands-on sort of boss who wouldn't expect anything of anyone that he wouldn't do himself. Owen had needed his advice.

After he told him in confidence what the PI had said, Jim answered, "You're my top reporter, Owen. I'd hate to see you go out there on a whim. Nobody knows for sure what's going on inside Twin Jesters. Do you really want to risk your career—hell, your life! —for hearsay?"

Owen smiled. "Isn't that what we do?"

"I suppose, but this is different. This is outright dangerous."

"If I don't live for the scoop, then what's the point of living?"

Jim chuckled. "I guess you're right, and I won't stop you. You know that. After all, I have a business to run." He clapped Owen on the shoulder with a huge, weatherworn and scuffed hand.

"Thanks, Jim. I'll be careful, promise."

* * *

Owen took another swig of brandy.

"You're going to be one ecstatic snoop when you receive my email, Sam. You too, Jim," he thought aloud as he swirled the remainder of the drink in his glass, then finished it off and shouted for another. The warm-bodied drink helped deaden the pain in his face, body and hands—especially his hands, which were hard at work typing an email to the private eye.

* * *

Dear Sam,

You were right. Merciful God, were you right! It's true. All of it—every last blood-soaked detail from the past to present regarding the Man-Eating Fucks. But there's more, much more, and only you, the government and I know exactly what's going on at Twin Jesters. However, we'll change that. I have the proof you need attached to this email.

Upon escaping Twin Jesters, I was followed to the town's borders by the Fuckers, as they've been so grossly named. They almost got me, but I managed to make it to safety, to a pub I know. Still, I fear they are lurking outside, waiting to tear the flesh from my bones and the organs from my body.

I may wait it out here until daylight. The landlord is a friend.

This danger is also the reason why I've decided to email you from my current position. I don't want to die without someone else knowing the truth. After I've sent this, I plan to communicate with my editor, whose contact details can be found at the bottom of this correspondence.

You may want to speak with Jim should something happen to me.

Before I go into what happened at Twin Jesters, I need to tell you what I know about the Man-Eating Fucks and the town itself, for Twin Jesters is steeped in a bloody, violent past.

First, the name: Twin Jesters is an odd name for a town, isn't it? There's a reason for that. And the place is hardly a town—before the evacuations, some 452 people lived there, and now less than half remain. It's said that fifty or sixty of the escapees are in critical condition and won't last the week. But I digress. Let's get to the history of the place.

The town didn't exist until after the Roman garrison departed the isle in 410. At the time, Wales was divided into a number of separate kingdoms, the largest being Gwynedd in northwest Wales, and Powys in the east. Glywysing, or Glamorgan (Morgannwg) as we know it today, was a much smaller kingdom in modern Gloucester, ruled over by King Glywys.

According to twelfth century sources, after King Glywys died, his kingdom was divided into seven cantrefs, and each of his sons received one. These were a form of medieval Welsh land divisions, often ruled jointly by the head of the family or sometimes treated as appanage subkingdoms.

This is where it gets really intriguing, Sam. I never knew so much about Welsh history until I started digging.

Pawl, son of Glywys, settled in the cantref named after him (Penychen), and built a castle there. The land held great economic potential, and Pawl sought to develop it into a market and farming town. Construction was finished in the year 510. He named the new settlement after his twin jesters, Ddu and Coch, which translates to Black and Red. I can only assume their names were derived from the colours they wore.

This pair didn't look like your typical clowns of the day. Most jesters of that era wore brightly coloured costumes comprised of bells, tassels and three-pointed cloth hats. They looked gaudy and told jokes. Not these two. In the scant records that mention them, they are depicted as looking sinister. Even though it was the medieval period, and everything was ghastly and frightful, this pair took the biscuit.

Their black and red costumes were meant to evoke terror and blood. They both wore half-masks similar to the one made famous in The Phantom of the Opera, and the halves were said to interconnect when the two were placed together. On the exposed sides of their faces, black daubs of make-up shrouded their eyes, and white make-up was applied over their lips to give the impression their mouths were full of razor-sharp teeth.

Their make-up is worth commenting upon. With modern cosmetics, their look can be achieved with ease, but in the year 510, it was quite a feat.

The two men were said to be brutally strong. When they weren't in costume, they went about bare-chested, exposing tattoos that snaked around their torsos. And instead of a marotte with a carved, smiling head on it, they carried shrunken human heads impaled on a spike.

There was nothing funny at all about the jesters. They looked more like executioners than clowns.

* * *

Owen stopped typing and pulled away from his laptop.

His brandy sat untouched. He picked it up and took a small sip, starting to feel light-headed. Replacing the glass on the coaster, he sorted through the files at his side and fished out the blown-up image of Ddu and Coch.

A fresh shiver ripped a path down his back.

He resumed typing.

* * *

There's hardly any information to be found on the jesters. I don't even know if they were real twins. All I do seem to know, which I've taken from history books and the local mythos, is how they came into Pawl's care, what they did, and their fate.

By all accounts, Pawl was a generous and sympathetic ruler. He is said to have found the twins in the wilds just outside the settlement that would become Twin Jesters. At the time, Ddu and Coch were youths, and Pawl, thinking them to be orphans, took them in and raised them as his own.

Then, one night, for reasons which have since been lost to history, the twins are believed to have gone on a killing spree. In the span of three nights, the pair is said to have slaughtered half the town's population. Among their victims was Pawl himself. Grisly as the murders were, the killings had been conducted in such a way that conclusive evidence could not be raised against the twins. Furthermore, a desire among the ruling class to sweep things under the rug helped ensure the twins would not be brought to justice.

Clwyd, Pawl's cousin, was next to rule over Penychen, which meant that the youths fell to his care. There was peace over the next ten years, though the town never fully recovered from the massacre. A curse had descended upon Twin Jesters.

Crops fared worse from season to season until eventually the yields were not enough to support the population. Each generation of calf was thinner than the previous, until at last the livestock failed to produce live births. Calves emerged stillborn from their mothers' wombs.

Eventually, the town came to be shunned. People wouldn't go near the place for fear of the curse attaching to them.

It was not long before trouble struck again.

Over the course of a week, there had been a rash of house fires that had resulted in several deaths. The guilty parties were never identified. This was going on amid mysterious infant deaths— children as young as the newly born were found murdered in their baskets where they slept, their throats cut. The terrified villagers demanded justice, which came swiftly enough. Just as tensions were approaching a boil, Ddu and Coch were caught in the act of starting a barn fire. In the minds of the townspeople, evidence of the twins' recent crime was enough to make them responsible for the previous arson attacks as well. In addition, the depravity of their offenses made it a foregone conclusion that they must also have been responsible for the infant murders.

With the evidence stacked against them, the twins were summarily declared guilty of their crimes. Clwyd ordered their deaths by hanging in the town square. Their bodies hung from the gallows for a week, at which point they were cut down and their heads were impaled on pikes with a message nailed to their foreheads:

Dyma beth sy'n digwydd i lofruddiaethwyr
(This is what happens to murderers)

Sam, I must digress for a moment and bring us back to the present.
I think the Man-Eating Fucks have somehow summoned the ghosts of Ddu and Coch, but I don't know why . . .

Chapter 8
Now

Owen relaxed in his seat, expelled air through his nostrils in a noisy fashion, ran his hands through his hair and picked up where he'd left off.

* * *

I think the Man-Eating Fucks have somehow summoned the ghosts of Ddu and Coch, but I don't know why they would do such a thing. To become more powerful? To dominate? So many questions I'll never have answered . . .

Anyway, I'm detracting again.

Ddu's and Coch's heads remained on the spikes until their flesh, eyes and tongues had been pecked away by carrion birds, until at last the bone weathered, cracked and fell apart.

But even in death, the village would not be free of the jesters' curse.

Almost as soon as the twins' rotted remains hit the earth, the town was beset by all manner of disasters: swarms of rats, floods, disease, famine—death. Not even Clwyd, who had ordered the jesters' executions, was safe from the curse. Within months, he was found dead, his severed head impaled on a pike.

The string of disasters proved to be too much for the townsfolk to bear, and the village of Twin Jesters was ultimately abandoned. It remained that way until the tenth century, when Gruffydd ap Llywelyn used the ghost town as a garrison during his conquests against the English, and later, his home. Legend has it that he chose to settle here after a vision in which he beheld a pair of jesters who persuaded him that the town would be the site of a great victory.

He saw it as a blessing, Sam.

A fucking charm, of sorts.

Gruffydd ap Llywelyn had thought he'd been touched by God.

Goddamn idiot!

When I looked into Gruffydd's life, I turned up some interesting information you won't find in most history books. The official story is that Gruffydd allied himself with lfgar, son of Leofric, Earl of Mercia, who had been deprived of his earldom of East Anglia by Harold Godwinson and his brothers. They marched to Hereford and did battle against a force led by the Earl of Hereford, Ralph the Timid. Gruffydd destroyed them, then sacked the city and crushed its motte-and-bailey castle. Shortly afterwards, lfgar was restored to his earldom and a peace treaty was concluded.

What the historians won't tell you, however, is that two jesters were often seen on the battlefields helping Gruffydd and his army defeat the opposition. Wherever the jesters were spotted, the battlegrounds were always a scene of great bloodshed, even by medieval standards.

By 1056, Gruffydd had seized full control over Morgannwg and Gwent, along with extensive territories along the border with England. After another victory at Glasbury, the English finally recognized his sovereignty as the King of Wales. Gruffydd then returned to Twin Jesters to rule over his newly acquired dominions.

By this time, though, Gruffydd was a changed man. The town—or perhaps the influence of its jesters—was turning him into an overconfident warmonger. All he could see was power. Gruffydd was blinded by it, and through his victories, he'd started believing his own hype.

Some five years after establishing his rule, Gruffydd received another vision from the jesters. Following their advice, he reached an agreement with Edward the Confessor, but the death of his ally lfgar in 1062 left Gruffydd vulnerable once again. In late 1062, Harold Godwinson obtained the king's approval for a surprise attack on Gruffydd's court at Rhuddlan. The general consensus is that Gruffydd was warned of the attack in time and escaped out to sea before he could be captured, but that's a lie. Gruffydd was slain at Twin Jesters during Harold's surprise attack, his head impaled on a pike in the town square. With his death, the land of Wales fell and was annexed into England.

The rest is history, as the kids say.

People will believe what's been recorded in books, of course, but local Welsh historians will tell you otherwise. And, from what I've witnessed tonight in Twin Jesters, I believe the rumours, Sam. I'm not easily spooked, but I'm positive on this one and I hope I can convince you.

Others, too.

There's darkness at work here. Twin Jesters is cursed by Ddu and Coch, who still roam, their reign of terror unending after Gruffydd's death.

Harold Godwinson, who orchestrated the attack on Gruffydd, died in Pawl's castle at Twin Jesters. He was murdered, his body mutilated nearly beyond recognition.

The town was destroyed in a massive fire one hundred years after Harold Godwinson's conquests. It lay in ruins for two centuries, then was rebuilt by a businessman who sought to exploit the surrounding natural resources. The atrocities started back up again: murders, rapes, plagues, deaths . . . The jesters' doings? I think so. There are reams of blood-drenched stories about the place the historians all disregard as local myths.

You're probably wondering why I'm telling you all this. Tonight, with my own two eyes, I saw the fools of yesteryear, and I believe they've brought the threat you spoke of to Twin Jesters, a town that's seen peace, bar for the odd incident here and there, for the past five hundred years.

Why has it started again? While I can only guess, here goes:

This year, 2080, marks the town's anniversary of being the oldest in South Wales. The townspeople have begun celebrating with street parties, fun and games. Even the local brewers got in on the action by brewing a new beer for the festivity: Weeping Fools.

Plus, the restoration of Pawl's castle has been completed.

When two jesters turned up for a party, one wearing black, the other red, nobody suspected a thing—that is, until the killing started.

A few days ago, I spoke to one of the survivors, a Mr James Gogwin, who's currently laid up in the hospital with minor injuries. He told me the week leading up to the festival, which had been planned to span from late Friday evening through to Monday afternoon, was "pleasant and peaceful. Nothing seemed out of the ordinary.

"It was your average working week," he continued. "When Friday rolled around and the party kicked off, everything ran smoothly. And then, on Saturday afternoon, as people took to the streets to continue enjoying their town's activities, a pair of fools strolled into Twin Jesters with a bunch of naked people caked in mud and leaves. They looked like feral cave-dwellers."

I didn't have to push Mr Gogwin for answers.

"At first, we stood about, laughing and joking, thinking the jesters had been hired by someone

from within the community. We didn't think anything of it, you know? The nakedness was inappropriate because there were small children present, but I thought it was part of some strange act. Besides, you couldn't really see their privates—the filth and greenery hid their modesty. They were led by these clowns, who were juggling flamin' daggers whilst riding unicycles. When they themselves got closer—and I don't mind telling you this—I almost soiled myself."

Before I could ask why, Mr Gogwin continued.

"They were . . . dead—behind the eyes, I mean. There was no colour to their faces, even though they wore make-up. The laughter all around me turned to gasps. The children started sobbing, screaming and pointing as the jesters snarled and snapped their teeth, which looked like needles; hundreds upon thousands of needles, all stained red. Then they started throwing their burning blades. Mrs Salls, who was standing next to me holding her granddaughter to her chest, caught two daggers in her eyeballs, which exploded like water balloons. A third, fourth, fifth and sixth thunked into Olivia, the child, pinning her to her grandmother as she wailed, bled and burned. Pandemonium ensued. A stampede erupted as burning bodies hit the ground one after another: men, women, children . . . When the jesters ran out of knives, they unleashed the cave-dwellers, who started attacking people by . . . eating them. Flesh, tongues and eyes were torn from p-people. Their skin . . . devoured—"

Here, Mr Gogwin broke down, refusing to speak further. I had to find others willing to open up, thinking it would be easy, but most refused, except for a young widow, a Ms Peterson, who'd come face-to-face with the "cave-dwellers."

"I wouldn't call them cave-dwellers," she told me. "They looked more like cannibalistic freaks to me—things that live deep in the woods or underground. They snatched my Lilly from my hands"—Lilly was Ms Peterson's six-year-old daughter— "and tore the flesh from her face. One of them ripped her leg off—it took me days to . . . wash her blood from my—my hair."

I didn't want to push her, but she continued once she'd composed herself and stopped crying.

"There were loads of them—fifty or sixty. Maybe a hundred. I don't really know. The streets became chaos, and I found myself ankle-deep in bloody water that had body parts, organs and party food floating on it. It was like something out of a horror film. When I got to the town's border, I saw the police arriving—they had a helicopter in the sky. I was told by others that the army would eventually turn up, but I'm not sure."

After getting all I could from Ms Peterson, I went to the police station for more information but didn't turn up much—they were tight-lipped about the whole thing. They also denied the army's involvement, even as they escorted me off the premises. I was lucky to escape their clutches with my camera, notepad and laptop.

* * *

Owen stopped typing, his fingers aching. As he sipped his drink, he read through the email, making sure all information was present and correct.

"Another, Owen?" Rodney yelled over.

He looked up, startled, and shook his head. "I'm feeling dizzy."

That roused a few titters from the men propping up the bar.

Owen ignored them and went back to his PC.

* * *

These "cave-dwellers" are your "Man-Eating Fucks," Sam. I found pictures of them in old newspaper clippings at the library. Do you think the jesters brought the tribe back to life? What if they can't be stopped? Are there more? Maybe the jesters conjured up a new clan of Man-Eating Fucks based on the history they know about Bridgend?

Whichever may be the case, you were right about us sitting on something huge!

Don't bother returning my email, Sam, as I want to speak with you face-to-face. I need to get everything straight and down on tape if I'm going to write about it in the paper, though I might leave out the part about seeing ghosts.

Having said that, I could mention them and say that someone could be masquerading as Ddu and Coch—that a couple of local nutters want people to believe the history. Then again, do I want a straitjacket as an early Christmas present? No, leaving the jesters out is for the best.

Anyhow, I need to tell you about what happened at Twin Jesters tonight.

* * *

Again, Owen stopped typing.

Maybe I'll have that brandy after all, Rodney, he thought.

He got the barman's attention and asked for a double.

"A double-double?" he called back.

"Please, Rodney," Owen said, voice wavering, and he failed to see the rotund landlord walk over and clamp a meaty hand to his shoulder.

"Are you fine there, lad?" Rodney asked.

"Ye—"

"I've never seen you this . . ."

"This what?" Owen's guts knotted and he feared they would fall out of his anus if he didn't clench.

"Like—like you've seen a ghost. You're as white as a sheet, Owen."

"It's nothing—"

"You never put brandy away as you're doing this evening. Is something troubling you? Is *someone* giving you trouble?"

Owen shook his head, took his drink and swigged a mouthful. "I promise you, everything's okay."

"Well, if there *is* anything I can help with, yell. You've been a loyal customer over the years, and I'd hate to see anything bad happen to you."

He gave a half-hearted smile, even though he was genuinely pleased by Rodney's concern. "Trust me, please."

The man nodded and lumbered to the bar. As Owen watched him go, he noticed some of the barflies looking in his direction. They were smirking.

Nosy fuckers.

Owen gave them an aloof, distasteful look before shaking his head and dropping it back to the laptop. His eyes travelled along the last few lines he'd written. He took a small hit of brandy and placed it to one side.

The shakes had subsided.

The ice-vipers that had nestled in his guts had melted and burned away.

He took a deep, shaky breath.

* * *

I have to admit, I wasn't going to go tonight, Sam. I saw it as a wild goose chase. Not only that, I was worried I'd get myself into a heap of shit. But hell, how could I not? I'm a journalist. A "hard-nosed" one at that, remember? In my twenty or so years of covering news stories for various papers, never, ever have I seen or heard of anything like I have tonight. Hell, I've never taken such a risk before.

I've wished for excitement, even thinking about moving to a large city—

Ah, I've gone off on a tangent again . . .

I went to Twin Jesters with an open mind, putting the eyewitness reports down to some sort of mass delirium or madness that had been contracted from a gas leak or virus that had wormed its way into the town. I even swept aside what you'd told me, Sam.

How wrong I was! I'm also glad I decided to pick up my reporting equipment and head out there—even if it ends up costing me my life.

The army are out there.

Or were, rather.

My first thought was to walk to Twin Jesters, but I decided against it last minute, thinking I might need a fast getaway. I'd almost laughed at that. The smile was soon wiped from my face when I was met by armed soldiers blocking the town's main entrance.

"This is a government zone now, sir—you'll have to turn around and go back," I was told. Normally I would have pushed, tried worming my way in with a silver-tongued response, but I felt threatened by the GI Joe wannabe, who had three others with him.

They loomed over me, Sam, and the one who'd spoken to me kept his hand on his holstered handgun the entire time. I didn't utter another word. Instead, I left and searched for another way in, but was met by the same resistance.

I had one option left: I ditched the car and used the night as camouflage. When someone wants to gain access to somewhere badly enough, they'll find a way. And so I crawled through a sewage pipe like a rat, popping up in the middle of Twin Jesters.

The lengths we go to . . .

* * *

A genuine laugh escaped Owen. It felt good, even though it attracted the attention of Rodney and the bar bozos. He gulped some brandy and avoided eye contact.

* * *

Even though the stench of shit was overpowering, I could still smell the charring of flesh, which is unmistakable to me as I worked four summers at my dad's crematorium when I was younger.

It was all around me, filling my nostrils.

Tears stung my eyes.

The heat within Twin Jesters was staggering.

Within seconds, my shirt matted itself to me and my forehead was like a burst dam from the sweat.

I shot to my feet, unloaded my camera, and started sneaking around. It didn't take long for me to locate bodies that had been burned by the army. Some were still alight; others were burned-out husks.

I feel sick thinking about it.

I'm not ashamed to say that I vomited all over a flaming corpse.

Hell, when I was being chased, I wet myself, and that's a hell of a thing for a grown man to admit. But I think anyone would have, had they come face-to-face with what I did.

After following a trail of scorched remains, I ran across the soldiers doing the burning. They were kitted out in suits that made them look as though they belonged on a space program, with flamethrowers in their hands and petrol tanks on their backs.

It was crazy.

There were five of them in total, and they were guarded by three soldiers brandishing automatic weapons.

Sounds like something out of a film, doesn't it?

Believe me, it's not. I was there, and I probably still smell to high heavens of human waste and smoked barbeque. That's probably why I'm getting such strange looks here at the pub.

Twin Jesters looked war-torn. Cars and buildings were riddled with bullet holes. I even saw a tank stalking the streets. Craziness.

Had I been caught, I fear I would have been shot on sight. Hell, if we go public with these pictures and stories, I could end up in jail. I'm not sure what scares me more: the fate of Bridgend as a whole, me dying, or being incarcerated for treason. They'll probably throw me in a deep, dark hole beneath London to rot.

If you don't hear from me in a day or so, make sure you get all this out there—don't let me die in vain.

Once I'd captured enough images of the soldiers participating in body-burning, I moved around the town as stealthily as possible. Where no soldiers roamed, the place was a ghost town— hollowed-out buildings and empty houses with smashed windows and missing doors. Some structures had even collapsed, spilling their bricks and mortar into the streets.

A cloying, thick-as-soup dust hung in the air and the multiple fires cast searing, wavering and bottomless shadows. I heard their snarls—the

Man-Eating Fucks'. I was terrified, Sam, but nothing could prepare me for the sight I was about to witness.

Towards the back of Twin Jesters, where the land runs out and a river cuts through, soldiers were digging a mass grave. Bulldozers were ploughing dead and burned bodies into it; there must have been fifty or sixty being dozed.

I've also included those photos.

Before the soldiers could finish burying the townspeople's remains, the Man-Eating Fucks attacked. They came out of the darkness all shadows and teeth, and tore through the military before they could react, let alone get a shot off.

In minutes, the bulldozer and digger sat idling, their drivers devoured. And when they were finished . . .

* * *

Owen grabbed his brandy and drank the remainder greedily. Some of it spilled out of his mouth and splashed into his lap.

* * *

. . .they were led into the heart of the town by Ddu and Coch.

I swear I saw them.

It wasn't a trick of light or anything such, Sam. They were there, with God as my witness, and they led the charge like a pair of demented dragoons minus their horses. I even took photos.

Ddu and Coch saw me, too, even though they stood at an impossible distance and I was shrouded in blackness. They pointed their fingers and let out a deafening cry, wail, screech—no human has ever produced a noise like that—which I took as a battle cry.

Blood trickled out of my ears and nose; the shout was that powerful.

And as I retreated, taking as many snaps as I could, I saw more and more Man-Eating Fucks spill out of the foliage at the backs of those advancing. It was as spectacular to watch as it was terrorizing.

I ran, screaming, with piss trickling down the legs of my jeans.

When I bumped into soldiers, they tried stopping me, but, by then, I was a gibbering, crying wreck.

They soon lost interest in me as shots rang out from behind.

Somewhere in Twin Jesters, a siren began to wail.

"Here they come!" someone bellowed.

More gunfire.

The reek of cordite was choking.

Before making a dash for the bridge at the town's edge, I stopped and looked back. The carnage was horrendous. The Man-Eating Fucks, which I could then see plainly, were hideously disfigured monsters. There's no other word for them, and seeing them in full fight, with blood, guts and gore decorating their chops and chests, was far-fetched, but I was witnessing it.

Flesh was torn away, along with privates and eyeballs.

And the screaming, Sam; God, the screaming—it'll haunt me forever.

When the remaining soldiers were torn through, the jesters and Man-Eating Fucks set their sights on me, and that's when I fled to this pub.

The jesters didn't follow. I had a gut feeling they wouldn't, but why? Are they trapped there?

How do we explain everything if nothing's found in Twin Jesters tomorrow morning? Will the bodies of the soldiers have disappeared? Will the government then level the place with bombs and explain it away as a gas leak or some such tripe?

Before I sent this email to you, I read through it and realized I waffled far too much, but I needed to tell someone all this. I was worried I'd take the knowledge to my grave.

Anyway, I'll be in contact soon.

Best,

Owen.

* * *

He packed away his laptop and camera, sucked the dregs out of his glass and returned it to the bar to settle his bill.

The barflies gave him a fleeting look.

Outside, Owen glanced at the bridge. His nutsack shrivelled and he pulled his coat's collar around his neck a bit tighter.

He heard their hisses and catcalls from beyond the darkness.

"Going to pull your tongue out through your arssse, sssnoop!"

The icy threat cut him to the marrow. He turned from the pub and made his way towards home.

Chapter 9
Then

*W*hen the police finally gave up searching the woods, we were free to go about our business. I would have been happy to stay put, but the mass hunt, and possible police reports, kept people out of the woods.*

No stray dog walkers. No campers. And no children playing. Not that many ventured this far . . .

It meant, once our food supply—which was good for a few months—ran out, we'd starve if nobody ventured out here.

Luckily, I already had a plan in place, but was forced into enacting it earlier than I'd hoped. I'd wanted the boys and Cerberus to grow that little bit older first.

I didn't let the lack of food allow me to hit the panic button immediately. No, we hunkered down, with the summer months ahead of us, and carried on as we were. In the daytime, I took one of the boys out hunting whilst the other looked after their sister.

We'd go looking, miles some days, for someone to kill and take back to our home. All our attempts proved useless, which started to worry me when we were down to a few weeks' worth of food.

"What will we do, Mama?" Tempest asked.

"We'll go on the blood and flesh of animals if we have to, boy. Only for a short while, until I can get my plan right in my head."

"But Mama, the animals don't come around here anymore . . ."

There was nothing I could say. He was right. Ever since I'd settled in with my babies and started eating human meat, killing and butchering what wildlife I could, the animal kingdom had seemed to sense death and danger. They'd fled the area.

Even the trees and shrubbery, for some strange reason, had wilted and not grown back. For four summers now, not a blade of grass, leaf or bush has blossomed. I can't remember the last time I heard a bird sing in the branches or saw a sly old fox sniffing around outside the cave looking for a piece of meat. When they did, they were easy pickings.

A slice of fox had been among Typhoon's favourite snacks as a baby.

Anyway, even if there were animals to eat, it wouldn't do. There's not enough on such small bodies to go around, and deer, sheep, horses and the like are rare out here.

No, it needed to be human.

Also, the boys craved it, now they'd been living off it the past few years.

There was nothing for it. My plan would have to be put into motion.

So, that night, I sat Tempest and Typhoon down and told them what would happen in the coming days.

* * *

Hydra, whilst nursing Cerberus, walked out of the cave in search of her boys. They were nowhere to be seen. A smile played across her face.

Boys will be boys, she thought, looking up at the trees to see if they were playing their monkey games.

Nothing.

Behind her, beyond the mouth of the cave and to the left, a campfire raged. Pots and pans filled with boiling meat sat atop a mesh wire above the flames—their supper.

"Tempest!" she called, giving it a couple of seconds before calling again. "Typhoon!" A minute or so passed. "Come on, boys. Your food's almost ready!"

Cerberus made small sounds.

"Don't make me come out there and get you. Do you *hear* me?!"

I hope they haven't ventured too far. I know how they get when they're playing...

"*Boys*?! Home. *Now!*"

Foliage rustled somewhere close by.

A twig snapped.

"Tempest? Typhoon?"

No reply.

Maybe it was too soon to allow them to go out wandering and playing. What if the police are still searching, but on a smaller scale?

Hydra knew she was letting her imagination get away from her.

"If you're trying to sneak up or scare me in any way, it's not going to work. Now, get in here or you're going to feel my wrath, damn it!"

She stepped farther from the cave, into the dying afternoon sunlight.

Laughter echoed in the distance.

"Typhoon? Tempest?"

When she heard the boys whoop and cheer, her heartrate settled. Even though she knew they were more than likely safe and capable of taking care of themselves, they were still young.

Anything could happen, but they have their father's blood coursing through them.

"Coming, Mama!" Tempest called.

"You're still *it* after food, Temp!" Typhoon shouted.

Hydra laughed. She'd taught the boys a handful of childish games last year when they'd complained of being bored. She didn't see why not. After all, why weren't they allowed a normal-ish childhood? They didn't have to hunt, kill and sharpen their skills all day, *every* day.

Maybe in Skull's day, she thought. The name brought a vivid image of the man to her mind and a longing to her heart and loins she thought would never fade. *No man will ever make me feel the way he did. The dominance, force and power he showed.*

"No, Ty. You have to stay *it*. You lost," Tempest argued back.

They leapt over logs, ducked low branches and smashed through bushes as they charged closer.

"Bang, bang. You're dead!" Tempest called over his shoulder, pointing a plastic gun at Typhoon. Hydra had found the weapon after killing a family in the woods a few months ago.

"Stop yap-yap-yapping and get your arses inside. *Now*!" Hydra demanded, removing the smile from her face. Even though she was amused by their antics, she still had to rule them. "I have something important to talk to you boys about after supper."

"What, Mama?" Tempest asked, his breath hitching.

"Never you mind now, boy. Get in there." She gave him a kick up the backside to get him moving. "You too, lad. Or do you want some too?" she asked Typhoon.

"No, Ma."

"Next time dinner's ready, you best both be closer to home so you can hear me, or Cerberus and I will be picking the meat off *your* bones!"

The boys scuttled inside with their tails between their legs.

Hydra allowed herself another smile before wiping it off and stepping inside behind them.

The boys kicked each other under the makeshift dinner table as they shovelled their mother's offering into their mouths.

"How many times do I have to tell you both? *Manners*!" Hydra slammed one hand down on the table whilst slapping Typhoon on the back of his head with the other and staring through Tempest. "And slow. Down. Do you want to choke? *Do* you?!" She gave the boy another smack.

"No, Mama."

"Good. Now get on with it."

They ate the remainder of their food in silence.

Twenty minutes later, with the last of their meals finished, Hydra called the boys to the fireplace outside where she sat nursing and feeding Cerberus.

"Come and sit by Mama, boys."

Still wary, Typhoon sat at a distance. Tempest, a little braver, settled himself close to Hydra. Neither boy spoke, keeping their heads lowered, their eyes fixed on the ground.

"We're moving." Hydra hadn't known where to start her pep talk, so she'd decided to be up front and blunt. They'd understand. They'd have to.

"Where, Mama?" Tempest asked.

"To my old house—"

"In the *real* world?!" Typhoon's eyes bugged.

"Yes, boy."

He gulped.

"But won't there be people there?" Tempest looked confused by his question.

Hydra nodded. She'd known this talk would come one day, and now that it was here, she was dreading having to spill the whole ugly truth. "Before I continue, there's something important I have to tell you, which won't change a thing between us, I promise. I'm only telling you because you have a right to know."

She saw the worry in their eyes. It killed her.

Her bottom lip trembled, so she bit it, keeping herself together. "I'm *not* your mother. Not your *real* mother, anyway."

Their mouths opened as Tempest and Typhoon looked at each other. Nobody said a thing, with the crackling fire filling the void.

An owl hooted.

"You can ask me—"

"Who *was* our mother?" Typhoon asked.

"A lady by the name of Eight-Ball. Skull—"

"You told us about them before. Said she was your sister," Tempest said.

"She was, sort of. I saw her as one."

"Skull was our *dad*?" Typhoon asked.

She nodded. "I don't want anything to change. I've brought you up as my own." Hydra thought the tears would come for sure now, but then the boys huddled closer and put their arms around her.

"You *are* our mother. And we love you."

"Agreed," said Tempest.

She hugged them furiously. "My real sister lives in my home with the man who used to be my husband."

"We will go and live with them?" Typhoon asked.

"Where is your house?" Tempest inquired.

"In a place called Twin Jesters. And no, we won't be living with them."

Before telling the boys her full plan, Hydra laid all her cards on the table, informing the boys of how she'd been captured by Eight-Ball and Skull. She didn't want any secrets. Not anymore.

They didn't bat an eyelid.

"Tell us what we will do, Mother," Typhoon said.

"We're going to go to the house and ask them to join us. If not, we'll kill them."

"Are there children?" Tempest asked.

Hydra nodded. "The same will happen to them. Tomorrow night, we'll leave for the place and do what we must. For now, no more questions. Go off and play. Enjoy the woods whilst you can."

The next day, Hydra cut up the last of the food, bagged it and gathered a large supply of water. Around six in the evening, she saddled the boys with their provisions, covered the entrance to the cave, removed the fire and cleaned away any trace of their presence. With Cerberus strapped to her back, she led her small tribe from their home and out of the woods. A long walk awaited them.

After a few hours of hiking, they bordered the edge of the woods and 'real' world, and so Hydra brought them to a stop.

"We rest for a while. Eat and drink, boys. Cerberus needs feeding, too."

"How far is the house after we leave here?" Typhoon asked.

"Another two or three hours of walking, son. We'll make plenty of stops."

"No need," Tempest said. "We're fit enough. Don't worry."

"I might need to feed your sister again."

Once Cerberus had finished her food, Hydra got them moving.

"We need to be careful in the open like this. Stay close, and in the shadows. Nakedness is not acceptable, and if someone should get close enough to see you—" She stopped herself from saying it. "Just do as I say."

The boys remained silent.

By the time they left the woods, it was past eleven p.m. The streets were deserted. Still, Hydra led them through side avenues and alleys as they pushed towards their destination.

Come midnight, Hydra found herself on her old street.

Not a jot of longing, remorse or nostalgia rattled around inside her brain, heart or guts as she stood face-to-wood with her front door. All she could think about was gaining control over the home. To take it by force, if need be.

How will he react to seeing me after all this time? Will he be terrified by my appearance?

Who gives a flying fuck? He's been nailing my younger sister!

She recalled when she'd found out about the betrayal as she raised her hand to hammer the door's knocker.

* * *

Days after Skull's death, Hydra, or Paula as she'd been called back then, had had a moment of clarity.

"I want to go home to Tony," she'd cried, huddled in a ball.

She'd been scared.

Her mind snapped back the other way: *If I had my medication, I'd be okay.*

During her moment of lucidity, Paula ventured out of the woods and found her way home, surprised by how easily she achieved it. After finding her old street, remembering which number she lived at, Paula went there, finding Tony standing outside the house.

Her heart swelled.

"Tony . . ." she whispered.

Close to her husband, getting out of a car, were her sons.

Paula smiled. Tears slid down her cheeks.

She held her arms out, ready to step from the shadows naked, filthy and bearing children, when she saw *her*, the woman who walked up behind her sons and put her arm around them like a loving mother.

A rage flared in Paula, for the woman was her sister.

"Fucking whore!"

How could he have—Maybe she's just helping—

And then the woman embraced Tony. They kissed. Everyone seemed happy.

They've already forgotten about me. I'm dead to them!

She'd known things had been on the rocks between her and Tony, but she never thought he didn't care.

Did he move that bitch in as soon as I was gone?

Paula hadn't known, but she'd intended to find out. One day.

* * *

I guess today's the day, she thought, finished slamming the knocker.

"Little pigs, little pigs . . ." she whispered. From somewhere inside, a light flicked on, and it shone through the panes of glass in the door.

"Who could it be at this hour?" a muffled voice said.

"I hope it's not the police," someone replied.

"You don't think Michael's been in trouble again, do you?"

A bolt unfastened.

Locks clicked and clacked.

The handle depressed.

A snarl-smile plastered itself across Hydra's face as she drew the knife from behind her back.

Cerberus continued to sleep against her cleavage.

"Look, if this is—*Jesus*!" Tony fell backwards, the door handle slipping from his grip.

Hydra put her foot over the threshold, pressing her toes against the cool wood. Thanks to the parting between the jamb and the door, she could see her husband crawling away from her on his arse by using his hands and feet.

She kicked the door in, the chain busting free. Brass links flew in all directions. "Honey, I'm home!"

"W-who are *you*?! Lucy, call the—*argh*!"

She stepped on his hand. Bones cracked. She smiled. "Don't you recognise me?"

"Tony? Tony? What's going—*fuck*!" Lucy turned tail and ran back upstairs.

By now, Tempest and Typhoon were inside with the door closed.

"Look after this piece of shit, sons, whilst I go and take care of the bitch."

"Yes, Mother."

"Don't hurt him. *Yet*. Drag his arse into the living room and gag him. I'll be right back."

Hydra un-strapped Cerberus from her chest, set the child down, and bounded up the stairs, taking them three at a time like some wild-eyed jungle cat, her knife clutched between her teeth.

Her hair flailed.

She growled.

"Hello—" was all Lucy had time to say before Hydra stormed into the master bedroom and punched her sister in the jaw. Lucy's head snapped sideways. Spittle and blood spattered the curtains and duvet.

"Sleep tight, whore."

Hydra dragged the woman onto the landing. Once there, she checked the boys' rooms. Michael wasn't there—his bed was still made. Daniel, however, was sleeping.

Hydra decided to leave him. For now.

She grabbed her sister by the ankles and pulled her downstairs.

By the time she reached the sitting room, the boys had tied Tony to a chair and were beating his knees with a couple of rolling pins they'd found.

"Okay, you can stop."

Tony was gagged. Tears streamed down his face. His eyes bulged and the veins in his neck protruded as he screamed beneath his gag.

"Boys, tie this pig-fucking cunt up," Hydra said, pointing towards Lucy but not taking her eyes off Tony. "If I remove your gag, do you promise to be a good boy and keep quiet?"

He sat motionless.

"Nod if yes. Well?"

He finally nodded.

Hydra put a hand to the knot in the rag and was about to undo it. "You're sure I can trust you? Because if not, I'll have my boys kick you about the room until there's nothing left of you."

He nodded again.

"Very well." Hydra removed the obstruction and threw it to one side. "Don't you know who I am?"

"Some crazy fucking bitch I'm going to kill if I ever get—*argh*!" he cried when she twisted his balls in a vice-like grip.

"Be nice, or the same applies . . ."

"Okay, I'm sorry. I'll be ni—*Paula*?!" He stared at her, eyes bugging, mouth open.

"*Finally*. How about a kiss?" She threw her head back and laughed.

"My sis—*oof*!" Lucy cried as one of the boys punched her in the guts.

"That's enough, Tempest. Where's Michael?"

"At a friend's. I thought you were dead! Lucy and I—"

"Spare it. I don't care. I gave up on you, the boys, my family and the real world years ago. I have a new life. One you *can* be a part of, if you want. Lucy, too. I'll even allow you access to my cunt," she said, rubbing a hand between her legs and thrusting her hairy snatch towards him.

To her surprise, he didn't look away.

"You won't hurt us?"

Hydra shook her head. "Cross my heart..." She took one of her filth-encrusted fingers and made an *X* in the dirt on her chest. ". . . And hope to die." She smiled and bent close to her ex-husband. "What do you say?"

He turned his face from her and nodded. "Okay. What do you want us to do?"

"*Argh*!" Lucy screamed. "He does not—"

Hydra nodded to Tempest, who planted his huge fist into the woman's stomach, stealing her air.

"Best keep my cunt of a sister in line, or I'll cut her into tiny sections and feed her to you. *Comprende*?"

"She'll be good. Don't harm her, please. I can help you more than you think, Paula, I'm sure."

Hydra had Tempest stand down. "Paula is dead. It's Hydra now. And what do you mean?"

"First, tell me what you have in mind with Lucy, the boys and me."

She eyed him with caution. *If he thinks he can worm his way out of this somehow, he's sadly mistaken.* "You mean *my* sons," she said.

"Jason is *ours*. Mine and Lucy's."

"Who? I didn't see another boy upstairs."

"He's sleeping in his basket by my bed."

"Interesting . . ." she said more to herself. "We'll get to that. What I want is for you and Lucy to move to my old home in the woods and fuck like rabbits. We need more numbers for this clan of ours. I'll live here with the children, and, as the normal ones grow into adults, they'll be sent into the world to fend for themselves and help continue the growth of the tribe. They'll never, *ever* forget who or what they are."

"You want them to live as woods-like people in the real world?" Tony asked.

"It's their best way of survival and continuing the family. Now, will you join us, or do I butcher you both and take everything anyway?" She stuck her tongue out and placed it against his jawbone. Hydra then dragged it up his face, slowly, before removing it.

He gagged but nodded.

Hydra looked at her sister, who whimpered and settled.

"I should rip your cunt off and shove it down your throat," she whispered. "You're so lucky I need you."

"I said we'll do it. There's no need—"

"What's this help you can provide me with?"

He took a deep breath, let it out and sighed. "There's a cult in town dedicated to your tribe—family," he corrected himself. "They think people don't know about them, but a few of us do. They go off into the woods every full moon and do God knows what to try and raise your dead ones. I'm assuming that's who snatched you? The cannibals?"

Now it was her turn to nod. He'd caught her by surprise.

"I'm sure they'd be willing to help you— *us*!"

"What makes you so sure?"

"Because I'm good friends with their leader."

Hydra stood, smiling. "Is that so?"

Tony nodded.

"I want you to bring him here, now. *Tonight.* We have things to discuss."

Chapter 10
Then

The man before her, Tony Adrian Harris, had been her husband for many years. And, until recently, Hydra hadn't known he'd been fucking her sister behind her back for almost their entire relationship.

Her marriage had been a sham.

Bitch always had to have everything I had, or try and go one better, Hydra thought, glaring at Tony and Lucy, who were tied back-to-back. She felt nothing for them.

No, that was a lie—she felt *hungry* for them. And it was a good thing he was able to help in a way that sounded like music to her ears: a chance to grow the clan numbers in mass amounts.

"I'm sure he'll come here tonight, if you'll allow me to use the phone, Paula?"

She slapped him so hard across the face she thought his teeth were going to fly out of his mouth. "I won't tell you again. Paula is dead."

"Jesus *Christ*! I'm sorry. Don't—"

"Don't even think about telling me 'don't', Tony. Those days are gone, you piece of fucking shit."

"I'm so sorry, P—*Hydra*," Lucy sobbed. "I wanted to tell you, honest to Christ I did, but I didn't know how!"

"None of that matters now, but I'll kill you both if he"—she pointed at Tony— "doesn't fulfil his promise of a cult."

"I'm not lying!" Tony said. "They even have a backer you know rather well, Hydra. A money man who's been funding them since your disappearance . . ."

"Who?"

Tony's head lowered.

"Well?" she demanded.

"I—"

"Our father, Hydra. Daddy," Lucy said.

Hydra staggered backwards, into Tempest's and Typhoon's arms. They kept her upright.

"He pretty much knew who'd taken you after all the stories about the cannibals emerged and you'd been gone for more than six months. Rumours circulated . . . Then he discovered the cult."

"This fucking sect set up shop overnight or something?"

"No," Tony cut in. "They've been around since the first incidents, keeping a low profile until your father got mixed in with them."

"Stop beating around the fucking bush and get on with it!"

"It's all rather difficult to explain, Hydra. We need Joe here—he'll be able to tell you everything," Tony said.

"Who's he?"

"The cult leader—your dad's new best friend."

"Where's your phone?" Hydra demanded.

"On my bedside table. Bring it to me and I'll call him and your dad."

"You better not be trying to pull some dirty fucking trick, because I'll burn the house down with you all inside!"

"I'm not. If you get my phone, I'll put your doubts to rest. Please."

Hydra turned to Typhoon. "Go and fetch it." He nodded and left the room.

A minute later, Typhoon was back with Tony's mobile in hand. He offered it to his mother, who took it and held it up to Tony's face. "This right?"

Tony nodded. "If you could untie—"

Hydra shook her head. "Tell me who to call and I'll place the phone to your ear."

"Call Joe first. He'll be pleased to know about you. Not that your dad won't, of course."

She nodded, then scrolled through Tony's list of contacts. There was only one Joe. After dialling, she put the mobile to Tony's ear. It rang a dozen times.

"He's probably sleeping. Maybe we should try your dad in the meantime? You know how long his days get—he's probably still up, or at the office."

"Knowing Dad, yes," Lucy said. "He's still the same. Worse since Mum passed."

The news of her mother's death did little to faze Hydra emotionally. "Okay, I'll try him next." She scrolled through the list of contacts until she came across her dad, Luke Goodling, and hit Dial.

When it started to ring, she pressed the phone to Tony's ear.

You were never too busy for your business, colleagues, partners, trips away or fancy dinners, but you were for your family, Luke*! Probably only concerned about me because I was your property and you wanted it back. I doubt you gave an actual fuck about me.*

"Nope, nothing," Tony said. "*Shit.*"

"Not like Dad," Lucy stated.

"Is he still in banking?" Hydra asked.

Tony and Lucy nodded.

"We'll give it a few more hours and try them again. Don't mind if we make ourselves at home, do you?"

Lucy said nothing. Tony shook his head.

"That's what I thought. Boys, why don't you look around, see what you can find. I'm going upstairs to wake up my darling Daniel." She stared at Tony, thinking he was going to protest, but he didn't dare. Out in the kitchen, cupboard doors slammed, dishes broke, and food packages rustled. "Boys will be boys," she said, smiling and standing.

"What about my baby?" Lucy said.

"He'll be taken care of, don't worry. And it's not like he's screaming for food right now, is he? Breast?"

"Formula."

Hydra tutted. "Breast is best, dear. What's the matter, barren?"

Lucy's face darkened. "You always liked to humiliate me, didn't you?"

"I think you'll find it was often the other way around. Still jealous of these?" Hydra asked, pushing her large tits out. "Reckon it were these that caught Douglas' eye all them years ago." She smirked.

"Who?" Tony asked.

"A lad your darling wife was fucking in comprehensive school, until he came to ours one night and discovered Lucy's sister had a better rack. Those bee stings held you back, sis."

Lucy said nothing, just scowled.

"Now, be good while Mama takes care of her business."

As much hatred, rage and all the other destructive emotions she had coursing through her at that moment, Hydra couldn't help but feel love for her sons Daniel and Michael.

Her heart suddenly ached.

Where did that come from? The closer she got to Daniel's room, a tingling sensation in her nipples intensified. *That conversation with Lucy?*

Right then, Hydra knew her spoken threats towards her children were empty. There was no way she'd be able to kill her own kin, no matter what. *They're going to have to accept shit for how it is.*

When she reached the top step, her heartrate quickened. Tears formed in her eyes when the memory of returning to the house and seeing them all outside with Tony and Lucy flooded her mind again. And, even though she'd been livid at the time, she'd still wanted to run and throw her arms around the boys.

Never mind that now. She wiped the sliding tear from her face and walked stiffly along the landing, hoping not to wake her son and scare him. *The noise downstairs has probably already done that.*

Then she remembered how good a sleeper Daniel was. Michael, too.

They could snooze through a hurricane ripping the roof off the house. A smile played across her mouth. As she slipped past the master bedroom, her motherly instincts told her to check on Jason, and so she opened the door and stepped inside. Hydra found the infant sleeping, his breathing rhythmic.

"Bless." She checked to make sure nobody was watching—no weakness could be shown—and then kissed her fingertips and pressed them to the child's forehead.

Hydra tucked the baby in and left, continuing to her son's room. Before entering, she ran her hands over the brightly coloured tiles that spelled out his name on the door.

"He loved these when we first applied them," she whispered, recalling the memory: "*Mammy, Mammy! My door knows my name!*"

She laughed and wiped her fresh tears away, then tapped on the wood. "Are you awake, son?" She depressed the handle and opened it to a sliver. She heard her son's light snoring.

She couldn't fight her smiles as she eased her way into the room and crossed to Daniel's bed. He was lying on his stomach, face to the wall.

My bareness may startle him . . .

"Dan," she cooed. "Dan, my baby boy, wake up. It's Mammy."

"Ugh-ugh," he groaned, writhing.

. . . No, he'll see it's Mother and throw his arms around me . . .

Hydra put her hand out and softly shook him. "Dan, wake up. It's Mam."

"Ugh, stop it." He turned over and opened his eyes, followed by his mouth. He screamed, but only the once, as Hydra covered his gob with one of her filth-encrusted hands.

"It's me, Paula. Your mother. Don't you remember?"

He stopped yelling, his eyes going wide.

"Can I trust you not to scream?"

Daniel didn't react.

"Nod for yes."

He did.

"Good lad." Hydra removed her hand. "I'm home, baby."

"M-Mam? It's *really* you? I'm not dreaming?"

She nodded, smiling, holding the tears back. She knew what she had to tell him wouldn't be easy—about the changes he would have to face in the coming days and weeks. "Yes, it's really me."

Daniel threw his arms around her. "We thought you were dead." He sobbed like his life depended on it. "Where have you *been*?!"

"It's a long story, baby, but I'll tell you as soon as your brother gets home. Why don't you come downstairs and meet your new brothers and sister?"

"Huh?"

Hydra's smile widened. *How did he get so big?*

In that moment, Hydra almost forgot her new self and thought she could quite easily revert to who she used to be. But no, lines had been crossed, promises kept, blood spilled. Even if she wanted her old life back, Hydra knew it could never be. She wasn't the same person emotionally, or physically. She could snap and kill at any time. The boys would have to learn to cope with things, just like Tony and Lucy would have to if they wanted to continue living.

"Come down and say hello. And don't worry about how Dad and Lucy look—they're going to be fine. Promise."

"Mam, you're, erm, naked . . ."

"Don't be shy, come." She held her hand out and pulled Daniel up.

"B-but . . . *I'm* nak—"

"*Shh!*" Hydra held him close, pushing his head against her breasts. "There's nothing to be ashamed of, boy. Nakedness is natural." He squirmed at first, then settled against her warmth. "Now, come."

"Were you abducted by the people in the woods like Granddad Goodling told us?"

"Is that what he told you and Michael?"

Dan nodded.

"There's more to it than that. I'll tell you, but please don't be scared of Typhoon and Tempest—

they mean you no harm. They'll love you like I do."

Daniel screamed when he entered the living room and saw his father's and Lucy's bloody bodies tied to chairs.

"*Dad*!" he squealed, his prepubescent voice cracking.

Tony looked at him. "I'm okay, son. Don't be alarmed."

Lucy averted her eyes.

"What did you *do*, Mam?"

"Everything'll be fine."

When Tempest and Typhoon walked in, Dan gasped, shoving away from his father. He pushed himself backwards along the carpet by using the flats of his hands and his naked arse, giving himself mild carpet burns.

"Argh! *Monsters*!" he said, voice cracking.

"Dan," Tempest said, "I'm not going to harm you."

"Neither am I," Typhoon confirmed. "We're blood."

Hydra smiled.

"You could have warned the poor boy, Hydra!" Tony said. "And allowed him to—"

Hydra backhanded Tony across the mouth, dislodging more teeth, which skipped along the floor and pinged off walls. "I told you not to talk down to me or try and demand. The boys need to learn not to be shy."

Blood trickled down Tony's chin. "Sorry."

"Now, Dan, these are your brothers. And over there is your sister, Cerberus. Don't be scared. I know they look different, but they're just like you and me. They'll protect you to the death."

Daniel looked from them to her, then back to Typhoon and Tempest. When he got up, he covered his privates with one hand whilst extending the other in greeting.

Typhoon and Tempest looked at it, turning to their mother.

"Like this," she said, shaking Daniel's hand. "It means hello, boys. Now you do it, Typhoon."

He took Daniel's hand in his huge paw and lightly shook it.

"Good, that's great. Now you, Tempest." Once he'd emulated Typhoon, Hydra pulled them all close and gave them a hug. "I love my boys, and nothing's ever coming between us again."

When the front door was unlocked, pushed open and then closed, there was a collective sigh within the living room.

"Dad? Lucy?" someone called from the hallway. "You guys still up?"

Hydra nodded at Tony. "We're in here, son. Come in. Don't be . . . startled."

"What are you talking about?" Michael said, laughter in his voice.

"I'm home, lad." Hydra said.

"Who—*Mam*?!"

"Yes, Michael. Mam. Show yourself and give Mam a great big hug." Hydra heard his slow approach. "Nothing or no-one is going to hurt you. You have extended family waiting to greet you."

"We were told you were . . ."

"Where have you been, Michael? We were worried sick. Have you been out with those thugs again?" Lucy snapped.

"Shush!" Hydra hissed.

Michael walked into the living room and gasped at the sight of his mother's filth-encrusted, blood-spattered body. His jaw sagged. "Y-you—*Mam*!" He rushed to her and placed his arms around her, pulling her so tight to his body she thought he was going to snap her. "I missed you so, so much." Tears spilled down his cheeks and ran through her knotted hair.

Hydra thought her heart would explode. She was a tangled wreck of emotions. *Got to stay strong. Remain in control. Show no weakness.*

"Where have you been? Why didn't you come back sooner if you've been okay? Why?" His fingers dug into her back, and then his hands balled into fists. "You left us, and Dad married that fucking *whore*!"

"Michael!" Tony yelled.

"You little—"

Hydra looked down at her prisoners, silencing them. "Have you been acting out, boy?" she asked, pushing Michael away from her to stare him in the eye.

"Drink, drugs, gang-related incidents... The list goes on," Tony confessed. "I thought to enrol him in the army to see if that would straighten him out."

"I can change, Mam, now that you're back. I promise." For the first time since entering the room, his gaze found Typhoon and Tempest. "Who the fuck are those freaks?!" He ripped away from his mother, picked up the fire poker and swung it over his shoulder.

"Put that *down*. They're your brothers, Typhoon and Tempest, and that's your baby sister, Cerberus. She'll grow to be a strong, leading female of our people, son," Hydra said, stretching her arms out to emphasise her point.

"What are you talking about?" Michael asked. Tears flooded down his face. "You're scaring me. And why are you *naked* and dirty and covered in blood? What's happened to you—you're the same. You've been off your meds. We can fix—"

She held her hands up to stop him. "I've never been more *in* my mind, son. Honestly. For the past five years, I've been seeing more clearly than ever before. Come, Michael. You too, Daniel. Sit here. I'll tell you all about my wonderful adventure and what the future holds for us. It's exciting."

Her boys were sceptical at first but slunk to their mother and sat with her on the floor. Typhoon and Tempest did the same. When they were comfortable, Hydra told Daniel and Michael about her abduction, how she'd lived with Skull and Eight-Ball, what she'd become and what she expected of them.

"Our kind will punish the people of this town and the surrounding areas for what they did to our people, boys."

"You know Granddad tried tracing you through a secret cult dedicated to the resurrection of your fallen family?" Michael asked.

"*Our* family, son. No, I haven't had all the information yet. I'm waiting to get it from the horse's mouth, so to speak. Which reminds me," she said, getting up and taking the phone to Tony. "Let's try Luke again."

After dialling, Hydra placed the phone to Tony's ear. It rang a multitude of times before he shook his head. "The guy is either busy or sleeping."

"Since when did sleeping get in the way of his work?" Lucy muttered.

"Okay, let's give Joe's number a go."

"Can you untie us, Hydra? This is getting tiresome. We're not—"

Michael and Daniel gasped when Hydra struck Tony across the face. "I'll untie you when I'm good and ready." She placed the phone to his ear. After the tenth ring, Joe answered. He sounded irate from what Hydra could tell.

"Sorry to bother you at such an hour, Joe, but you're going to be glad I did . . . I have Hydra—*Paula*—here . . .Yeah, my ex-wife. She's standing right in front of me with her sons born out of the tribe you guys have been so desperately trying to unearth, or whatever the hell it is you do on a Friday night in your cellar . . . Look, get over here, *pronto* . . . What? He *is*?! Then bring him with you!" Tony pulled away from the phone. "He's on his way."

"Luke's with him?"

Tony nodded. "They'll be here soon. Can you please untie us now?"

Hydra turned her back on Tony and smiled at her boys. "Soon, we'll be more powerful than ever."

Thirty minutes later, Hydra heard the squeal of tires pull up outside. Four doors opened, slammed shut. This was followed by a rapid knocking on the living room window.

"Typhoon, Tempest—let them in," Hydra ordered, going into the kitchen and drawing the butcher knife and cleaver from the knife block. She ambled back into the living room, surprised that neither Luke nor Joe screamed at the sight of her or the boys.

Hydra stood face-to-face with her father and three other men, who wore robes. They had a crest on them.

"You must be Paula?" the man wearing a red gown enquired.

"*Hydra*, please. Paula's dead." She took the proffered hand, shaking it with a vice-like squeeze. "You're Joe, cult leader?"

"*Cult*? We don't like that word, Hydra. We prefer 'organization,'" he said, smiling.

"I see. And who are they?" She indicated the ones at Joe's back. They had their hoods drawn up; heads bent as if in prayer. "Disciples?"

"Yes."

She laughed. "Delightful. And have you people been sacrificing virgins and goats in my people's honour, or in the hope of raising their spirits or corpses from beyond the grave?"

"Well, erm . . ."

"There's no need to be shy. Just answer my question and take your eyes off my tits."

"This is utter madness, Paula. And put some damn clothes on, *woman*," Luke said, stepping up to his daughter and grabbing her upper arms.

Typhoon and Tempest growled, stepping forward.

"It's okay, boys. Stand down. I suggest you take your fucking hands off me, *Luke*, or I won't be responsible for my actions."

The look in her eyes told him all he needed. He let his daughter go, leaving behind finger impressions on her skin.

"Continue, Joe."

"I became fascinated with your people many years ago, when they were rumoured to be roaming the Welsh coastlines from the north to the south. Then I caught wind of them settling here, in Bridgend—"

"We all know the history. Get on with it."

"Fine, okay. I tried my best to seek your people out in the woods—I wanted to offer my help and services, to be a part of the clan. I have wealth, not to mention power, Hydra. I'm a pillar of the community. I could have kept your tribe safe. By the time I managed to track them down, they'd been killed, or so I thought.

"After your disappearance, I again went in search but couldn't find hide nor hair of anyone or anything. Months went by. They said you were dead. Over the years that followed, I heard of strange things happening in the woods and surrounding areas, and so, I decided to set up a group.

"There were many in South Wales, surrounding towns and boroughs who thought highly of your kin, Hydra. We dedicated time and searches to finding a survivor. And yes, we have practiced sacrifices. I'm heavily involved in the black arts. Not just me, but others in my organization. Your dad came to us hoping we could help find you. He funded us, not that we needed money."

"What is it that you do, Joe?"

"I'm a self-made multi-millionaire. I have most of South Wales in my back pocket: police chiefs, mayors, government personnel, money men . . . I have time, cash and resources to do whatever I want. If there's ever a problem, my influence makes it go away. People tend to think highly of you when you donate tons of cash to various charities and they name hospitals and children after you."

"Impressive, Joe."

"And I'm sure my organization, or family, can help yours flourish. I take it that's your plan?"

"Power and territory, too. I want to make sure my children, the ones like Typhoon and Tempest that have genetic failure, are safe after I'm gone. I made a promise to keep our kind ticking."

"This can be achieved, now that we have found each other."

"How many do you have in your power, Joe?"

"At current, we are a few hundred strong."

"How many of mating age?"

"Oh, I'd say eighty percent."

"Excellent."

"You know I can't let you endanger the boys' lives like this, Paula!" Luke said. "I only hired this madman in the hope he'd one day find you. Please, snap out of this and—argh-*ugh*!"

Hydra tore the butcher knife across his throat.

Blood squirted up her face.

Her father placed his hands to the gushing wound and stumbled backwards.

Tony, Lucy, Michael and Daniel screamed.

"Get him, boys," Hydra told Typhoon and Tempest.

Her sons pounced onto the dying man like jungle cats—they tore at him and sank their teeth into the soft, saggy flesh around his neck.

Ripping and slurping sounds ensued.

Hydra turned back to Joe amidst the carnage. "You won't disappoint me, will you?"

A smile spread across the cult leader's face. "Absolutely not, Hydra."

The two at his back flicked their hoods off and beamed. "Do you mind if we join in?" asked one of the twin girls, who couldn't have been more than sixteen.

"These are my daughters," Joe said, "and they've been eating human meat for years."

"Well, this *is* exciting. By all means, ladies—tuck in."

The women stripped out of their robes, revealing their slender bodies.

Lucy and Tony continued to shriek, but Michael and Daniel now looked on in awe as the girls knelt by Tempest and Typhoon. The four pulled at the man on the floor, ripping his clothes off. The boys had enough strength to tear flesh from the man's flabby gut, arms and sides, whilst the girls lapped at the blood and took offered strips of meat.

"I'd like my boys to mate with your fine girls, Joe. *Tonight.*"

Joe nodded. "I made sure they remained virgins. I knew this day would come. What do you intend on doing with them?" He nodded at Tony and Lucy.

"They'll be added to our army and used for mating and guarding purposes."

"You have a lair?"

"In the woods, far from here, and that's where I plan to take Tony and Lucy to breed. They shall live there, and I will remain here with my sons."

"Very well. And this lair of yours—can it be modified?"

"I'm sure it could. Why?"

"Good. Then we shall make a temple!" Joe said, laughing as he watched his children drain Luke's blood and greedily shove the man's offal down their gullets.

Chapter 11
Then

*I*t took a long time for the screaming and crying to stop after Tempest, Typhoon, Summer and Pixie (Joe's teenaged girls, whose names I learned later) devoured my father. Daniel and Michael were terrified. I knew they would be, but it was a good thing, and they got an early glimpse into what would be expected of them.

"Now you know what we are, what you'll become," Tempest had told the cowering lads, who yelled and cried alongside Lucy and Tony.

"We'll never be like that! You're crazy, Mam!" Michael had screamed.

"I want my mammy back," Daniel had sobbed.

Even when Luke's blood fanned out and ran beneath Daniel and Michael, they were too scared to move. They remained on the floor, holding each other and clutching Tony's and Lucy's legs.

Of course, Tony then tried the macho bullshit, but I'd beaten him and Lucy within an inch of their lives as Joe and the boys watched on.

I threw down my dominance in that moment of terror, buckling all those who would now swear their allegiance to me.

It took Lucy and Tony a couple of weeks to heal, but in that time a lot happened.

The next evening, Joe took me to meet with a few of his colleagues: bigwigs who helped run the organization, along with a few lieutenants that helped keep the disciples, or "followers" as Joe liked to call them, in line.

The meeting didn't go according to Joe's plan, because he hadn't been completely straight with me . . .

* * *

"Ladies and gentlemen, I would like for you to meet Hydra."

When Hydra first walked into the room, which looked like a boardroom in Joe's mansion, there was a collective gasp. This wasn't solely down to her nakedness and blood-stained appearance, but the fact that they *thought* they had a real-life cannibal before them, a member of the infamous tribe who terrorized and decorated many a coastal town, hamlet and seaside with guts and gore.

She was the sole survivor to the Sawney Bean clan.

It didn't matter that she wasn't a direct descendant by blood; it was enough that she had lived, survived, bred and killed with the cave-people of yesteryear. To these robe-wearing, rich cunts, she was a god among men and women. They would worship her.

"I thought you said she had sons, Joe?" an old man at the end of the committee table asked, standing.

Hydra had left Typhoon and Tempest at the house to keep an eye on things. Daniel, Michael, Lucy and Tony had been sedated, bandaged and locked in their rooms. Summer and Pixie helped guard them.

"They are at my home, taking care of business in my absence." She eyed the old fella, who sat back down under her intense glare.

"Yes," he mumbled.

"Any other questions? Do I have to *prove* myself?"

Joe's committee spoke among themselves.

"What's to discuss?" Joe asked. There was annoyance in his voice. "I'm the leader-"

"Yes, and you put us in place," the oldie said, indicating the three men and two women that sat alongside him, all of whom were of equal age, "to make sure things ran properly. Now, we're not suggesting she's a fraud, but I think *some* kind of proof is needed."

"You honestly think I'd drag someone in here from off the streets?!" Joe's mouth hung open.

"We know how bad you want this, Joe," a woman said, arching an eyebrow. "And if you want us to continue sinking our money into this organization, then I suggest you play ball. You can't make the calls without us. You understand that, right?"

"I *could* run this without your funding."

"Really? But isn't that *why* you came to us?" the old man asked.

Hydra looked at Joe. "I was under the impression you were the top man here?"

"I am!"

One of the other women scoffed. "You might be, but your money alone would not suffice, and we're in place to help make decisions."

"Plus, your pull wouldn't be as great without us. You know that, Joe. Most of your connections were our friends before they knew about you."

"Okay, okay, so I lied a wee bit when I told you I had *full* control, Hydra, but I do run the show to an extent. When I first put this thing together, I brought in these people, who were as fascinated about your folk as I am."

"But why?" Hydra wanted to know. "What could we possibly offer you?"

"There's a great deal of money to be made from people such as you," Joe said. "Not to mention dominance and authority. With our help, you'll be able to thrive beyond your wildest dreams."

"Do you know what I think, Joe?" Hydra said, picking up a knife that lay on the huge corporate table.

"N-no, what?!"

Hydra stalked around him with the blade at her side. "I think you've been looking for me, or someone in my clan, for your own hidden agenda. If I'm wrong, stop me."

"I-I . . ."

"Now, this goal of yours—to resurrect my fallen people, or whatever it is you're trying to do—isn't working, is it?"

Joe shook his head. "No, but—"

"Please don't interrupt me. You know I don't like that."

He nodded. "Yes, ma'am."

"You need the blood of a member, don't you?"

Joe's face flushed.

"Did you think I would let you kill one of my children? One of Skull's boys or baby girl? You see, she's mine. *Direct* blood."

The people around the table gasped.

Hydra grabbed Joe by the balls, squeezed and twisted.

"*Ugh!*" he cried, his legs buckling.

"Not enough that I let my boys fuck your girls, hmm? Or were you planning on using my blood and leaving me for dead?"

"P-*please*," he gasped. "You've got it—*ooh*—all wrong! And if you hurt me, you'll never get what you want."

She twisted his bollocks harder. "Who said anything about hurting *you*? I'll let you live, chop up your girls and mail pieces of them to you from time to time. I'll start with their faces."

"You wouldn't . . ."

"You saw how I dealt with Luke. You think I'd give a shit about people I don't know? And I don't care how loyal those girls of yours are— I'll still sacrifice them."

"*Argh!*" He gritted his teeth as she twisted, his lips pulled back. "You won't-"

"Get what I want? Do you honestly think I need you? And do you really think I'd want it at the cost of my family?"

"We'd only need *some* blood, as part of a ritual—nobody needs to die. Please, let me go . . ."

Someone behind the table cleared their throat. Hydra looked over her shoulder to see the committee staring at her.

"Must this *charade* continue?" asked one of the ladies sporting a necklace of fancy beads, which she twirled with a finger. "Your little stunt isn't fooling any of us, Joe."

Hydra let go of Joe's balls and turned towards the woman.

"And I wish you'd put some clothes on, lady!"

Hydra arched an eyebrow. "I thought you were looking for the genuine article?"

"Yes, we are, and you're clearly some trickster Joe's brought here to try and dupe us with, but I'm unclear—"

"What makes you think I'm a fraud?"

"The way you act, speak, walk . . . Did Joe black you up, or did you do it yourself?"

"You've been told I'm *not* blood. I'm Paula Harris, the female who—"

"Please, you don't except us to believe that claptrap you're selling. Paula Harris died years ago —the police confirmed it."

"It's all poppycock and you know it, Susan. All the scheming and dreaming we've been doing, and when I finally unearth a living tribe member, you try to do everything in your power to pooh-pooh it. *Why?*" He thumped his fist on the desk, making some of the cups and glasses wobble. Contents spilled.

"We have to be absolutely positive, Joe, and I think you've been fooled. I don't care what you're trying to spin. If this was concrete proof, why not get her to bring the sons? The daughter? Hell, if you were at her house, you could have brought along ID, proving to us who she really is. And, another thing: if she'd spent much time with the actual tribe, don't you think she'd be a little more . . . feral?"

The other committee members chuckled.

"She's got good points, Joe," the old man said. "And, as much as this fine young thing is good to look at, she's no flesh-eating crazy who could help our cause. I think we're done here, people."

"No, Phil, please. I thought my word and visual evidence would have sufficed, but I can get further proof."

"I'm sure I could provide that for you right now, Phil," Hydra said, smiling.

"Smirking, pleasant cannibals," Susan sneered. "What next—attack dogs capable of licking intruders to death?"

Another shockwave of laughter rippled around the room. Even Hydra managed a titter as she walked towards Susan. "You want proof?"

Phil, still smiling, nodded. "I think we'd all love that."

In that instant, Hydra's face changed to something beyond heinous.

The chuckling turned into a collective gasp.

Hydra grabbed Susan by the face, her thumb and forefinger and middle finger digging into her cheeks, and shoved Susan back towards her chair. With her free hand, Hydra held her knife overhead, the light from the bulb in the ceiling glinting off the steel. "I'll give you what you want, *cunt*!" she yelled in Susan's face, driving the woman into the seat.

Her head rebounded off the headrest.

"Help!" she gasped, but Phil and the others were in awe.

"Kill her!" one man demanded, grabbing his crotch. "If you are who you say, then slaughter her. Drink her blood and eat the flesh from off her bones."

"N-*no*!" Susan pleaded, throwing her arms up to cover her face.

Hydra's blade punched into the woman's chest and ripped downwards, shredding her white suit and skin alike. Her intestines slipped out and piled up on the floor. The woman's arms dropped, her elbows crashing atop the chair's padded armrests before flopping over the sides.

Susan's eyes crossed, her tongue lolled, and blood drizzled out of her mouth and nostrils.

Hydra didn't stop stabbing until she was breathless, the knife buckled and useless. She threw it to one side and savagely tore at Susan's ruptured flesh with her fingers and stuffed handfuls into her mouth as though she hadn't eaten in months.

Over the gratuitous sounds of scoffing, Hydra heard someone throw up.

Another begged for her to stop.

A female screamed.

"Okay, I think that's enough!" one of the men said, putting a hand to Hydra's shoulder. "We get—"

She turned on him with scores of skin dangling from the mouth—blood speckled her face. Hydra pounced like a jungle cat and landed on him. She wrapped her arms and legs around his body, holding him in place as she bit into his neck and ripped some of his veins out.

Blood squirted across the table and up windows.

"Christ, make her stop, Joe!" Phil begged.

Joe laughed. "I thought you wanted this?"

"Susan we could afford to lose, but not the whole damn committee!"

"Maybe you'll learn to trust me in the future, people. And if you don't play ball, this is what will happen to you."

Phil, along with the rest of the committee, hid behind Joe, who called upon Hydra to stop. "Please, Hydra. We're on your side. Well, I am," Joe admitted.

Hydra looked up, her mouth, nose and cheeks covered in dripping gore. Her jaw methodically worked at a piece of meat, her eyes moving between Joe and the other faces over his shoulders.

She walked up to Joe and jack-hammered his chest with a finger as she spoke. "*I'm* running the fucking show, you hear?"

He nodded, his chin touching his chest.

"Do the rest of you old cunts agree?"

They also nodded.

"Good. Now, I'm willing to get you the rest of the proof you need—"

"That won't be—"

Hydra backhanded Phil, knocking him to ground. "I'm talking." She heeled him in the balls before kicking him in the face, his head snapping to one side. "You'll get the rest of the proof tonight, then that'll be the end of your bitching and whining. You want what I have to give, to seek out my people and sell your soul in order to be a part of my family?"

The committee members, who were still standing, got to their knees.

Phil sat up, grovelled to her feet, kissed them and asked for forgiveness. "We'll be your loyal servants, Hydra," he snivelled.

She snarled, pulling her foot away. "Get! You haven't earned the right to touch me, not yet. Now, I suggest you worthless bags of shit get this place cleaned up and get over to my place by midnight—we have a lot of planning to do."

"What do we do with the bodies, Miss?" Phil asked, cowering.

"Cut them up into the smallest pieces you can and bring them with you. I promised the boys I'd get them a present." She looked at the committee. "Have I made myself clear?"

"Yes," they mumbled in unison.

"Good." She turned to Joe. "Next time, be up front with me, Joseph. I wouldn't want to have to rip your balls off and eat them. You want to be my friend, don't you?" She caressed his groin.

"*Ugh*, yes!"

"Have this lot over to me tomorrow, understood?"

"Yes, of course."

"I'll see myself out," she said, leaving.

The next night, fashionably early by five minutes, Joe and the rest of the committee arrived at Hydra's house. None of them wore robes.

"Who are they?" Hydra asked, indicating two new faces at the rear. They had Hessian sacks slung over their shoulders.

"Stephen and Greg. They're fellow followers, Hydra, and mean you no harm. They are simply drones—worker bees, if you would. They have in their possession the cut-up bodies of Susan and Andrew."

Hydra nodded, stepping to one side. "In," she commanded. When the two strapping men with the bags passed her, Hydra informed them to put their cargo down in the living room. "My boys will assist you."

Before she could close the front door, Hydra heard Typhoon and Tempest growling and talking, asking the men if their *treat* was in the bags. Seconds later, heavy-duty zips could be heard being pulled. This was followed by Lucy screaming.

The boys tucked in.

* * *

The previous night, after returning home with a small portion of meat skinned from Susan, Hydra had encouraged Daniel and Michael to try it.

At first, they'd refused, and hadn't spoken to her much since she'd killed Luke.

"If you don't eat it, you'll starve. Same goes for you and Lucy, Tony. Soon, you'll be living in the wild, and you'll need to keep your strength up."

Tony caved first, knowing he would be no good to anyone if he became weak. "Come on, Lucy, this is the only way to survive—you know Hydra won't allow anything else."

Nobody within the house had eaten in close to twenty-four hours.

"It's this or *nothing*!" Hydra boomed.

Lucy looked at her sister with hatred. "You'll pay for making us do this, Hydra."

"Get down on your knees and start eating, before I execute you like I did our pig father."

Lucy didn't need telling twice.

Michael and Daniel stood strong.

Their bellies will get the better of them in the end, she thought.

* * *

When Hydra walked into the living room, she found her boys, along with Lucy and Michael, tucking into the bodies of Susan and Andrew. A smile pulled across her face. "Brilliant. Enjoying, boys?"

Michael and Daniel ignored her, too engrossed in stuffing their faces.

"Some things will never change. Typhoon, Tempest, are you not partaking?"

"We'll let them have their fill first, Mother," Tempest said.

Typhoon nodded.

"How very thoughtful, boys. Right. Will you keep an eye on things?"

"Unbelievable!" Phil said. "This is truly a miracle."

"Are you all satisfied?" Hydra said.

The committee, including Joe, looked at her with awe. They smiled like children in a candy shop.

"Good, because we have business to discuss, people. Would you all like to follow me into the kitchen?"

Hydra marched the sect into the room and closed the door behind them.

"What are we here to discuss, Hydra?" Joe asked.

"The building of your new temple in the woods," she said. "It probably won't take much funding but will require a lot of manpower."

"We already have such a building, hidden away from the public eye," Phil said.

"This one will be different, as it'll also home members of my family who cannot stay in public light. However, Tempest and Typhoon, along with Cerberus, will remain here. The new temple will also act as a breeding ground and hospital. I want as many trained people living there as possible, along with guards—all of it. Understand?"

"May we add a prayer room and sacrificial chamber?" Phil asked.

"Anything you want, as long as this place is built deep into the mountain so our family will be safe to breed."

Joe turned to his council. They whispered among themselves.

"We agree," Joe said, "and will be happy to get this done as quickly as possible. Do you have somewhere in mind?"

"Yes. The cave I told you about—the one I've been living in. There's much room for expansion."

"This is in the woods?" Phil probed.

"Far in the woods, yes. I was lucky to find it. I've explored it a fair bit, and I'd say it goes at least four miles into the mountain before you pop out the other side. We could dig down, and also make multiple paths that branch off."

"Seems promising, and doable," Phil admitted. The other committee members nodded. "I think we need to see this site of yours, Hydra, to give us a better picture of what we're dealing with. Can you take us there tomorrow?"

"Of course, but I want construction to start immediately—before this week's out. I want my ex-husband and my sister—who he's fucking—up in the cave. It'll be their new home."

"We shall see what can be done."

"That's good to hear. I'd hate to be disappointed."

Early the next morning, Hydra ventured off into the woods with Joe, his committee and two drones so they could assess the cave and see what could be done with it.

After two hours of walking around, talking amongst themselves, Joe went to Hydra and told her that he thought the whole thing was a grand idea.

"I have plenty of people on the payroll who could turn this thing into a place before the year's out."

"That's exactly what I wanted to hear, Joe."

"I'll see if I can get workmen up here as early as this afternoon to check the place over."

"And your people will keep their mouths shut?"

"Oh, definitely. Most, if not all, are part of the organization. You have nothing to fear, Hydra. We will protect you to the death!"

* * *

Joe had been as good as his word. That afternoon, workmen turned up on site to make their plans. I'd stayed out of sight, not wanting to be seen by the drones.

It was impressive how they moved the materials and got the diggers and whatnot in. A lot of stuff was brought in by helicopter.

Money talks, and nobody came to investigate, not that anyone saw a thing that happened. And, after a year of digging and shifting half a mountain's worth of stone and muck, the cave was ready for the cult to build their rooms and lay their mark.

I did the same.

Tony and Lucy had already been settled at the new base for well over a year. They'd also made babies and put their own stamp on a couple of rooms and chambers found within the intricate layout.

Two years later, the temple/hideout was built. Babies had been born, and the whole place had been kitted out with beds, cots and all the rest of it. It was up and running and the clan was now more powerful than ever. With Joe's money, power and influence, there was no stopping me from doing what I wanted, and all I did was stay low and do my bidding.

My time to strike would come.

Chapter 12
Now

J im Hengroth couldn't sleep. He'd spent the last few hours tossing and turning whilst his wife Laura slept soundly by his side. But sleep wouldn't come for him no matter how much he'd tried telling himself that Owen would be in to work tomorrow; that the man would be first there, with the kettle boiled as usual.

He hadn't heard from Owen since that day he'd informed Jim about going to Twin Jesters. They were the best of friends. Not an evening went by where they didn't speak on the phone or communicate via text or email, and now four nights had passed in succession without contact.

This isn't like him. If he's found something, he would call. Hell, even if he hasn't found anything, he would contact me. And I'd be shocked if he didn't turn something up at Twin Jesters with all the oddity going on around the place.

Jim knew he was being silly, that Owen was a grown man and was probably busy or out cavorting at a favourite haunt, but something was niggling away at the back of his mind.

He grabbed his sports watch off the bedside cabinet and lit its face.

A lick past three a.m.

"*Ugh*, Jesus," he groaned.

With a huff, he threw the covers aside and got out of his luxury king-size bed. After replacing his watch, Jim plucked up his mobile and moved to the bedroom door, exiting with silence and stealth. In the kitchen, he made himself a mug of coffee and took it into his downstairs office and switched on his PC.

He took a sip of his black coffee, placed his mug on a coaster on his PC desk and sat in his roller chair. He wheeled himself closer to the computer screen and switched everything on.

"I'm being paranoid—maybe try his phone again?" he muttered as the PC fired up. He shook his head. He'd already rung Owen six times since leaving work and left two voice messages, one regarding his somewhat amusing visit to Liz at the Lamb and Flag: '*She's definitely involved with it all somehow, Owen. Just call it gut instinct, yeah? This old dog can still apply the pressure. Anyway, call when you can and I'll fill you in on the rest. Bye.*'

When he'd heard nothing by late evening, Jim had tried calling a few more times. Nothing. Then, before bed, he'd tried Owen's phone once more, his call going straight to voicemail. This suggested the mobile was off or had no signal. Either way, it left Jim cold.

Jim reclined in his chair and let his mind wander.

Maybe I should go to Twin Jesters and see if I can find him? He could still be there.

What if he's hurt, lying in a ditch, calling for help?

Stop it! The army's there.

What if they opened fire on him?

Now you are *being crazy.*

When his desktop popped up, Jim opened his web browser, calling up his email and entering the necessary codes and passwords to gain access. Within seconds, his inbox appeared onscreen and he noticed he had a new email from Owen. It had been sent five hours ago.

"Damn it!" Jim slammed his hand on his desk, making his mug rattle and coffee spill. "I should have checked earlier. Stupid, stupid, *stupid.*" He slapped his forehead as he muttered.

He opened the email and read it, mouth moving in silence as he nursed his warm mug, taking the occasional sip. His eyes flicked from left to right as he sped through the lengthy correspondence.

"Fucking *hell*!" He shot up out of his seat, his mug tumbling from his lap and smashing against the wood floor.

His eyes sought out the clock on his PC and then the time the email was delivered. *He might still be at the pub! I need to get my arse down there and pick him up.*

Jim rushed into the hallway and grabbed his coat from off the stand. He fished his car keys out of a bowl on a side table kept by the door and went to exit the house.

Should I leave Laura a note? No, there's no time! I'll ring her from the pub.

Jim unlocked the front door, stepped out into the cold night, and closed it at his back. His four-by-four sat on the driveway. He rushed to it, got behind the wheel and rolled down his drive, opting to start the engine once he was clear of the house.

"I hope to God he decided to stay put and not try to venture home."

Thirty minutes later, Jim pulled up outside the Pig and Pen pub, killed his vehicle's engine and got out. The building sat in darkness.

He looked at his watch. It was almost five a.m.

I have to try, no matter who I upset. I'm sure Rodney'll understand.

Jim strode over to the pub's main entrance and repeatedly hammered the door's metal knocker until a light burst to life in a window overhead.

He heard a voice. It sounded distressed, angry.

Doesn't Rodney own a shotgun?

"Someone better be dead or fucking dying!" Rodney yelled.

Jim stood back from the door.

Bolts and chains rattled.

"It's me: Jim Hengroth!"

"Newspaper Jim?" The door flew open, and out poked the barrel of a .410 bolt-action.

"I like to hunt game with this beauty," Jim remembered Rodney telling him one night whilst he and Owen had shared a drink at the man's ale house after work.

"Pfft, that things a pop gun!" Jim had replied.

Now, with the muzzle mere inches from his nose, he didn't think such a thing.

"What the hell—do you know what time it is? Is there a fire?"

"No, b—"

"Is someone *dead*?"

"No—"

"Then what do you want, Jim from the papers?" The gun's hammers were cocked. "Is this a ruse? You got men trying to get in the back way whilst—"

"Will you shut the fuck up and listen! Is Owen here?"

Rodney looked wounded. "Your fella from the rag?"

Jim nodded.

"He was earlier. Looked spooked. Why?"

"Is he *still* here, on your sofa or . . .?"

"No, he went on his merry way after a load of brandy."

"Oh, Jesus." Jim put a hand to his mouth. Tears threatened. He stepped from Rodney and looked behind him. In the near distance was a humpback bridge that led to Twin Jesters. "I have to go over there."

"Woah, fella. It's the middle of the night. Why not come in and talk about things over a whiskey, eh?"

"I really should try and find—"

"Look, you can't go padding around in the dark. You've got no light or coat, and you're in your pyjamas! Come in, have a drink and tell me what's going on. If you're no happier then, I'll help you with whatever's going on. Sound good?"

The sight of Rodney's bed-hair and sudden yawn broke Jim, and so he huffed and let out a chuckle. "I'm probably worrying over nothing. I'll take that drink, if it's okay by you?"

Rodney stepped aside and held the door open.

Rodney led them through the passageway and into the pub's lounge.

"It'll be warmer in here, Jim. The heat kicked in about thirty minutes ago."

When they walked through the entrance, Jim clapped eyes on the large room, and he couldn't ever remember wandering into this part of the ale house before. "You've recently decorated?"

"No, been the same in here for years. Make yourself comfortable. I'll fix us some drinks."

Jim took up a seat close to the bar.

Rodney reached for a couple of tumblers near the spirits. "Ice?"

"Neat, please."

Bottles clattered; liquid poured.

"So, what's happened?"

"You know about the unrest at Twin Jesters?"

"I've heard rumours, but nothing solid..."

Jim told Rodney how he hadn't heard off Owen yesterday evening, and how the man had gone into the town that was now supposedly sealed off by the police and army.

Rodney scoffed as he walked into the room with the drinks. "Come on, don't you think such a thing would be all over the news? I heard people there were hurt due to a gas leak or something. And I'm not surprised about Owen, man."

"What do you mean?"

"I told you, he was knocking brandy back like there was no tomorrow. He probably went home and collapsed."

Jim shook his head. "What time did he leave here?"

"Around ten, ten-thirty. Why?"

"That corresponds to the time he sent his email. His words were perfect—no mistakes, which makes me think he was sober. You said he was on edge?"

"He entered a little shaken but left happy. Tell me more about Twin Jesters. What's going on, exactly? Should I be worried?"

Jim decided to bite the bullet and speak about the email and its contents.

By the time he was finished, the bar owner looked jarred. "I think I need another," Rodney confessed.

"Me, too, but I don't think we should sit here wasting time. We need to get over to Twin Jesters."

"Call the police?"

"Whatever's being covered up, the police are in on it. I need to help my friend." Jim got up and walked towards the exit.

Rodney sighed. "Hold up, I'll come with you. You're going to need a jacket. We'll also need some light. Sun won't be up for another hour or so."

"We might need your gun too."

Five minutes later, with Jim outfitted with a jacket, they set off towards Twin Jesters. They had a flashlight each, with Rodney nursing his shotgun in the crux of his arm.

"I really don't think there's a point to this, but if it helps put your mind at ease, Jim . . ."

"It will. I just hope you're right about him sleeping the booze off."

"Pretty sure I am." Rodney lit a cigarette.

They pushed on through the darkness, over the humpback bridge and into the gloom beyond.

I bet he made his escape this way, Jim thought. *Poor fucker must have been terrified. He seemed shaken in that email.*

"The town is roughly a mile away, Jim. Think you'll be okay dressed as you are?"

"Just fine."

On the other side of the bridge was a narrow dirt track surrounded by fields, trees and shrubbery.

A cow mooed.

"Where the hell are we going?" Jim asked.

"This is the quickest way, trust me."

After walking for almost forty minutes, they reached the outskirts and spotted military and police presence.

"Jesus. You were right! What the hell is going on there?"

Jim ignored the question. "Do you know a sneaky way in or around?"

"I do. But it depends if we can slip past the first outpost—there could be guards everywhere."

When they got closer to the main road into Twin Jesters, they hunched down and used the green and trees as cover.

"Did you see the amount of army vehicles?" Rodney asked.

Jim nodded.

"Can't we just go up to them and speak of the situation?"

"From what I've heard, they'd gun us down on sight. Now, be—"

Jim stopped talking and stood.

"Get down or they'll see you."

"I don't think they'll see anything ever again, Rodney. Look," he said, pointing.

Rodney straightened up and peered in the direction Jim's shaking finger indicated. "What am I supposed to be seeing?"

"There, by the trucks."

Rodney squinted. There, in the dim, greying light of early morning, soldiers lay in the road. "What are they doing?"

"Come on," Jim said with a nod.

They approached with caution. Rodney readied his gun.

"There's nobody moving. No standing guards or anyone tending the fallen . . ." Jim's words trailed off.

When within touching distance of the military vehicles, they could see nobody standing guard to block their path into town.

All the soldiers were dead, their fatigues blood-soaked.

Most of them wore gas masks.

"What the hell?" Rodney asked.

A radio from inside a jeep crackled and spat. A voice came over the air waves. "Report back, unit 15. I say, report back. We've not heard from you in two hours."

The radio fell silent.

"This guy's missing half his neck!" Rodney cocked his shotgun.

The air stank of cordite and gun oil.

Spent casings lay scattered about the floor.

"Did the Fucks attack them, Jim?"

"Yes, I think so."

"We need to call someone! Come on. Let's get back to the pub."

"No. I have to find my friend." Jim made his way towards the jeep and poked his head inside. The console, dials and steering wheel were covered in blood, chunks of flesh and strands of hair. An unmoving soldier sat hunched in the passenger seat, his head resting against the dashboard. The eyeholes in his gasmask were shattered. A handgun lay on the driver's seat.

Jim reached a shaking hand out and unclasped the receiver from the radio.

Before he could press the squelch button, a hand gripped his shoulder.

A scream lodged in his throat.

"No, Jim. We can't alert them from here. If anyone should know we were out here, we'll be in a whole heap of shit."

"We'll be long—"

"Too risky."

"*Ugh!*" the soldier in the passenger seat groaned, pulling his face away from the dashboard. Blood trickled out of his gas mask.

"Oh, *fuck!*" Jim jumped back, catching his head on the doorframe. He tripped over his feet, glanced off Rodney and fell to the floor. "Shit."

Rodney raised his gun.

The private looked at them. His eyeholes seemed bottomless. He held a hand out, his voice muffled. "*Help . . .*"

Jim got to his feet and rushed to the other side of the vehicle and opened the door. Glass sprinkled the tarmac. "Can you stand?" he asked.

The soldier reached out and grasped Jim's arm. He dragged himself out of the jeep and slumped against Jim. "Get me out of here!"

"Okay, easy. Easy. Rodney, give me a hand, would you?"

The bigger man shot over to Jim and helped get the soldier clear of the vehicle.

"Take his mask off, Rodney."

When the private's headgear was removed, the extent of his wounds was revealed: chunks of flesh had been torn or bitten from his cheeks and half of his bottom lip was missing. Also, some of his teeth were gone. Those that remained were broken and misshapen.

How? He had his mask on . . . Jim wondered.

"They came from nowhere," the private slurred. Strings of bloody saliva clung to the remainder of his lip and drizzled down his chin. "There was so many of them." The fear and shock in his eyes spoke of hell. "Are the others dead?"

"Yes," Rodney said. "We need to get out of here, before they come back and attack us."

"They were wild, crazed killers. They were in front of us, behind, all around . . . I couldn't see them through the machine-gun smoke. I hid like a coward whilst my friends were killed. But then they found me and . . . I barely escaped their clutches. Oh, dear God!" He started weeping.

"He's cracking," Jim said. "Let's get him back to the pub."

Rodney nodded.

A snarl rumbled behind them.

"What was that?!" Jim looked over his shoulder. There was nothing but blackness.

Rodney stood and aimed his gun. "Get him to his feet. Start moving. I'll cover us."

"But—"

"Now, damn it!"

"Come on, let's move," Jim said, helping the soldier to his feet.

"Take my gun," the soldier told Jim. "From the holster."

Jim looked down at the man's belt and saw the pistol strapped to his waist. *Whose gun was that on the passenger seat then?*

Having fired guns at a shooting range on occasion whilst visiting the States, he drew the Beretta and loaded a round into its chamber. Jim then heaved the soldier up the road and into the bushes, joining the dirt track that would lead him back to the humpback bridge.

Behind, he heard the report of Rodney's bolt-action.

A heinous scream rang out.

Shit, shit, shit! Jim's mind screamed.

The sound of rushing footfalls filled his ears.

"Jim, where are you?"

Jim stopped and turned. "Over here, Rodney," he called, waving his arm. He then started walking again.

"Keep moving," the soldier urged.

Another gunshot from behind, followed by a second and third.

More tortured screams.

"We're not going to make it!" Jim blurted, his voice wavering. He felt like crying.

"Shut up and move."

The private suddenly felt lighter—Rodney joined them and threw the man's other arm over his shoulder.

"I *think* I got 'em all. There were more in the distance, though. I saw their eyes, red and glowing, but they were too far back to know which way we've come. They're cannibals, right?"

"Monsters, more like."

"What are you talking about, Jim?"

"There's no time to explain. Let's move!" Jim said, dragging the solider along as he upped his speed.

Fifteen minutes later, the humpback bridge came into sight.

The sun was almost at its zenith in front of them, its orange-red glow dangling over the roof of the Pig and Pen.

"If Owen went to Twin Jesters last night, then I'm assuming he called them out. They probably got him after he left my place," Rodney said. "Nobody—*nothing*— could have survived them."

"They're fucking evil," the soldier said.

Jim turned to the man, noticing for the first time that the soldier's surname was stitched into his fatigues. "Hodge?"

"Yes, sir?"

"What's really going on in Twin Jesters?" Jim asked. "Have the cannibals taken over? Are there evil jesters?" He felt foolish saying the latter. His face flushed.

"The cannibals—the tribe that terrorized—*argh*!" the man screamed as he was ripped from Jim and Rodney's clutches.

Cloth tore.

Bone snapped.

Blood sprayed across Jim's face as he stood staring, mouth agape.

Rodney raised his gun and fired, but the bullet was lost among the pack of large, disfigured people at their backs. The ones at the front foamed at the mouth and slashed clawed hands at them. All the while, the ones at the rear of the mob mauled and devoured Hodge in great big bloody batches.

Hunks of meat were torn from him as he screamed.

Jim reacted and shot, hitting one of the closest to him in the chest. The monster stumbled backwards and flopped to the ground.

"*Move!*" Rodney yelled, firing. "Over the bridge. Quick, Jim."

A heinous scream rang out.

When they got to the other side, Jim turned to cover Rodney, who'd fallen behind.

"Come on! They're on your arse."

Rodney, wheezing, chugged closer. "Jim, behind you!"

Jim swung around; his world slanted. Something heavy crashed against his face. He flipped over the bridge's low stone wall and crashed into the water below.

Semi-conscious, he watched, helpless, as the things swarmed Rodney and ripped into the landlord. His gun, pointed skyward, fired.

Jim tried to grab hold of some reeds on the embankment to stop from floating away, but it was useless. As he continued downstream, he was finally able to manoeuvre onto his stomach and swim.

When water became shallow, he got to his knees and crawled out of the stream. Panting, he collapsed into the mud and grass and lay there, his chest hitching.

Tears came.

"It true, all of it—everything Owen said in his email." He gasped, spitting water and slamming his fists against the ground.

When he regained control over his breathing, he clambered to his feet and staggered through the shrubbery.

I don't think I'm that far from the pub.

His feet squelched as he walked with the morning sun at his back.

I need to be careful—they're probably looking for me. They won't want me surviving to blab.

Jim swatted low branches out of his way as he marched forwards.

"I don't fucking believe this. Laura! Oh, *fuck*!"

He patted the coat down and found his mobile in a side pocket. He opened it. Nothing happened when he hit the power button.

"Frazzled," he muttered, replacing it and continuing forwards. And then he saw something ahead, close to the floor. He stopped and stooped. Whatever it was, it wasn't moving.

He got closer, being as quiet as possible.

Is that . . . a body?!

Jim could hear flies buzzing, the sound of squelching—which wasn't coming from his footwear.

"Oh, Christ!" He covered his mouth and swallowed his vomit.

A carcass lay before him, face down. Birds perched on top of the body—some tore at the dead person's flesh.

Jim stuck a foot out and toed the body so that it rolled onto its back.

Jim's mouth hung open.

Owen lay dead before him.

A couple of crows fought over a plucked eyeball.

Jim was powerless to stop the spew.

Chapter 13
Now

Betty watched from a gap in her curtains. There were soldiers everywhere—on the streets, in houses, down alleys—fighting her family.

Those fucking jesters have ruined everything! I should never have summoned them, and I banished them too late.

"These fuckers think they can come here and kill my blood? My family? My flesh?" She scrunched the net in her hand. "They shall die for this, now that our secret is out."

To look at, Betty wasn't a formidable woman, with her four-ten height and rotund frame. However, what she lacked in stature she made up for in temper and power, making her a fearless female and tribe leader.

She turned to her son, Igor, who stood at an incredible seven feet, three inches.

"I want you to rally every member of the clan you can and get them down from the hills and deepest, darkest parts of Twin Jesters. I want the streets to run red, Igor. Do you understand me?"

"Yes, Mother."

Betty picked up her rolling pin, which lay by her telephone, and began beating her open hand with it. "If they come knocking here, they'll die."

"We heard them talking about bombing the town, Mama."

"Don't worry. We have the bunker. They won't kill us *that* easily!"

"Maybe we shouldn't have listened to the clowns, Mama . . ." Igor's head lowered, his chin touching his chest.

"What did you say, boy?" She got closer to her son and looked up at the towering mass of meat. "Are you questioning my leadership? It was Hydra's plan to take over as much land as possible—to stamp out the fuckers who tried suppressing us. It's *ours*, and it's not like they can stop us, even if they do drive us out of Twin Jesters and Bridgend. We're *everywhere*!"

Betty would never admit it, but she knew he was right. And, deep down, she knew they could never win if the entire army came rolling in.

"But the only ones left like us are here, Mama. The others in the world are normal—there's no saying they've kept up *our* way of living."

She turned her face, teeth bared. "Watch that tongue, boy. You know damn well our kind can't get away from what they are on the inside no matter how the world tries to change them. Look at Liz—she's not turned. Never will. It's in here"—

she pointed at her head— "and here," she said, indicating her heart.

"Yes, Mama. I know you're right."

"Now, go do as I tell you, or I'll wrap this piece of wood around your head!" Outside, an explosion rocked the glass in the window frames. Gunfire and screams erupted. "Go! *Now!*"

Betty watched her overgrown son lurch off and disappear into the kitchen before turning to look down at her phone. *Maybe I should get Liz out here after all, especially if her position has been compromised. Damn it!*

She picked up the receiver and cast her eyes over the various photos of fallen family members until her sight landed on Hydra's. She felt the dead woman's presence wash over her, as though her spirit was trapped within the bricks and mortar of the family home.

Would you be proud of what we've accomplished? she wondered, her other hand hovering over the keypad.

* * *

After Hydra's death, Betty's mother Agnes built on what was left behind. She grew the family bigger, stronger, using Hydra's old home as HQ.

Over time, breeding stamped out most of the imperfections. Some of the normal children, when old enough, left for jobs in nearby cities, towns and countries far away. Now and then, however, a mutant-looking baby would happen along, and they'd be put to work with the other oddities, or drones. Their job was to protect the home and scavenge by night.

As the clan got bigger, they needed more houses and space, so they killed, cut up, and devoured their neighbours.

When people came looking, nothing or nobody was found.

The years rolled on, and the ownerless homes were put up for auction. More and more money had come in through the normal members who held jobs and the oddities' nightly raids, and so Betty was quick to purchase the abandoned properties. Suspicion fell on her, but there was no evidence to suggest she or her family had done anything wrong. They were respected within the community.

As dubious as it looked, she'd got away with it, and so the eldest, normal-looking children who'd remained in Twin Jesters soon occupied the new homes, taking with them a share of the mutant members. This eased the burden on Betty, who had Igor and a few others to look after.

Soon Betty had enough cash to buy more homes and the pub for Liz's parents.

Hydra's plan of taking over as much land and property as possible was slowly working. And, thanks to the town's checkered history, the odd person going amiss here and there wasn't uncommon.

"It's not *that* strange at all," a neighbour had once informed Betty. "Every so often, there's a spate of disappearances and whatnot." The woman's voice tapered to a whisper. "They say Twin Jesters is cursed."

Unsure of what the lady had meant, Betty looked into the town's history, finding it to be a bloody, brutal affair. Her interest in the jesters spiked, and so, thinking they could help speed up Hydra's ultimate plan, she decided to summon them via black magic she'd been taught by various clan members. Over the decades (or so Hydra had spoken of in the family bible), the tribe had dabbled in the mystic arts: voodoo, spiritual magic, a secret occult who helped build a cave in the hills and quadruple their numbers, and all the rest of it. Being descendants of Celtic warriors, with rumours of a splash of druid blood mixed in, they were able to do unspeakable things with their dark powers if performed correctly.

Betty had dug deeper, researching the numinous arts, finding people with druid blood who could perform magic that could call on spirits of the long deceased. Personally, she thought it a pile of mumbo-jumbo, but was keen to try.

As much trying as she did with virgin and goat sacrifices, Betty couldn't summon the jesters, and had given up. Then, roughly a year or so later, Ddu and Coch turned up out of the blue, knocking at her door one evening.

They're hideous! Betty had almost shrieked, moving away from the open door. Even though they'd looked startling, she hadn't been frightened of them, and, in some weird way, had been excepting them.

They had stood in the doorway, towering above her, silent except for the jingle-jangle of their bells. They stank of earth. Of death, blood and decay. They had wry smiles on their faces, and when they spoke, their voices were soft, delicate.

"You seek us out, Betty?"

Not even them knowing her name had unnerved her. "Yes. I need your help in fulfilling a . . . plan. It involves much blood and death. Something you're much accustomed to, no? I'm sure you'll enjoy what I have in store."

But of course, the jesters hadn't needed much persuading. Where there was mischief to be caused, they wanted a part of it. They'd replied with grins, exposing rotten, broken, bent teeth.

"Won't you come in? I have a lot to tell you," Betty had said, holding the door wide for Coch and Ddu.

It had taken Betty a spit over two hours to fill the jesters in on what she wanted. And then they'd left, disappearing into the dark, foggy night without a word. However, the deal proved a grave mistake. Whereas Betty had wanted people picked off one by one, slowly and methodically, the jesters had had a massacre in mind instead . . .

* * *

Betty shook her head. *Get your mind in the here and now, woman! Nothing can be undone, that's for damn sure. And it's not like everyone in the family knows. Only Igor, and he wouldn't go telling on his mum. Not if he knows what's good for him.*

With trembling fingers, she punched Liz's number into the keypad. When there was no answer after the twentieth ring, she hung up and tried again. And again.

"Fucking hell!" Betty slammed the phone's receiver into its cradle and stared out the window. There were troops moving in her direction. "*Shit!*" She was about to call her son but remembered she'd sent him to get reinforcements. "They're *dead* if they come here," she muttered, taking up the rolling pin and clobbering her open hand.

A fierce knock rattled the front door.

"If there's anybody in there, I suggest you open up, or we'll shoot the door in!"

Betty's heart thundered in her chest. She was frozen to the spot. *What to do, what to do?*

"You have until the count of three, and that's one . . ."

Weapons cocked.

"Two . . ."

Betty approached the entrance to the hallway and peered around the jamb. Through the frosted glass in the front door, large silhouettes loomed.

"Th—"

"Don't shoot, I have children in here!" she lied. "I'm coming. Wait, *please.*"

"Hurry up, woman, or I'm going to riddle this door with lead."

"Just a second." Betty put the rolling pin to one side and ambled down the hall. She reached out with a shaking hand and grabbed the locks. As she was about to disengage them, a blast rang out, followed by rapid gunfire. Screaming, she threw herself to the floor and covered her head, thinking bullets were going to smash through the glass and hit her.

"Get over there and stamp that out!" a man shouted beyond the door. "Quickly!"

Feeling foolish, Betty got to her feet and again went for the locks.

"If you're not opening, I'm blasting!"

Betty unlocked the entrance and greeted the masked men with a smile. "Yes?"

The lead soldier gripped her by her jumper and pulled her out onto the stoop. "What the hell are you still doing here? This place has been evacuated. Don't you know what's going on? People are being butchered out here!"

Betty saw red and shoved the soldier's hands away. "This is *my* home, and me or my family aren't going anywhere, you hear?!"

"If you don't, you'll be blown to bits. We're detonating this town in thirty minutes. We're overrun."

Over his shoulder, Betty saw her family tearing up a group of soldiers. It was hard keeping a smile off her face.

"Sir," a young soldier at the man's back called, putting a hand on his superior's shoulder. "We have problems."

"What is it, private?" The officer turned. "Oh, fuck!"

Betty's family were finished ripping up their victims and now had their sights set on the men before her.

"There's only a few of us left, sir. What do we do?"

"Everyone, inside!" the leader screamed, pushing past Betty.

"*Hey*!" she tried to protest, but the dozen army men were already inside her home. Before closing the door, she warned her kin off and smiled. *This lot's not going to know what's hit them,* she thought, engaging the bolts.

"Get the door barricaded, men!" the officer yelled.

"I'm sure they—" Betty again tried to protest but was pushed out of the way. Her furniture was upended and shoved against the door; her main window covered.

"Check all back doors, windows and the rooms of this place. Make sure we're safe. Hawks, get on the radio."

"Yes, sir!" Betty heard a man call from somewhere.

"Now wait a bloody minute!" Betty found her voice. "This is *my* home, and you can't just come in here and throw your weight around."

The officer ignored her and stepped closer. "You said there were children?"

Betty couldn't see the soldier's eyes due to the lenses in the mask being tinted. *He thinks he can intimidate me?* "I lied. Shoot me."

He got closer still, his breathing eerie through the mask's vents. "Don't tempt me, bitch. I've had a stressful day, and I don't handle hostile environments well."

"Why don't you get out? Your threat is on the streets, in Twin Jesters, not in here."

"This is a government issue, and we can do whatever the hell we want, woman. Now, is there anyone else in the house, a possible threat to me or my men?"

His hand lowered to his holstered handgun.

He means to kill me if I lie or don't answer.

There were others in the house, but they would be hidden by now: in the walls, under the floorboards, in the attic, in the bunker . . . Her kin could smell trouble a mile off, and so she was confident when she answered, "No. I'm alone."

The hammer clicked on his gun.

He knows I'm lying . . .

She gulped and tried to remain calm.

"You're with them, aren't you? I knew something was wrong about you," he whispered.

His gun cleared its holster.

"*Sir*!" a woman yelled.

The officer's hand froze, his gun unmoving.

"The house is clear, sir. Nobody here but her."

He holstered his weapon, his eyes never leaving Betty. "You're lucky."

"I have nothing to hide," she affirmed.

"We'll see about that." He turned his back and addressed his troops.

Betty's heartrate slowed. *As soon as Igor gets back, we'll get rid of them.* "Excuse me. Do you mind if I use *my* phone?" she asked the man in charge.

He turned to look her up and down.

Why don't they take those stupid masks off? There's no gas or disease here.

"Who do you want to call?"

"My daughter. She's probably worried sick if this madness is on the news."

He nodded. "It's not, but go ahead."

"Thanks." She turned and walked to the phone. Picking it up, she punched Liz's number into the keypad and waited. After the fifth ring, it was answered. "Liz?" she whispered. "Thank God! I've been trying you non-stop. Look, I do think you should come out here after all. As soon as you can. I have the army here. You're not safe there on your own. We can use the bunker . . . Igor is out gathering reinforcements. I know what I said earlier, but I've changed my mind. Get here by midnight."

Betty hung up. "Would anyone like tea?"

"This is a life or death situation!" the officer snapped. "Now, shut up and get out of our sights."

"Rude fucker," she uttered. "That black heart of yours will taste just fine . . ."

"Excuse me?"

"Nothing."

He then went back to ordering his personnel around. "I want you on the upper windows, laying down fire. Same at the back and front. I also need someone on the doors. Let's get this place secured so we can bunk down and wait for the cavalry, people."

"Sir?"

"What is it, Hawks?"

"The radio . . . It's dead."

"How the fuck can it be *dead*?"

"It's not detecting a signal, sir. It's like..."

"Like what? Spit it out!"

"Like we're in a black hole. There's . . . *nothing*."

"That can't be. Keep trying, damn it!"

Soldiers rushed about the house, and soon Betty heard crashing footfalls above—dust worked free and sprinkled her face. Spluttering, she remained calm and kept a lid on her temper.

She smiled. *I just knew they wouldn't be able to get a hold of their base.* A giggle escaped her.

"Something funny? My men are dying out there, and all you can do is *laugh*?"

"It has nothing to do with that. It was something my daughter said, actually."

"Still nothing with the radio, sir. It's of no use."

"Well, make it of use, Hawks. You're the fucking radio tech!"

"Sir, the threat seems to have retreated," a voice called from upstairs.

"Keep your eyes peeled!" the officer replied, going to the window and peeking from behind a board that had been placed over it. "Hmm . . . What are they up to?"

Betty took the opportunity to move to the back of the house and look out the kitchen window. There was no sign of Igor. *He'll know there's trouble here, surely? Damn, I didn't think this through at all.*

Gunfire erupted from behind Betty, startling her.

"*Argh*! I'm hit!" someone cried.

"Neutralize the threat!" the commanding officer bellowed.

Bullets tore up the kitchen floor around her and thudded into the cupboards, shelving units and fixtures. Glass and china alike exploded.

From the other room came agonized screams.

"Fucking traitors!" a new voice stated.

The stench of cordite and oil filled the air, catching at the back of her throat. Betty gagged, wheezed and coughed. A thick fog surrounded her.

What the fucking—

Betty thought she was going to collapse. Her eyes filled with tears, blurring her vision. She got down on her hands and knees and sucked at the cleaner air.

She started to hyperventilate when slugs punched holes into the kitchen floor close by.

The game's up. We've been rumbled. Did they spot Igor out there? Did they try coming in off the streets?

Rushing, crashing footfalls assaulted her ears. She screamed and covered her head.

"*Die*, motherfucker!" a woman bellowed.

Something ripped.

Spilling, splashing sounds ensued.

Rapid gunfire erupted. Bullets stitched the wall at Betty's side and bits of plaster, tile and wiring came loose.

"*Stop!*"

A door slammed against a wall.

The sound of her drooling, bloodthirsty drones filled the inside of her head.

More ripping, tearing sounds, which were followed by munching and chewing.

Someone somewhere slurped liquid as though they were trying to get the dregs out of an empty cup with a straw.

"There's too many! Re—*argh*! Out the back!"

Betty thought her heart was going to smash through her ribcage and flutter away. She looked up in time to see the commanding officer standing in the doorway, his mask gone, his uniform ripped, bloody claw marks adorning the chest area.

"You fucking *bitch*!" He cocked his gun and raised it.

At his back, soldiers scrambled and shoved him out of the way. His burst of fire went wide, taking apart a cupboard filled with plates and bowls.

Betty got to her feet and ran towards the living room, brushing shoulders with the troops that scrambled out the back door, where they were greeted by Igor and a band of killers, who tore them asunder.

Before Betty could step foot inside the lounge, she was pulled back by her hair. A pistol shoved against her temple. Through blurred eyes, Betty saw a number of figures standing before her.

"Get the *fuck* back!" The gun's muzzle pushed tighter to her temple. "I'm walking the fuck out of here and this town, and I'm taking this bitch with me. And if any of you traitor, hillbilly, interbreeding fucks try to stop me, then I'll fill this cunt full of lead!"

Betty's vision cleared. Masked soldiers stood in front of her, pointing their assault rifles in her direction.

They were flanked by her drones from outside and from within the home. Their smell was overpowering—their naked, filth-encrusted bodies didn't yield a strip of clean skin.

They were hungry.

Some gnashed their teeth; others snapped their jaws.

Tongues lolled.

Their bloodshot eyes were banshee-wild.

They advanced, forcing the commanding officer to step backwards, taking Betty with him.

"I said stay back!" He pressed the gun tighter to Betty, forcing her head to bend.

"You're hurting me!"

"I should shoot you in the fucking face. You got my men killed."

"You shouldn't have come here. You don't belong. This is mine and my family's town, bastard."

"Shut up, shut up, shut up!" he screamed in her ear. Phlegm plastered the side of her face. "Get back!"

"Let me go and I'll spare you," Betty said.

"You think I'd trust a piece of shit like you?"

"I'm the leader. They'll listen to me. You can't win, no matter how many tanks, guns and soldiers you send. We're too strong, and we're everywhere; all around, above and under you. You won't see us coming. Nobody will. Our time has come."

"You won't be saying that after we bomb you're fucking arses!"

"Ha! Please. We will flee to our bunkers, hills and woods. Nothing can stop us. *Nothing* and nobody! Go ahead, drop your bombs. See what happens."

"Crazy fucker." He edged out of the room and into the kitchen.

Her drones and the three military men followed.

The traitorous soldiers baffled her. *Who are they? Drones dressed as troops?*

The officer's feet crunched annihilated glass and china as he shuffled backwards.

Her clan ambled forward.

She screamed when he removed the gun from her temple and put a bullet through the forehead of one of the soldiers mixed in with her lot.

"I'm being serious. *Back*! Or I'll kill more of you."

"You don't have enough ammunition to kill all of us, sir," one of the remaining troops said.

Betty's kin continued to close in, flooding around their fallen.

His gun kicked to life again and again, dropping two more.

The back door burst open, forcing the man to turn.

Igor stood there with his bloodied pack of drones, some of whom were holding offal. Others had tendrils of skin and bits of guts hanging from their mouths.

"Sweet Jesus . . ."

Before he could get another shot off, the drones that flanked him closed in and pulled him off Betty. They ripped the gun from his hand and dragged him to the floor.

Betty stood over him and stared him in the eye as Igor and the rest tore his clothes off and raked at his skin. Searching fingers invaded the man's anus, mouth and other orifices. His tongue and penis were stretched and pulled free. The eyeballs were next, and it wasn't long before his stomach was pulled open and his guts feasted on.

Turning her back on the carnage, Betty, on wobbling legs, pinballed out of the kitchen and into the living room where the remaining soldiers were.

"Who are you?" she asked.

They both turned to her and removed their masks. They held no deformities.

The one in front, who had 'Hawks' written on his chest, smiled and spoke for the rest of them. "Don't you recognize us, Betty?"

She shook her head.

Hawks' smile grew and a laugh escaped him. "We're family!" he stated. "All of us." He indicated the female troop at his back and the one dead on the floor. "Bastard killed our brother."

"B-but, you're not *my* children."

Hawks laughed again. "No, of course not—we're too old. Agnes was our grandmother, Aunt Betty. She sent our parents—your siblings—out into the world before you were born, so you wouldn't know us. Sorry we couldn't come to the rescue sooner, but we didn't want to cause too much suspicion."

"You were killing soldiers on the streets?"

Hawks nodded. "Plus, I'm the radioman. As much as they wanted backup, I told them the radio was down."

Now it was Betty's turn to smile. "You're going to be a great asset, boy."

"Oh?"

Betty nodded, cackled, gathered her clan and laid down her plan.

Chapter 14
Now

Jim screamed and stamped, scattering the crows off Owen's body. Tears and vomit covered his face. With the crows gone, Jim got on his knees and scooped Owen into his arms.

"What the *fuck* did they do to you, friend?"

He looked at his ex-employee and saw the birds had pecked most of his face away, the eyes gone—the sockets bottomless wells of black ink. Owen's teeth were visible through large holes in his cheeks, and some were missing.

There was bruising around his throat and his head flopped around, suggesting his neck had been snapped. His eyes bugged; his tongue lolled. His clothes were shredded, revealing claw and bite marks all over his body.

Poor bastard. Whoever did this will pay, Owen.

Jim placed Owen's head on the ground, got to his feet, and scooped the reporter off the floor like a sack of spuds, placing him over his shoulder.

With the morning sun beating down on his back, he headed back in the direction he'd come.

It took him over an hour to get to the pub, thanks to the things from Twin Jesters lurking in the bushes.

As he cowered, they baited Jim by whispering threats and telling him they could smell his blood, sweat and piss. When they couldn't find him, Jim moved until it was time to cower again.

When he reached the pub's door, Jim kicked it in and closed it behind him. The lock was smashed, useless. He put Owen down on one of the benches before going behind the bar to look for a phone. In his search, he discovered another one of Rodney's guns.

Christ, how much protection did he need?!

Jim took the shotgun, along with two full boxes of ammunition, and placed it on the bar. Not finding a phone, he snatched a brandy glass off a shelf close to the optics and poured himself a double.

When he'd drained the glass, he poured a second. Then a third.

He wiped his mouth clean, loaded the gun and headed for the door.

"Damn! What am I going to do about locking—then again, does it matter? I need to get the fuck out of here and over to that lying sack of shit at the Lamb and Flag. Going to end that bitch, but not before I get her to tell me where the leader of her tribe hangs out."

His eyes widened when he saw hideous men and women stalk out of the bushes and head towards the pub.

"The *fuck*?!"

One of them pointed at him.

Another licked its lips.

"Gonna pull your insides out, *fucker*!"

Jim pushed a table up against the door.

This won't keep them out for long.

He rushed through the pub to the back door, finding it bolted. Jim looked out the window and saw more of the disfigured people coming that way.

They're surrounding me. Before moving, he tested the door's sturdiness. He couldn't budge it. Jim moved back to the bar and spotted the ones up front trying to force the door open.

"Back, or I'll shoot!" he commanded.

They continued to shove and push, the table scraping along the floor.

Jim fired. His bullet tore through the thick wooden door. One of them screeched—the noise was like something he'd never heard before. Blood splashed against the window.

Not sticking around to see what would happen next, he gathered up the ammunition and headed out into the hallway.

Up!

The front door crashed open. They entered the building with a snarl and a snigger.

Jim headed to the second floor and into the master bedroom, where he found Rodney's mobile phone on a nightstand. He snatched it up and placed it in his breast pocket.

They were on the stairs, climbing slowly.

Jump out a window? And break my legs? No chance.

Peeking over the banister, Jim spotted three ascending. He put the gun over the rail and fired, taking the lead cannibal out—the bullet crashed through its skull and sprayed its brains over the wall. The others screamed and beat their chest before bounding up the stairs.

Jim ran for another set of steps, leading to the top floor. When he reached the landing, he moved underneath the hatch in the ceiling and pulled on the cord. The small door fell downwards, the ladder lowering. Jim snapped its legs into place and climbed. After gaining entrance to the attic, he turned back to pull the ladder up, but a cannibal got a hand to it. Jim put a bullet between its eyes.

When the ladder was back in place, Jim secured the hatch.

There's no way they can get to me now.

He relaxed, pushed away from the dropdown door and pressed his back to a wall. It was sweltering inside the confined space.

Jim removed the mobile phone from his pocket and switched it on. No signal, and the battery indicator was flashing.

"Who am I going to call anyway? Well, the wife would have been a starting point." He shook his head. "I never thought this morning might be the last time I'd see her." Jim slammed his fist against the floor. "*Fuck!*"

Someone is bound to happen along soon and scare them off. Like regulars.

"Going to get you!" one of them said, scraping its fingernails along the hatch.

A shiver inched its way up Jim's back, and icicles stabbed at his scrotum, shrivelling his privates. "Not if I get you bastards first!"

Not willing to just sit there and hope to dodge his demise, Jim got to his hands and knees and searched through the various boxes Rodney had stored in the attic. He used the mobile's light to aid him.

Hopefully I'll find something of use before the battery dies.

He shifted boxes out of his way and opened others, spilling their contents over the floor.

"Come on, got to be . . . *Ah*!" Jim scooped a torch up and tried it. He was surprised when the thing burst to life. "Excellent." He pocketed the phone and used the torch instead.

When he got to the back of the room, his gaze fell on a large Jerrycan.

"And what do we have here, then?"

Jim went to the red container and tried lifting it, but the twenty-litre receptacle wouldn't budge. Fluid sloshed around inside it.

"This could be my ticket out of here."

As he dragged the can from its space, he saw another box, a plastic one, hidden behind it. Jim placed the fuel container to one side and pulled the new container from its space. He opened it.

"Oh, Rodney—I could kiss you!"

Inside was shotgun ammo, gloves, rope, canned food, a lighter, batteries for the torch, a lantern, first aid kit and other bits and pieces needed for a survival kit.

"I wouldn't have taken Rodney for a survivalist nut!"

Jim gathered the stuff and put it in the middle of the room with the Jerrycan. He scanned the attic and found a rucksack peeking from behind a support beam. He grabbed it and started filling it with the items he thought he'd need.

"*Wait!*" Jim looked up at skylight. "If I could get up there, I could light up those fuckers below."

His ingenious plan couldn't have come at a better time, as he heard hands yanking at the attic's trapdoor.

"Big mistake, fucktards."

Jim uncapped the Jerrycan and found the lighter, putting it aside for safe keeping. He then picked up the rifle, loaded it and kicked the hatch open, seeing cannibals below riding piggyback.

"Not so stupid, are you?"

He opened fire, shooting two and killing one outright.

More of them rushed up the stairs and lunged at the door and ladder, trying to get purchase.

When he'd cleared enough of them, Jim grabbed the can of fuel and poured it over the injured and those who kept coming.

"Like rats out of a fucking hole!"

After dumping enough diesel onto the unsuspecting victims, he ripped a strip off his shirt, set fire to it and threw it. The fuel went up with a quiet *woomph,* instantly engulfing everything around it.

The creatures shrieked.

Some ran; others hit the floor and rolled, trying to douse themselves.

Whole place is going up!

Jim threw the rucksack on his back, shouldered the gun and stood on the plastic box he'd found. This gave him enough height to reach the skylight.

Jim pushed it open and hoisted himself up onto the slate.

Below, aflame cannibals ran from the pub and into the bushes.

"Burn, you bastards!" he screamed. "That's for Owen and Rodney."

After securing one end of the rope around a chimney stack, Jim decided to go off the left-hand side of the pub, which was clear. Smoke now billowed out of the building, and he knew he didn't have much time before it collapsed.

He threw the rope over the side and watched it hit the gravelled floor to the car park before abseiling down.

Car keys?

He patted his pockets and found them in his back one. Jim fished them out, unlocked his car and threw his newfound gear on the back seat.

"Where now? Twin Jesters? No—Liz. That bitch needs to die."

He started his car and put it in first.

I can't just walk in there shooting the place up?! Jim stared at himself in the mirror. He looked wild. *Can I*? He took a deep breath and looked out the driver-side window. The cannibals had retreated altogether. *What if I go to Liz tonight? Wait for her to lock up and finish what Sam started*? He smiled, liking the sound of that.

Releasing the handbrake, Jim powered his car from the pub and headed home. If he was going to carry out his plan, he'd need to think of something to tell his wife, for she wouldn't approve. Jim also needed a hot meal in his belly and a shower.

* * *

Since the call from Betty, Liz had been in a panicked state, not being able to concentrate on anything.

Get through tonight's shift, then I can get me and the girls out of here, she thought, serving a pint of beer to one of her regulars. *Thankfully, it's been pretty quiet so far. Let's hope it stays that way!*

Liz had argued with herself—after Betty's call—that the best thing to do was pack up and leave right then and there, but she knew it would have caused suspicion, especially since the newspaper guy had been sniffing around.

Should have killed the fucker where he stood! She gritted her teeth, fearing they would shatter if she didn't ease up. *If he comes back, I'll do him in.* The glass she was holding slipped from her hand, hitting the floor and bursting into a puddle.

"*Shit*! Oh, man. Fuck! Sorry, Jonesy," she said to the man she'd been serving.

"It's okay, beaut."

"Bollocks. I think that's the first beer I've *ever* spilled."

"What's up, Liz? You seem distracted tonight. Not yourself at all," he said, his gaze drifting down to her exposed cleavage, thanks to her low-cut top.

"You know it keeps the barflies coming back for more!" her brother used to say. "Keeps them drinking, too!' He'd flash his teeth. *Yeah, and you loved getting your hands all over them too*, she thought, smiling.

"That's what I like to see, Liz." Jonesy smirked, taking his fresh pint. "Always nice to see a pretty gal beaming."

"Thanks, Jonesy. Been a lot on my mind today," she said, mopping up the spilled beer and shattered glass.

"Oh? Anything I can help with?" he asked, pocketing his change. His eyes were still fastened to her tits, her nipples now jutting through the thin fabric of her top.

"Not really, no. But thanks for the concern."

He was standing right there, wasn't he? Looking at me with accusing eyes. He knew, from the off, there was something wrong here.

"You know, if someone's giving you a hard time, me and the boys will be happy to help you sort them out," he whispered in her ear, his arse hovering off his barstool.

The 'boys' he referred to were also in the pub. At current, they were playing pool and darts around the other side of the bar. They were a rough bunch who ran small-time business rackets within the area. They went by the name Hooligans, and Jonesy was the fearless leader who thought a lot of himself.

Liz managed a smile, and then an idea hit her.

"Well, there's this guy…" She stopped talking and forced tears down her cheeks. She turned her back to Jonesy, playing him.

"Hey, what's going on? You can tell me, sweetheart."

She felt his hand on her shoulder and smiled. "The rotten bastard killed my brother," she said, getting closer to Jonesy. "They got into a row over money and this . . . this bastard killed him. I would go to the police, but I haven't got enough proof."

"Who is he? Does he drink here?"

"He's been in once, but I don't think you know him. He goes by the name of Jim Hengroth."

"Hengroth? Hmm, name rings a bell. Got a photo, number or address for him?"

She shook her head. "He said he was going to come back here to kill and rape me and burn the place to the ground. I'm so scared." Liz was visibly shaking.

"Not on my fucking watch!" Jonesy got up and walked around the bar to Liz. He put his arm around her, and she put her head on his chest. "You want my help?"

She could feel his erection poking against her thigh.

Men are so easy to manipulate.

Liz looked around the room. None of the other customers were paying attention, as the TV was on and they had their eyes glued to a football match that was unfolding. Every now and then, there was a cheer or words of annoyance.

"I'd love your help, Jonesy." Liz slid her hand down his chest and placed it close to his manhood. She felt his body twitch. *Will he want me to pay in kindness? Well, doesn't matter if he does.*

"Okay. Is there someplace we can go to talk about this?"

"I have to tend the bar, Jonesy."

"You'll only be five minutes. I just need to talk to Spurs about this, and I'd like you there when I do."

"Fine. Give me two minutes, and meet me in the lounge," Liz said, pulling away from him.

Jonesy went back to his seat.

"I have to go and change a few barrels and get some stock for the bar," she announced. "Does anyone want anything before I go? I'll be about fifteen minutes."

"Pull us a pint, Liz, please," an old-timer asked.

"Bitter, Emerson?"

"Yes, love."

"I'll pop it on the bar for you, Em. We'll sort payment out when I get back."

"Okay, hun."

Liz grabbed her keys and made for the door. When she got to the lounge, she found Jonesy and Spurs, his second-in-command, standing in a darkened corner. They were whispering and laughing.

"Ah, there she is. I was just filling Spurs in on what you were telling me, Liz."

Spurs was a brute of a man, well over six feet, five inches tall and close to three hundred pounds of meat and muscles.

I could feed my family for a year on that big bastard, she thought. *And it might very well come to that . . .*

Like the rest of the Hooligans, save for Jonesy, Spurs wore a leather biker vest that had a massive patch on the back with their elite name stitched across the shoulder blades in arched lettering. Under the word was a drawing of a man sporting a multi-coloured Mohawk and wearing chains around his neck—his torso heavily tattooed, his nipples and ears pierced.

Spurs was bare-chested, and when he walked, the spurs on his boots chinked.

He stuck his hand out for Liz to shake, as though they were meeting for the first time. He had a strapping, teeth-exposing smile on his face, and a gold-capped tooth winked at her. "Hi, darlin'," he said, his words smooth.

He's a grinning crocodile, she thought. Liz had heard many stories about him. Spurs was an enforcer to end all enforcers, and ate his victims' hearts.

She had to admit, it made her wet for him.

He'd be a perfect partner for breeding. Big, strong and best of all, fucking Looney Tunes.

His long, lank and black-as-coal hair flanked his face, and his pale-blue eyes peeked through the thick, unkempt ringlets.

She took his hand, trying to appear unimpressed. After the friendly gesture, Liz crossed her hands over her chest, stuck a hip out and bent one knee. She sighed. "Well, what can you guys do to help? I don't want the police—"

"Wow!" Jonesy said. "Nobody's going to know you're involved."

"And I suppose you're going to send this big lug over there?"

"Hey!" Spurs stepped forward.

"Sorry, I'm just rattled," she lied. "This guy really spooked the fuck out of me, guys." Liz turned the waterworks on again even though there was no need—she had Jonesy right where she wanted him.

"And I told you nothing is going to happen to you. But before I do anything, I want you to fill Spurs in."

Liz turned to the enforcer and spilt her guts about Jim." After he said what he had to, he threatened me."

"With burning the pub?"

Liz nodded.

"Okay, how do you want to play this, Jonesy? We can't have Liz being pushed around—not on our turf."

Inwardly, Liz smiled. *I should have asked for their help sooner.*

"There's one other thing. I need to get to a family member in Twin Jesters later this evening, after locking up. I was wondering if you boys would escort me there?" She bit her lip in a provocative way.

Spurs looked her up and down. It was clear what he was thinking.

Jonesy cleared his throat. "I'll need some form of payment . . ."

"Well, I don't have much money, but I'd be happy to pay you boys in kindness?" She winked at Spurs. "At the same time . . ." It was her turn to linger.

Spurs turned to Jonesy and smiled. "I'm pleased with that offer, boss."

"I bet you are, son. Okay, you're on, Liz. Do you know if this Jim character is a lone wolf?"

"Meaning?"

"Did he threaten to come back here with 'the boys' or anything like that?"

"No, not at all."

Jonesy nodded. "Spurs, round the guys up and see if you can find out where this fucking punk lives. Didn't you say he works for the newspaper, Liz?"

"Yes." She gulped. "What will you do to him?"

"Tear his fucking heart out," Spurs jumped in, and then he laughed, which was loud and braying, making her wince. "If he works for the paper, he should be easy to find, boss."

"His name's Jim, right?" Jonesy wanted to know.

"Correct," Liz replied.

"Okay, Spurs, away you go, and take Knucklehead and Berserko with you. Once you find his home, come back here and report to me—I don't want you doing *anything* until I know what's what. Got it?"

Spurs nodded. "Can I check his home out, see how the land lies?"

"Yeah, of course, but straight back here before anything else."

"No probs." Spurs walked towards the door leading to the bar, looked back, and flicked his tongue at Liz. A shot of excitement pulsed through her.

"He's a wily one. I have to keep his chain tight."

Liz smiled. "I bet, Jonesy."

"Now, how about a little bit of payment before the boys get back, huh?" He got closer to her and put his fingers through her soft, walnut-coloured hair. "You smell delicious. I bet your pussy tastes damn good, baby."

She didn't resist or back away. "You'll find out, but not right now. I have a pub full of people to serve. I'm sure you can keep your trouser snake under control until you've taken care of business?" She winked, stroked his face and left the room. When she got back behind the bar, Liz found she had punters waiting to be served, and saw Spurs and his men leave.

Excellent. With Jim out of the way, the clan and I should be fine. I'm sure Betty is crushing the threat her end.

* * *

When Spurs, Knucklehead and Berserko left the pub, they jumped on their bikes.

"Where we heading, Spurs?" Knucklehead asked, slurring his words as he put his German helmet on. This wasn't due to him being drunk; Knucklehead always slurred his words due to being kicked in the head by a ram when he was a boy. The doctors told his mother he should have died but informed her that he had a skull as thick as a sheet of metal.

It wasn't just impaired speech he lived with either. Knucklehead's jawline was fucked up. A dent graced his forehead and a dashing scar ran from his hairline to his Adam's apple.

He's an oil painting of beauty, Spurs thought, looking at his life-long friend, who he'd never insult or make fun of. *The man kept me sane in prison. I owe him my life.* Someone once had name-called Knucklehead in Spurs' presence, and they'd paid dearly. *Not on my watch. Ever.*

"Remember Squealer McGee?" Spurs called over.

"Simon?" chirped the rotund Berserko, who was crazier than a shit-house rat. His level of insanity never failed to impress Spurs.

"That's the fella."

"Fuck, I've not heard of him in a dog's age!" Knucklehead confessed. "He's not still giving people up, is he?"

Spurs nodded, then laughed. "He sure is. Some pricks never learn, right?"

Berserko shook his head. "I would have thought the heavies over on the west side would have wiped his fucking arse out by now, considering he gave up most of the mob bosses ten years ago."

"I think Jonesy's been keeping him ticking. He's been a good informant to us over the years. Knows every fucker in the damn borough!"

"Got a mouth like a fucking foghorn," Knucklehead said.

Spurs laughed. "Come on, let's get over to his place. I'm sure he'll be happy to flush this Jim dude out for us."

The men laughed as their hogs pulled from the kerb.

Twenty minutes later, Spurs and the boys parked outside a ramshackle building that looked ready for dynamiting.

A solid gust of fucking wind would blow this shithole down, Spurs thought.

"Nobody fart!" Berserko said, as though reading Spurs' mind.

"*Ha*!" Knucklehead chortled. "Little pigs, little pigs . . ."

Spurs shook his head as he dismounted his bike. He slipped his helmet off, put it on his seat, proceeded up the side of the building (which was an alleyway) and knocked on the heavy metal door.

An echo from the other side assaulted his ears.

Spurs looked at his watch. *Almost ten p.m.*

Before Simon 'Squealer' McGee had turned stoolpigeon for the police and everyone who threw cash his way, he'd worked as an accountant for the big boys of the criminal underworld. When his boss and best friend of thirty years was caught for killing and racketeering, it looked like everyone was going down with their warlord.

But not Squealer. He gave everyone up, including members of other gangs and petty crooks. After that, he stuck close to the police and gave them anything and everything they wanted in return for his safety. Not that he needed it, as he had thugs like Jonesy and others who were happy to look out for him.

Should the heavies come looking, they were sent packing. And, after a few heads, toes and fingers were returned to said troublemakers' money men, they started leaving Simon alone.

"Squealer, it's Spurs. Open the fuck up, man!"

"Cold enough to freeze the balls off a brass monkey out here, dude," Knucklehead commented.

"Man-up, fella," Berserko told him.

"Shut up, guys!" Spurs interrupted. "I can't hear if he's coming or not. Squealer!" Spurs thumped the door repeatedly with his fist. "Come the fuck on. *Jesus*. You best not be tugging your goose in there, dirty little fucker."

"Isn't he married?" Knucklehead asked.

Spurs looked at him. "No woman would marry *that*! He wanks off more than a twelve-year-old lad, Knucks."

The three men laughed.

"I'm *coming*!" Squealer yelled from somewhere inside, provoking the men to laugh harder.

"I hope he means to the door," Spurs managed, starting them off again.

Heavy-duty chains rattled on Squealer's side of the entrance. "Spurs?" the man said through a yawn.

"Yeah. Open the hell up."

"Do you know what time it is?"

"Fuck the time! Your skills are needed."

Squealer muttered something unintelligible. He then pulled the door open. As he did, he popped his glasses on and pushed them up the bridge of his nose.

Spurs shoved his way past the man and walked into the room that lay beyond. It brought to mind the inside of an abandoned factory.

"Hey!" Squealer protested as Knucklehead and Berserko did the same. "I didn't invite you guys—"

Spurs held up a handful of money. "I need to know the whereabouts of a Jim Hengroth. He works the local newspaper."

"Works it? He *runs* it."

"Don't get smart, Squealer. Just give me what I want, and we'll be on our way."

The informant grabbed the wad of cash and closed the door. "Stay here, I'll be right back."

"What, no offer of tea?" Berserko asked.

Squealer looked over his shoulder as he climbed a set of steel steps to the second floor. "No. Kitchen's closed, fellas," he said, then disappeared out of sight.

They talked amongst themselves for twenty minutes before Squealer reappeared with a ledger of sorts.

"Right, okay—I have the man's work and home addresses, including contact numbers for both, and his mobile."

"Is he married? Kids?" Spurs said.

"Married his sweetheart twenty-odd years ago."

"That's excellent," Spurs said, smiling. "May I?" He stuck his hand out for the book.

"You'll return it in the same condition?"

"Of course. What type of reprobate do you think I am?"

Squealer eyed the burly man over the rims of his glasses. "Am I supposed to answer that?"

"Give me that!" Spurs snatched the information and looked through it, finding Jim's home address. "Excellent." He snapped his fingers and ordered his men to roll out. "I'll be back with this before morning."

"Great, I can't wait."

"Yeah, and get the fucking pot on," Berserko informed him.

"What can I say?" Spurs said. "The boys like their tea."

And then they were gone, on their bikes and tearing down the road.

* * *

"Don't argue with me, Laura—pack!" Jim told his wife, raising his voice. "You're not safe here."

"Please, Jim, tell me what's going on. You're scaring me."

"You don't want to know, trust me. Now, help me pack your bag," he instructed, shoving some of her clothes into a large holdall.

She sniffled, walked into the on-suite and gathered up some toiletries and other bits she thought she'd need. "How long do you want me gone, Jim?"

He could tell she was pissed, but he didn't care. This was for her own good; people were dying. "A few days. Until things blow over."

"What *things*?" Laura put her belongings into the bag Jim was packing and went to grab a few more items of clothing, such as a jacket and boots.

"Look, I'm not getting into it with you now. You're going to have to trust me, okay? I'm probably overreacting, but I don't think so. I want you gone, now, to your mother's. You'll be safe there."

Laura sighed. "Okay, fine. You win."

Jim stopped packing and got up from his crouched position in front of the bed. A bedside lamp was burning within the room, creating their only light. Laura looked tired in the weak glow, her long black hair a twisted shock. She had bags under her eyes, her cheeks sunken.

"You're beautiful," he whispered. "And I fear I've dragged us into a world of shit by poking my nose where it didn't belong."

"Jim, you're a reporter. It's what—"

He shook his head. "You know I don't go out into the field these days. Besides, I should have known better—Laura, Owen is *dead*. Butchered."

Her hands went to her mouth as she gasped. "D-dead?"

Jim nodded. He could feel the colour draining from his face. "I should have discouraged him . . . I was bloody stupid."

"Shh!" she cooed, throwing her arms around him.

She smelt like freshly picked flowers. Jim buried his face in her hair, filling his nostrils with her clean aroma. "What have I done?" He was borderline blubbering. "I had to k-kill today. Many . . . *things*." He felt her tense up. His grip on her tightened, crushing her breasts against his solid chest. His fingers dug into her back. "You don't have to worry: they weren't human. Well, to look at, maybe, but not in the sense of how a normal human mind, heart and person works, babe. They don't have the same ways as us."

"Who doesn't, Jim? Who have you killed?" She seemed to relax.

She has a right to know, he thought, *and what if I never see her again after tonight?* And so he unloaded everything onto her.

"Christ, Jim . . . You have to go to the authorities."

"I'm worried they'd lock me up in a deep, dark hole and throw away the key, Laura. Or kill me . . . I need to go to Twin Jesters and take the bastards out. For Owen, at least."

"That's suicide, Jim. You can't. I won't let you." She pushed from him and frantically beat her fists against his chest, her hair whipping about her face.

"Laura, stop it!" He grabbed her wrists and forced her from him, pushing her onto their king-size bed, where only hours ago they'd made love. "I'm going. End of. I have to try and stop this bloody madness before it spreads further. God knows what they're capable of."

"Go to the police. Or ring them at least. You could do it anonymously."

"I will, but not yet. I need to get out there and see what's what. I'll ring them then, promise," he lied. "Now grab your stuff, coat and car keys. We need to go. Pronto."

"What's the mad rush?"

"Haven't you been listening? Besides, I'm worried they may have followed me or something. I know, silly, but still. You didn't see these things, Laura. They could smell and sense my presence. It freaked me out." He moved to the bedroom window, parting the curtains. "Something tells me they won't leave the safety of their town though. Yet, we can't take that chance."

"I'm ready." Laura threw her holdall over her shoulder.

Jim turned to her and smiled. "This will all blow over in a few days. Something like this, like those creatures, can't go undetected for too long. The army'll sort it out, I'm sure."

"Then you should leave them to it, Jim. Please. For me?"

He lowered his head. "Sorry."

Laura sighed. "You better give me a kiss, then, since your mind's made up."

Jim went to her and held her. "I love you more than life, baby," he whispered in her ear. "I'll be fine. I'm wily." He almost laughed at that.

"Bye, Jim." She left his embrace and exited the room without looking back.

Jim sighed and dropped onto the bed. *What the hell am I thinking? Idiot.*

The sound of the front door's locks clacking brought him out of his thoughts. The door slammed. The knocker rattled.

Slowly, he stood and went to the window. He saw Laura taking big strides towards her car, keys in hand. Jim put his fingers to the glass and sighed, misting his vision.

"Sorry," he muttered. He was about to turn when he saw a large figure step out of the bushes and approach Laura from behind.

"Oh, Jesus!" Jim's hands fumbled as he tried to open the window, but he was too slow in warning

Laura. She was engulfed, arms wrapping around her body, pinning her limbs to her side. She was dragged from Jim's sight. "Fuck, fuck, fuck!"

He rushed to his side of the bed and crammed his feet into his slippers, dashed out the room, down the stairs and threw open the front door. He was about to step into the cold night to go to Laura's aid when a hand smacked against his chest. He was shoved backwards. Hard. He hit the deck and slid along the wooden flooring.

"Evening, Jim," the huge thug dressed as a biker said, towering over him. "You've got a pretty wife."

Two others filed in behind the mountain of a man, who held Laura captive.

"Who are you? What do you want?"

"I'll answer that," another man said, stepping inside and smiling. He removed a cigarette from his mouth and blew smoke out of his nostrils. "We've come here to teach you a lesson. It's not nice to threaten women, Jim."

"I-I don't know what you're talking about. Please, let my wife go. She—"

"You're going to tell me you didn't tell Liz you were going to burn her pub down with her inside?" the smoker said, removing his coat.

Then it all clicked into place for Jim, who realized he and Laura were in big trouble.

Chapter 15
Then

They'd beaten Storm to within an inch of her life.

It was miraculous she'd still been breathing, let alone had the foresight and fight left in her battered state to crawl out of her burning house. It was beyond thinkable. It was extraordinary, yet ludicrous.

Storm should have been brain damaged—a cabbage in a wheelchair for the rest of her life. Her head, face, chest and most of her body was caved in. Chunks of flesh were missing from her torso.

No, she shouldn't have been in a vegetative state, but dead on a slab inside a metal box at the mortician's office, alongside her mother and daughter. But she wasn't.

She was alive.

When they'd rushed Storm into A&E, the surgeon, Dr. Fields, had had little hope for her— she was nothing more than a bloody, broken lump upon a hospital gurney. Deep, violent cuts adorned her abdomen and inner thighs, with strips of skin as lengthy as eight inches missing from her buttocks, left breast and shoulder blades. Patches of her skull were visible due to where chunks of hair had been pulled out. Her eyes were blackened and closed, her jaw and nose smashed. He'd never seen anything so horrific, brutal.

Sure, he'd treated victims who'd been attacked with knives and guns, others who'd been involved in bar fights or set upon by thugs, gangs or burglars, but nothing compared to the savagery Storm had undertaken.

"What happened?" Fields asked.

"We found her like this, outside her burning house," one of the ambulance drivers said.

"The police think it was a robbery gone awry," the second paramedic stated.

"Good grief!" a nurse shrieked.

"Get her down to theatre this instant. She's lost a terrific amount of blood."

Before she made it to theatre, Storm's body started to convulse.

"We're losing her!"

They fought to keep her alive.

A nurse held her hand.

"You're going to be fine, sweetie."

Storm gargled and spat something unintelligible. She repeated the word, and the nurse bent closer.

"What's she saying?" Fields asked.

"I'm not sure, but it sounds like 'revenge'."

Nothing was thought of it.

After making it through her operation by the skin of her teeth, Storm was placed under observation until she pulled out of the danger zone. Once in the clear, she was moved to a private room to finish her recovering process. She then underwent months of physio and reconstructive surgery to rebuild her face and body.

When all was said and done, Storm didn't like what she saw in the mirror. A different person resided in the glass. She also felt changed inside, but not for one moment did she think she was hideous or monstrous—looks had never bothered her—and, in time, she would learn to live with the scars.

Not that she planned on living long.

Revenge, she thought, lying awake one night in the hospital bed as heavy rain assaulted the window. *Revenge*. It was a word she'd clung to during her recovery period. *I'll hunt that cunt down and kill her and her family. I don't care how long it takes or if it costs me my life—that would be a small price to pay.*

She balled the bed sheets in her hands. *I swear, God as my witness, she's dead. I'll start my preparation as soon as I get out of here.*

Gone was the broken girl who couldn't be bothered to get out of bed or eat. She'd been replaced by something cold. Only hatred lived within her now, and the need to hurt the people who'd crushed her world kept her motor ticking.

Weeks later, she was discharged, and she rented a small place for a couple of months so she could establish her bearings.

To her surprise, Dr. Fields visited to make sure she was okay and said he would drop in on her from time to time to see if she was coping.

"Yes, that's fine. Tea? Coffee?"

"Tea, please. Listen, I know you have a health visitor coming by once a fortnight, but I thought I'd see you for myself."

For the first time, Storm noticed he was much younger than what she'd first thought. *Can't be much older than thirty.* His manner was soft and delicate, with real concern in his eyes. "Thanks." She smiled. "Something you do for *all* your patients?"

"No. I have to confess, you intrigued me. Your courage to keep on fighting when you were so close to—"

"I thought I still had something to fight for, forgetting, in my beaten state, that my child and mother were gone."

"What will you do now, Storm?" he asked, switching subjects.

Tears trailed down her face.

Revenge. It burned at the back of her mind. She stopped crying. "I'll probably move from here in time," she lied, sensing a spark between them. *Something could easily form between us, but I won't let anyone else get hurt.* Storm then told him that he needed to leave because she had things to do.

He tried hiding his disappointment, placed his empty mug in the kitchen sink and left with a smile on his face. "I'll call again soon."

But he never did. The hint had been taken. And, as much as it saddened her, Storm knew it was for the best.

Shortly after this, with the money she'd been left by her dad combined with the insurance pay-out, Storm bought herself a small place not far from her old home. It was a risk staying in the area but, if she was going to follow her plan through, she needed to be close.

One afternoon, whilst out walking, Storm went to see her old home, finding nothing but a blank spot, some rubble and diggers.

Looks like they're getting ready to clear and develop the site.

Whilst sifting through debris, she was fortunate to find a few blistered photos of Stevie, her mother and her dad, which she kept along with a few other personal items pulled from the blackened rubble.

Storm kept to herself, stayed in and shopped out of town where nobody knew her.

"We can relocate you?" the police had offered.

She'd declined, changed her identity and appearance, and kept her head down.

With the cash she had left, Storm had a multi-gym installed in the house and bought weights, a speedball and punch bag.

In the evenings, she went swimming. By night, she jogged the dark, desolate streets and surrounding areas.

It took months for her to rebuild any form of strength, stamina and core power, having never been that fit a person anyway. However, she stuck at it and ate healthy.

The scars would never heal, but her body could be whipped into shape.

Along with exercising, Storm invested in a multitude of classes and clubs: Pilates, driving, yoga, archery, knife-throwing, karate, shooting, hunting and trap setting, tracking and a multi-weather/terrain survival course. Equipment was purchased including tents and camping gear, a compass, maps, binoculars, Bowie and Buck knives, a hunting rifle and a variety of other things she thought she would need to live in the woods.

I could be gone for years. Doesn't matter—no one will miss me.

Whilst in training, preparing to face the long, hard challenges ahead, Storm kept an eye on the news. Not just locally, but across the country—she had a gut feeling the cannibals were still in the area.

They're not going anywhere soon, she thought. *Paula knows the place too well. No, she'll sit around and wait until her children are old enough to move them. Why wouldn't she? She thinks her threat is dead.*

She could also have more babies by now.

Good. I can make her suffer before ending her.

Five years passed before Storm was finally ready to venture into the woods to hunt down her prey.

* * *

Storm double-checked her equipment as she packed it into two large camouflaged rucksacks she'd bought for the occasion. All the while, her radio/scanner, which was tuned in to the police band, crackled and spat information.

So far, like the last few years, nothing had turned up.

Fuckers are hunkered down, gathering their strength. Well, I won't allow it to continue. It ends this time. For good.

Storm placed her gear into her newly purchased four-by-four and got behind the wheel. The first part of her plan was to drive out to the tunnel to see if she could find Paula or unearth clues to her whereabouts.

When she left her home, dawn was breaking.

The drive took less than an hour, the roads deserted.

Not bothering to unpack her stuff when she arrived at her destination, Storm sought out her powerful flashlight and trekked, with caution, the short distance from where she'd parked on the dirt path to the bricked-up mouth of the tunnel. The structure was barely visible due to the foliage that engulfed it. After the attacks, the council had abandoned their plans to reopen it, and so it had been left to rot.

"Ugly fucking thing," she uttered, clasping the torch to the utility belt she wore around her waist, which also held her Bowie knife and crackling radio.

By now, there was enough light in the sky for Storm to be able to see the surrounding area and what she was doing. She didn't know what she expected to find after so many years but clung to the fact that there *might* be some clues—a hint to where they had gone.

"I could smash my way into the tunnel and walk to the other end? No, that's a stupid idea. If anything should happen . . ."

What if they're in there?

Storm put her hands to the bricks and pushed with all her might. They didn't budge. Giving up, she stepped back and looked at the brickwork—it was fully cemented.

She shook her head. "Nobody's entered the tunnel from this location. Besides, would they really come back here?"

It was doubtful.

Christ, they could be anywhere *by now.*

As fruitless as it seemed, she knew she couldn't give up, and so she spent the next few hours investigating the area around the tunnel, venturing deeper into the woods and circling back to her starting point.

Nothing.

Not a shred of evidence uncovered.

Now what, Dr Watson? She sighed. *Come on, we knew this would happen—can't be dismayed at the first hurdle.*

Closing her eyes, she threw her head back and took a deep breath. Storm made her way back to her four-by-four, got in and drove to the next location on her list: the opposite end of the tunnel.

The other side was trickier to negotiate. The closest she could park to the tunnel was in Treherbet, a town a few miles away.

"Chances are I won't find anything, so I may as well travel light," she told herself, making sure she had her knife, flashlight and radio.

Like the other end of the structure, this end was also bricked up tight. Nothing dislodged when pushed.

"I guess that puts that notion to bed. There's no way they're hiding in there." Storm put her back to the bricks and looked at the looming woods before her, knowing she would have to venture into them if she were to find Paula. "This is one of the last places they would have been."

Not letting the situation daunt her, Storm swept the area in search of clues and went into the woods a short distance. She hadn't expected to find anything, and then she came across footprints in some mud. They were headed in the direction she had come from.

"And what do we have here?"

Storm walked farther, finding more tracks hidden beneath foliage that she brushed aside with her thighs as she went.

After a few thousand feet or so, the tracks ended abruptly.

"*Fuck*! Now wh—"

Her words trailed off when she spotted muddy prints on large rocks that continued for a couple of hundred feet before ending.

What do I do now? These tracks could belong to anyone. *Keep going in a straight line—something might turn up? Wait, what about my stuff?* Storm looked up at the sky. Her natural light was starting to wane.

She decided to press on. With her newfound skills, she could withstand a cold, damp night in the woods. Besides, she had her flashlight, and if push came to shove, she would easily be able to make it back to her car.

If nothing turns up in an hour or so, I'll give in, head back to the jeep and try again in the morning.

The farther she progressed, the steeper her climb became, sapping her of energy.

Storm stopped, bent over and placed her hands on her thighs. After a few deep breaths, she pressed onward, thankful when the ground started to even out. By the time she reached the zenith of the scale, it was almost too dark to see, and so she resorted to using her flashlight.

The beam swept this way and that as she hunted for more footprints or tell-tale signs. But nothing revealed itself.

This is pointless. I can't—

Up ahead, Storm saw large, looming silhouettes. A grey, cloud-scattered sky studded with stars acted as its backdrop.

"Hello," she whispered, forging forward. "And what's this?"

Stealthily, Storm sneaked through the foliage, staying low, and crept up on the large log cabin. No light came from inside. There were no bikes, horses or any other mode of transport fit for this terrain.

That doesn't mean there's nobody home...

When she got closer, she killed the flashlight, stopped and listened.

For the first time, she realized how quiet the woods were and how utterly alone, small and helpless she felt. The odd rustle of leaves or hoot of an owl startled her, but she kept her cool and vigil over the structure to see if anyone would come, go or light the joint up.

Storm decided she needed a closer inspection.

Upon reaching the four steps leading to the porch, she took them and risked peeping through one of the main windows that looked in on what would have been a living room. The space was empty, the floorboards exposed.

She relaxed. *Not out of the woods just yet, though.*

She allowed herself a smile.

Stepping past the door, with one hand on her knife, Storm trekked to the large window on the opposite side of the porch. On gazing in, she sensed it would have been the home's kitchen, but no appliances could be seen in the bare room.

How odd . . .

Storm walked around to the back of the place with urgency, no longer worried someone was home. The rear entrance was open and off its hinges, the pane of glass in its centre covered in spider-web cracks.

"Anyone home? Hello?"

She stepped over the threshold. A board creaked and a rat squeaked as it scurried off into the shadows.

"I'm not looking for trouble."

Through the kitchen windows, Storm saw lightning rip the clouds apart. A moment later, thunder rumbled, and the first heavy drops of rain fell, pattering the tiled floor underfoot.

"Huh?" Storm looked up. Most of the roof was missing.

I guess I don't have to worry about the three bears showing up any time soon. Danger could be lurking, though. If not the cannibals, someone who's stumbled across the place, like me.

The Bowie was now clear of leather.

It felt good in her hand.

"If there's someone here, make yourself known, please. I have a knife."

More lightning. Thunder followed a second later.

Storm couldn't hear herself think over the noise of the rain.

She switched on her torch and swept it around the kitchen. There were tell-tale signs of someone having been here: empty cans, half-drank bottles of pop and pots holding human waste.

"Ugh, *fuck*!" She moved into the living room, finding it empty save a couple of tatty sleeping bags and more bare food containers. "Doesn't look like anyone's been here in a while," she muttered, bending to inspect the bedding, which was covered in mould.

Satisfied, she moved to the front door and turned the handle. Locked.

"Brilliant."

Her torch's beam found a door in the corner of the room. It stood ajar. She stepped over to it and pushed it open with the butt of her light. On the other side was a staircase leading downwards.

"Anyone there?" The top step groaned as she placed her foot on it, and she used the handrail to guide her. "I'm coming down, ready or not."

Storm could hear the faint sound of dripping water.

When she stepped into a puddle, she shrieked, pulled back and went up a couple of steps.

"Christ, what was that?"

She pointed her flashlight to the staircase and saw that most of it was submerged beneath dirty water—branches, leaves and other bits and pieces floated on its surface.

Probably safe to say there's nobody lurking down there. Not unless they have diving gear.

After closing the basement door, Storm went back into the kitchen and shut the rear entrance the best she could.

This will be a good place to spend the night, she thought, heading into the living room and sitting with her back against the front door. *First thing tomorrow morning, I'll pick the trail back up and go from there.*

She closed her eyes and drifted off to sleep.

Chapter 16
Then

Storm awoke to the sound of scratching. It was urgent, violent.

"*Huh*? What—who's there?" Her eyes shot open, her hand darting to the Bowie knife that lay by her feet.

At first, she thought it was coming from behind the front door, and so she turned her head and pressed her ear flat against the wood.

The scratching came again.

Her ears pricked.

It's coming from the kitchen. The back door?

When she sat up, a new noise sounded.

Voices?

The cannibals?

Her insides went cold.

Getting to her knees, Storm crawled across the floor to the kitchen's entryway and peeked around the jamb, into the room. From where she spied, she had a perfect view of the back door. It was being shunted. Before settling down last night, she'd pushed the dining table against it.

"I think someone's in there, Brian. Sure I saw 'em through the window. Sleepin', they were."

"You need to stop drinking so much, Stan. It's starting to affect your eyes. And brain!"

"Nothing wrong with my peepers, mate. And if there *is* someone in there, how comes we can't get the door open?"

"Something's probably fallen against it. Hell of a storm last night."

"Yeah, well, can you get us inside pronto or not? I want me some rabbit stew."

"Might have to break a window, Stan. It ain't budging. Here, hold my bag." Storm heard the rattle and clink of bottles.

"What ya doin'?"

"Stand back, Stan the Man," Brian said.

A figure loomed outside the kitchen window, whom she took to be Brian. When he pulled his arm back behind his head, she saw the large stone he held.

"*Shit*," was all she had time to mutter before the rock smashed through the window, sending shards of glass into the air and scattering across the floor.

"Watch climbing through there—"

"Well, I'll be!" Brian said, poking his head through the blown-out window. "Looks like you were right, Stan—someone's here."

"Told you, didn't I? How can you tell?"

"They've barricaded the door." When Brian turned his head, Storm pulled from the entryway and hid behind the wall. "Come out. We're not looking for trouble."

No way, she thought. He had distrust in his voice.

"I'm going in, Stan."

Storm looked to the front door, knowing it was locked. Her gaze fell on the large window beside it. *If I jump through it, I'll cut myself to ribbons.*

"Go around front, Stan. Make sure they don't escape that way with our stuff."

Stuff? Storm looked at the sleeping bags and other bits scattered across the floor. *They've been using those godawful things?* Her stomach lurched. Now, in the light of day, she saw bugs worming, crawling and slithering around inside the beds.

Footsteps approached the front.

The one at the kitchen is on his own. I should rush—

Booted feet landed on the kitchen floor with a heavy thump.

Fuck, too late.

She brandished the knife and decided to show herself, thinking the impressive blade would be enough to scare anyone off.

"I suggest you back off!" Storm said, stepping into the room.

When Brian cocked his rifle, Storm's jaw dropped open, her mouth forming a perfect *O*. She backed up until her arse shunted the front door.

"Holy *shit*. Get in here, Stan. I found our culprit."

"I didn't steal *anything*. I just stayed the night, that's all." Storm held her hands up. "Please, lower the gun."

Brian was shorter than Storm and wore a tatty, moth-eaten beanie hat. He didn't have sideburns, suggesting he was bald underneath it. His clothes, which were mere rags, were caked in filth and stank to high heaven, much like their owner.

His face sported an unkempt beard decorated with food particles.

Dead rabbits hung from his belt by a cord, and a small hunting knife clung to his opposite hip.

"Drop the steel and we can talk about it."

"I can't get in!" Stan called.

"Climb through the kitchen window."

By the time Storm had sheathed her knife, Stan was in the room. He was a carbon copy of Brian: ragtag clothes, scruffy beard, bald. He wore no hat. A knife dangled from his belt.

The only difference in the pair Storm could see was Stan was slightly taller and had a scar running across his chin.

If they didn't have that gun, I'd be able to take them both.

"Now, unhook your knife belt and kick it over to me."

Storm narrowed her eyes. "Not a fucking chance, Stinky."

Stan laughed.

"Shut. *Up!*" Brian yelled at his friend.

"Come on now, Brian. We don't want to go hurting the girl. She said—"

"I told you to keep quiet. Get her steel."

"Touch me, and I'll kill you," she said, looking at Stan stony-faced.

"She's feisty, I'll give her that," Stan said, making his way towards Storm. "I just want the blade, baby." He got closer and held his hand out. "Come on, give it up."

"I wouldn't mind a piece of her fine young arse."

Stan laughed, stepping into Brian's shooting field and blocking Storm. She rushed forward and drove the heel of her palm into Stan's nose, shattering it, shoving bone into his brain.

Before his carcass collapsed, Storm shoved him backwards with all her might, sending the dead man crashing into Brian.

The gun fired, the bullet ploughing into the ceiling as Brian stumbled backwards, hitting the deck. Stan fell on top of him.

"Ugh-*argh*!" he screamed.

Storm walked over to Brian and placed her foot on his rifle, pinning it. "Let it go."

He looked at her, teeth bared. "Fuck you, *whore*!"

"I'm guessing you were going to try that, and look where it's got you? How many others have you attacked?"

"You *killed* Stan."

"Better him than me. If you let me walk with the gun, I'll let you live. Deal?"

"And if I don't?"

Storm drew her knife. "I'll cut your throat and take it anyway." She winked at him. "You pricks messed with the wrong girl."

He nodded. "Have it." His grip on the weapon released.

When she bent to retrieve it, she pushed the knife close to his face, never taking her eyes off him. With the rifle in hand, Storm cocked and pointed it at Brian as she backed out the kitchen door.

She half expected him to push Stan off him and make a play for her, but he didn't move. Storm shouldered the gun and climbed out the window, not looking back as she jumped to the floor with a grunt.

"Shit!" she howled, landing awkwardly, her legs going out from under her. The rifle slipped off her shoulder and slid along the floor, burying itself under a fall of leaves.

"Now you're going to get it!" Brian appeared at the window, his blade drawn. "Going to cut you open like a little piggy and fuck your tight arse, bitch."

Before she could get a hand to her Bowie, Brian leapt out the window and was standing over her. His booted foot stepped on her sheathed knife.

"Not so fucking tough now, are you?"

He punched her in the face, bloodying her nose.

Double vision set in.

Storm shook her head, grabbed his foot and shoved him off-balance.

"*Argh!*" he screamed, somersaulting backwards. His head connected with a log, silencing him.

She bounced to her feet to attack, her knife drawn and ready to be plunged. Storm fell on him to drive the steel home, but Brian rolled away and slammed his forearm into the back of her head.

Storm grunted, but his blow had little impact.

"Fucker." She clenched her jaw until it clicked, her teeth exposed. "Going to kill you, *motherfucker*."

He ran at her, knife raised.

She ducked. The top of her head rammed into his guts, and she flipped him over her back.

"*Ooph*!" He hit the ground with a dense smack. Air rushed out of him, leaving him winded. Brian coughed and held his hands out in front of him. "P-p-please," he wheezed. Tears streamed down his face.

"Who's not so tough now, bitch? I've had enough of men thinking they can treat me however they fucking please."

"N-n—"

Storm stamped her foot into his face until it was nothing more than a gooey, soggy mess under her boot heel.

She didn't bother covering his body or hiding it

The wildlife will hopefully take care of him. Stan the fucking Man's, too.

After grabbing what she needed, Storm pressed on. Now that she had a gun, a couple of extra knives, spare ammo and skinned rabbits for food, she didn't think she'd need her gear from the car yet.

If I don't find anything after today, I'll turn back for my stuff.

Forty minutes after leaving the cabin, she came across a stream, washed herself down, drank some and got moving. At one point, she found pitched tents and camping sites, but not a living soul.

You'd never catch me camping this deep in the woods. Hell, you'll never catch me doing such an activity, full stop.

Another few more hours of pushing deeper into the woods and Storm had found no sign of life. No paths, no tents, no footprints—nothing. Also, the overhanging branches had become so dense, natural light was blocked out.

Maybe I should turn back? I could get lost easily. Nah, I have my compass and training. Besides, I've walked a straight—

Her chain of thought was broken when she came up against a rock face. "What the fuck?" Storm stepped back and looked both ways. There appeared to be no immediate way around. "Hell. Now what do I do? Could take me hours to walk around this thing."

She put her hand to the wall and found deep grips.

"I'm sure I can scale this baby," she muttered, looking up. "It's not that high."

Not wanting to stand still thinking about it, she started climbing, her hands and feet finding purchase like an expert.

Who would have thought that rock climbing course would come in handy?

Storm grunted out a laugh and was surprised when she reached the top with minimum effort. Once she hoisted herself up and was able to stand, she looked down. *Going to have to find another way down . . . Don't fancy breaking my neck, back or legs. Nobody would find me.*

"Now, where was I?"

Turning, she moved forward, pushing her way through thick bushes and foliage.

Like a goddamn jungle!

When she got so far, she stopped, out of breath and sweating. Storm slapped at flies on the nape of her neck, legs and arms.

"This is pointless, man. I have—what was *that*?"

She pricked her ears and controlled her breathing.

Somewhere in the distance there was a rattle of pots, pans and cutlery.

Campers?

With caution, she moved on, making as little noise as possible until she heard a woman speak.

"Think we'll see that fucking bitch any time soon?"

"Come on, now—don't talk about her like that. I thought you were over it?"

"I am, but I still don't like the way she treats us, especially with everything we do. She's always been the same, even when we were children."

"She could have killed us. You know that, right? The woman I knew has long gone. I'm surprised she spared us."

"Using us as baby-making machines wasn't bad enough? Why don't we run?"

"How?"

"We could if we wanted to, Tony. Or do you still have feelings for her?"

Storm heard smacking.

"Don't talk like that! I'm only doing this for the children, damn you."

"I'm sorry."

"It's fine. But yes, I think we'll see her soon. She's not dropped us some supplies in a few days."

When it went quiet, Storm continued to walk forward. Twigs snapped underfoot, and she winced in apprehension of being heard.

But she needn't have worried, as the people started speaking again.

Nice and easy, baby, she told herself.

Then the trees and foliage thinned, and Storm could see movement up ahead, directly in front of her.

"Well I hope you're right, Tony. She seems to be leaving it longer each time. I'm hungry. So are our children."

"We don't know her circumstances, though, do we? You've seen what she's got to deal with. Can't be easy getting the things she needs for herself, let alone us."

"*Always* protecting her."

"Don't start that bull—"

A baby began crying.

"*Fuck!*" the woman screamed, startling Storm.

"Calm—"

"Stop telling me to fucking calm down, Tony. She's hungry. Not like you give a shit."

"Give her some of—Did you hear that?"

Storm cursed herself for treading on a thick, dry branch, which made a deafening sound.

"Probably wildlife," the female said.

"Go and check on the baby. I'll have a nose."

Storm parted the foliage in front of her and saw a large man sitting by a campfire close to a cave's opening. He was naked and scruffy. Dried blood graced his cheeks, chin and lips.

He's eaten recently.

The man, whom Storm assumed was Tony, rose from the tree trunk slowly, making a grab for something. When he brought his hands up, he was clutching a large fire axe—the steel head was encrusted with red. Strands of flesh and hair clung to it.

There was even dried blood up the handle to the hilt.

"Bring the gun, woman," he said, moving his head from left to right, right to left. At one point, he was staring straight at Storm, but he couldn't see her due to the green coverage.

"You and your gun," the woman muttered.

"Just what the hell is that supposed to mean?"

"You couldn't hit the back end of a bar with that old thing."

His face turned scarlet and the veins in his neck protruded. "Get the *fucking* gun!"

"No need—"

"Why not tell the whole fucking world I can't shoot for shit? Anyone could be close by."

The woman held her hands up. "You're a regular sharpshooter, sweetie," she said, smiling.

"Don't be so goddamn patronising, bitch. Do as I say."

"How did she ever live with you . . ." the woman muttered.

"What you say?" Tony turned his back to Storm, and she used his distraction to pull back.

I can't take them yet. I need to know more, Storm thought. *I'll come back later tonight, once I've had some food and it's dark.*

Moving backwards, Storm stepped on more branches, twigs and dried leaves.

"There's definitely someone out there watching," she heard Tony say. He sounded distant. "Come any closer and you're going to get shot. Get the fuck away from here. Now!"

"It might be Paula."

Storm stopped walking.

Did she just say what I think she did?

"*Hydra* would have alerted her presence, stupid. And I told you to get my gun."

"I'm going to stick my foot up your arse if you keep talking to me like that."

"What did you just say?"

Storm heard the slap of flesh on flesh again, but she didn't care. *So this pair* do *know Paula, but who are they? They don't look like cannibals, and they couldn't have been a part of Skull's tribe. How do they fit in? Have these poor people been hoodwinked into joining up? Forced to do what Paula says? No, I can't see that. Nothing is holding them here. Maybe they're family?*

Her mind reeled with questions.

"The woman did ask Tony if he still had feelings for 'her'. Did she mean Paula? Was Paula his . . . wife?"

When Storm had retreated far enough, she turned and made her way back to the rock face.

Once she'd gathered some kindling and rocks, Storm built a fire and cooked one of the hares she'd been gifted.

Do I go in all guns blazing? she thought. *No, I need to take one of them alive at least. I need answers. If Paula isn't there, then where? Is there more than just Paula?*

Her mind swirled as she ate.

What about the baby?

Kill it. It'll only turn into a monster.

The fire warmed her face as she stuffed rabbit into her mouth.

Maybe shoot him—Tony. The woman will be easier to handle.

She liked that idea. The man was big and had an axe, plus a gun. Even though he'd been declared a poor shot, he was dangerous. Storm had to put him down first.

As the sun started to set, she checked the rifle and made sure her knives were secured at her hip. Getting up, Storm left the rabbits, thinking she would return to this spot later, and left the fire to burn itself out.

Retracing her steps, Storm found their hideout with ease. When she was close enough, she stopped and parted the branches before her. The campsite was quiet. Neither Tony nor his woman was in sight. Their fire had dwindled.

Storm cocked the gun.

She stepped through the foliage and into the makeshift camp. In the poor light cast by the crescent moon, Storm could see camping equipment placed close to the cave's entrance, along with a pile of clothes, shoes and other accessories. There was also a makeshift washing line to the far right of the site. Something hung on it.

Those aren't clothes . . . Storm thought, moving closer for inspection.

Strips of flesh, human and animal, clung to the dirty rope, the ends of which were tied around thin trees some thirty feet apart. Maggots and other beasties scurried, crawled and slithered over the meat.

Storm turned from it and gagged, her stomach flip-flopping.

These gross fucks are getting it.

Walking towards the cave, she made sure the rifle's safety was off and a round was loaded in the pipe. Storm unclipped her flashlight and clicked it on.

Before she could enter the 'home' and fill it with light, she heard footsteps.

Storm killed the torch.

"Thought I heard something, that's all," someone said. It sounded like Tony.

Calm, Storm took up position behind a large boulder, rested the gun on top of it and lined up her crosshair with the cave's entrance.

The glow from within brightened by the second.

Footfalls grew louder, followed by the rattle of something.

What is that?

The glow from the cave burst into the open. "Someone out here?"

"Now you're going to get it, you bastard," Storm uttered, pulling the trigger. Her shot went wide, killing the light Tony held.

"Fucking *hell*! We're under attack—"

Storm cocked the gun and fired a second time. Her shell found its target, propelling Tony backwards and into a tumble.

"*Argh*! I'm hit . . ."

More light came rushing towards the cave's opening.

"Come and get it, *bastards*." Storm clenched her jaw. "That's it."

"Stay d-down—they've got a gun," Tony warned. "Holy shit, the blood's pumping from me."

Storm's third shot missed its crouching target and ricocheted off a wall.

Gunfire was returned.

A bullet whizzed over her head and smashed through the trees.

My gun smoke has given my position away.

"Who are we shooting at?" a new voice asked.

"There's someone over in those trees, John."

Cocking her gun, Storm popped her head around the boulder and shined her torch in the direction of the other light—two people stood close to where she'd shot the first.

Before she could lower her gun and fire, they shot at her, their bullets tearing into the rock, throwing up dust.

Her heart lurched.

A breath caught in her throat.

"Come out. We won't hurt you!"

Where have I heard that *before?*

"Please, hold your fire. I'm out of ammunition," Storm lied.

"Then get out here," the same person said.

"Tony, you okay?" the second man asked. No answer. "You murdered Tony, friend! I say we kill the bastard, Clive."

"That's down to her inside, John."

I haven't heard their feet moving. They must be in the same spot. "Please, I'm out of bullets. I'm coming out."

"Throw your gun over here."

Storm did as instructed, making sure it didn't go far from reach. "See. Don't shoot, I'm standing up."

Light was thrust in her direction.

"You got any more guns?" John asked.

"No, I swear."

"John," Clive said, "frisk her whilst I keep a light on her."

"You got it."

Excellent. Storm drew her small hunting knives and steadied herself. When John got close enough, she threw one knife. The haft flipped over tip and sank into his forehead.

Before his body could hit the deck, Storm threw the other blade at Clive and dived for the rifle.

"Motherfucker," Clive screamed, the steel lodging in his shoulder. He attempted to pull it free, but the sudden explosion of gunfire had him running for cover. But he didn't make it. A slug tore through the back of his knee, sending him to ground in a sprawling mess.

Storm broke cover and walked over to him.

He flipped onto his back and held his hands up. "What do you want?" Like Tony and John, he too was naked and covered in muck and greenery.

She drew a bead on his forehead.

Piss shot down his thigh.

"How many inside?"

"T—t—"

"You're lying." She cocked the gun.

"Four."

"How many grown men?"

"Three."

"The woman's the fourth?"

He nodded.

"Who are you? Why are you here?"

He pulled a knife from behind his back and sprang from the ground.

Storm put a bullet through his left eyeball. "They *never* fucking learn."

Loading another shell into the rifle's chamber, she made her way into the cave.

Chapter 17
Then

The cave had definitely been modified.

It was intricate, with many tunnels leading in multiple, misleading directions with dead ends.

Storm was lost. And even though she had nerves of steel these days, it unnerved her. The darkness played its tricks on her mind. From where she stood, she made circles and lit the cave with her torch beam, pushing the inkiness back.

Within the tunnel she could hear unearthly sounds, along with a constant dripping of water and other noises that were heightened in the stillness of the dwelling.

The rest of those fucks must be around here somewhere, she thought, pointing the light towards the ground and seeking out a piece of slate. Storm tried marking the wall with it, but it was too dark against the stone to make out.

"*Fuck*! If only I had a loaf of bread—I could leave a trail of breadcrumbs." A small laugh escaped her as she backtracked up the path she'd wandered down, and her joyousness almost turned to floods of tears when she noticed she was at the main entrance again.

From where she stood, she could see the three men she'd killed before entering.

"Christ. At this rate, I'll be going round in circles all fucking night."

Storm turned from the dead men and lit the passageways in front of her. She'd already taken the middle route, which had led her in multiple directions before bringing her back to the starting point. She had just investigated the left path, to the same result.

"Guess it's the right one. What if that one brings me back here? Give up and go the fuck home!"

No, I'll pitch camp outside and wait for them to come to me . . . They'll have to sooner or later.

With a huff, Storm aimed her torch in the direction of the right passage and slowly sloped down it. She stopped herself from screaming or reacting when rats scurried past, their swishing tails brushing against the lower portion of her legs as they went.

Deep, unseen pools she trod in threw water up her boots and found its way inside, soaking her feet.

She soldiered on.

Twenty minutes later, thinking she was getting somewhere, Storm stopped in her tracks when she came across a fork in the passageway. One led right, the other left. Also, the path she was on continued ahead.

"Great, now what?"

Storm edged over to the passageway branching off to the right and shined her light down it. The path bent around a corner.

Hmm . . . She stepped into the opening. *I can always turn back if I don't think it's right.*

When she rounded the corner, Storm's feet went out from under her and she fell face-first into a void. The drop was short, but she landed awkwardly, twisting her ankle as she crashed to the stony dirt floor.

"Aw, *shit!*"

A single tear slid down her cheek.

Unfolding her bent leg, she assessed the damage by rotating her foot. She winced, pulling her lips back and exposing her gums. After a few more turns, the tenderness eased.

No breakage, thank God.

Storm looked up and used her flashlight. She'd fallen maybe six feet into a hole with a circumference half its depth. She swept the light in the direction she was planning to head. The tunnel had come to a dead end.

I wonder if they were trying to dig their way through here? Plausible, I guess.

She stood and brushed herself down. Storm placed her hands at the top of the hole and heaved herself up and onto the path. It took her less than five minutes to get back to where she'd branched off, and she took the left tunnel.

Bats squeaked overhead. More rats scampered underfoot. Storm pushed on, knowing she'd wasted a terrific amount of time.

If I'm to catch this lot napping, I need to find them, fast.

Storm walked with determination, her face set, but her resolve quickly turned to further frustration when she ran across a blockage in the form of a flood.

Well, that's this way—

In the distance, beyond the water, Storm could see what she thought to be a pinprick of light. She got on tiptoes and eased herself as close to the water's edge as possible.

There's definitely something on the other side, but how do I get there? Maybe the water isn't that deep?

Storm shined her torch over the flood. It spanned as far as the eye could see and touched either side of the tunnel. She looked down at her feet, her skin growing cold and the hairs on her arms and neck standing to attention at the thought of wading.

After a few shaky breaths, she inched forward, her feet sinking into the coldness. It slowly rose to her ankles, then her knees, until the water was up around her waist. When it climbed to her tits, her nipples instantly hardening, she was all for turning back, but the water level didn't rise more.

As she got closer to the ever-growing light on the other side, the water started to drop until it was back below her knees. She yelped when she stepped into a pothole and crashed into the water, causing a wave of ice-coldness to wash over her, soaking her hair to her skull.

When she resurfaced, spitting water, Storm rushed to the other side as quick as possible. On dry land, she checked her equipment before plodding along the path. The light she'd seen was bright enough to hurt her eyes, and so she switched off her torch and attached it to her utility belt.

Won't be needing that.

The glow from down the tunnel lit her path, and the closer she drew to it, she discovered it was flaming torches affixed to the walls that were casting the blaze. As she passed them, warmth licked at her cold wet body.

Her sodden clothes stuck to her like a second skin, her feet squelching within her boots. By the time the tunnel opened into a room, her arms were bone dry.

"*Wow*! What's this place?" she muttered. The space resembled a temple with pews whittled from trees. There was an altar. The walls were decorated with fancy cloths that displayed an insignia.

A stone slab rested in the corner of the room. It was covered in stale blood. Dried pools and splatters of the stuff stained the floor and walls. Storm went to it, putting her fingers upon the granite. Some of the blood was still wet. In the middle of the stone, her digits found rough grooves. On closer inspection, she saw the emblem from the walls carved into the rock.

"It's their symbol. They have a *cult*?" The thought made her sick. "The bastards have gathered disciples. What the actual fuck?! That's why they were outside! There could be more of them. Much, much more. A fucking army."

"Who's there?" a voice whispered in the darkness.

Storm froze, her heart hammering. She scanned the area and decided to hide behind the altar.

Soft footfalls approached.

"Tony? Clive? Is that you guys? Everything okay up front?"

Storm drew her knife. She chanced a look around the altar. The large, temple-like room was empty, still.

Then, a shadow crept up the wall close to the entrance. Footsteps grew louder.

"Guys? Are you in there? Guys?"

Storm kept her eyes on the entrance. A lone, skinny man holding an axe entered her field of vision. She almost pulled back out of sight but didn't.

I can take that scrawny sack of shit.

He stepped deeper into the light. He was naked. His short, fat prick stood on end, and his greying thatch revolted her. Still, she kept her focus on him and his slow approach.

"I must be hearing things in my old age."

The man turned and started to leave. She dashed from behind the podium and put her knife to his throat. Startled, he dropped his weapon. As the teeth of her blade bit into his neck, his piss splashed against the floor. His body trembled.

"Don't hurt me," he pleaded.

"Shut up," she said, "or I'll kill you where you stand. Where's your leader?"

"Who are you?"

"Answer my question, damn it!"

"Our leader doesn't stay here. This is *our* home. It belongs to the drones."

Storm pressed the steel tighter to his neck. "So where's your leader? And where's everyone else in here?"

"I can't tell you about our leader because I don't have that kind of information. You must believe me."

"Then take me to someone who *does* fucking know!"

"No, I cannot do that, either. It's against the oath I took."

"What are—"

A robust elbow ploughed into Storm's guts, taking her wind. The old man, as decrepit as he looked, held a lot of power in his broken-down frame.

The blow propelled her backwards, and she tripped. Storm crashed to the ground, her knife slipping from her grasp. It skittered across the floor and slid beneath a pew, out of sight.

"*Shit!*" she gasped, rolling onto her back.

"Argh!" the old man screamed, raising his axe overhead as he stumbled towards her. As he brought it down, she flipped to the left. The blade missed her by inches.

As he tried to hoist the axe again, she lashed out with her boot and crushed his dangling nuts against his thigh. He buckled, crashed to his knees and lost his weapon in the process. As his hands went to his hurt, he vomited.

Instead of going in search of her knife, Storm picked up his axe and swung it underarm, pinning the man's hands to his privates. Blood rushed out of his mouth and dribbled down his chin, spattering his chest.

The man gave out a low groan and slammed against the floor. He twitched once, and then lay still. A pool of blood fanned beneath him. Storm couldn't help but laugh at how he was positioned, thanks to the axe: his arse pointed skywards, as though he was waiting for a fucking.

Storm grabbed the scrawny man by his brittle wrists and dragged him behind the pews near a corner, thinking his body would be safe there.

Now what?

Look for the rest of them murdering bastards!

Storm gathered up her gun from behind the altar and was about to head out of the room when she heard approaching footsteps, chanting and screaming.

The fuck?! Is that heading my way? You got to be shitting me.

An eerie squeaking and thin mist filled the corridor. *What am I going to do?* She searched for another way out, but there wasn't one.

The footfalls grew louder, as did the screaming.

Hide! Storm went back behind the altar and took aim with her rifle. From where she was perched, she had a clear killing field. She cocked the gun. "Come get it, fuckers."

When half a dozen cloaked figures entered the room, dragging with them a nude teenaged girl, Storm retreated into the shadows. They hadn't spotted her.

Probably because they have their heads bent in prayer, she thought.

She took them in: apart from one who wore red, they were dressed in black gowns that reached their ankles. Hoods covered their heads. The one in crimson held a book in one hand, whilst his other swung a censer that emitted billowing scented smoke. He mumbled something unintelligible as he ambled towards the granite slab Storm had investigated earlier.

The robed people stepped closer. Their gowns bore the insignia found on the walls.

"Lay the sacrifice on the table, disciples," the one in red said, voice deep like a man's.

The girl writhed, her blonde hair thrashing as she tried to lash out with her hands and feet. But she was held too tightly. Five figures wearing midnight black hoisted her into the air and placed her on the granite. A rattling sound ensued.

What are they doing?

They shackled the youngster in place.

The five drew their hoods back, revealing crude wooden masks in the shape of imp or demon faces. The man in red removed his head covering, unveiling a deer's skull mask.

"Pray with me, oh brothers and sisters, as we summon the ghosts of those who have fallen. And in doing so, we shall sacrifice our virgin offering to appease them."

Not on my fucking watch, Storm thought, about to raise the gun.

"We call upon you, Skull, Bone, Cue-Ball..." the psychotic priest said, reeling off the names of the cannibals who had captured Storm, killed her family and friends, and cut a path of destruction through her hometown.

"We offer you this gift . . ." The man splayed his arms, spreading incense smoke and casting shadowy hands over the secured girl's tits. ". . . in the hope of resurrecting you so you may walk the mortal world again."

Storm noticed a pendant the shape, size and colour of a heart hanging from around the leader's neck. It looked real. She gagged but raised her gun and lined him up in her sights.

"Pray with me, oh brothers and sisters—let your voices and appreciation be heard, as I take this, the ceremonial blade and place it above the offering's heart."

I'm about to open up a world of shit! she thought, watching as the tip of the eight-inch knife poked at the girl's skin. Before the priest could press down on it, forcing it through the flesh and breastplate, Storm fired—the crack of gunfire was deafening. Her bullet went wide.

A buzzing sound assaulted Storm's ears, but she cocked the gun and fired at the leader again. Her shot drilled through the centre of the deer mask, embedding in his forehead. A squirt of blood erupted from the mortal wound. The blast propelled him back against the wall, his arms flapping, the book and censer lost. He slumped down dead.

A collective gasp emitted from the followers, their heads turning in Storm's direction. They drew back their robes at their midsections to reveal sheathed machetes.

"Shit!"

One by one, the disciples removed their weapons and stalked in her direction, raising the impressive blades above their heads.

"Stay back!" Storm demanded, jumping from behind the altar, her rifle trained on them. "I have enough bullets to kill you all twice over."

They halted.

She gulped. A trickle of sweat slid down her forehead. *If they rush me, I'm done for!* "Let the girl go."

One of them laughed. "You're not quick enough—"

"Hey, that's the police officer's daughter!" a voice at the back stated.

The others turned to look at him before refocusing on Storm.

"Are you?" the one who'd laughed asked. "Huw Davies' daughter? Storm, is it? We thought our leader'd *killed* you!"

"You thought wrong, dickhead." Storm fired. The slug ripped through the guy's mask and smashed his brains out the back of his head, coating the ones behind him in gore and splintered bone. He hit the deck, twitched, and died.

She reloaded. "Who's next?"

"Help me!" the girl on the table screamed.

"Get the fucking bitch!" a disciple yelled.

When Storm was about to fire again, the gun jammed, forcing her to grab the weapon by its barrel, turning it into a tool fit for bludgeoning. When the first machete wielder came at her, her karate skills kicked in, and she was able to block the attack with the gun's butt whilst lashing out with her booted foot.

Her toes connected with her assailant's bollocks and a satisfying crunch ensued, bringing a smile to her face as he went to ground. Her victory was short-lived, as a second blade came down in her direction, throwing her into quick action.

Storm sidestepped the knife, which was close enough to slice through her top and break skin. Blood spurted. She gritted her teeth. Storm forced the butt of her rifle into her attacker's face, smashing through the mask and flattening their noise. This drove them backwards—they toppled over a pew and crashed to the floor.

After a quick inspection, Storm settled on the fact they were down and out because of the way they were lying on their head. *Their neck's gone.*

Before the first aggressor could recover from the kick to the balls, Storm picked up a dropped machete and decapitated him. His head rolled along the ground until it thumped against the slab holding the frantic girl.

The remaining three held back.

"I don't want any part of this!" the one to the left said. She took her mask off to reveal flowing red hair and a pretty face. "I never wanted in on this to begin with, Ted."

The one Storm assumed to be Ted raised his face covering and glared at the redhead. He looked much older than the woman. "Shut up, fool!"

His daughter? Storm wondered.

"Will you pair get with it!" the third said, not taking their eyes off Storm.

"No, Dad. I can't. I feel sick. Please don't make me do any more horrible things. What would Mum think?"

Ted grabbed his daughter by the arm, causing her to yelp, and dragged her close to his face. "You don't *ever* mention her again, little bitch!" He then pushed her away and slapped her face. "I'll deal with you later."

"Not with me around you won't, fuck-face. Why don't you come and pick on me?" Storm suggested.

"Let's get her, Ted," the remaining cloaked figure said.

Ted slipped his mask down and went for Storm with the aid of his companion. "You're not leaving here alive, hear me? There's an army of us. You *can't* win."

"He's right. You have no idea what you've got mixed up in, Storm. You should have died. If you come quietly, our master might spare you and allow you to be sacrificed to our gods."

She almost laughed. "You pricks have any last words?"

"Ha—"

Ted's laughter was cut short as Storm's thrown rifle smacked him in the face, knocking him off-balance. This gave her the opportunity to go for the remainder with the machete.

Steel clashed, sparks flew.

"Give it up, bitch! You can't wi—*argh!*" the other man cried as she grabbed his balls and twisted.

"Let's see if I can't pop 'em, eh?"

"Get—*ugh!*" He started to vomit, which ran down her arm. When he dropped his knife, Storm let go of him and drove her machete through his chest, forcing him back and out of the room.

"Eeee-*argh*!" Ted screamed as he charged her.

Storm spun around, delivering a whirlwind kick. The flat of her foot slammed against his jawline. His head snapped violently to one side, breaking his neck. Ted continued to move forward until he crashed into a wall.

"*Daddy*!" the redhead sobbed.

Storm readied herself for the girl's attack, but it never came, and so she relaxed.

"I'm not going to try and hurt you," she cried, her shoulders hiccupping. "I'm s-s-sorry for my father—for all of them—he wouldn't have meant it. He was forced into joining, along with a few others."

"Look, I'm going to need your help, but first, we need to free her," Storm said, indicating the girl on the slab. "Do you have a key for her restraints?"

"No, but Pablo should. He's the one in red."

Storm stepped to the fallen man and searched his person, finding a set of keys around his neck close to the dangling heart. "I'm going to need you to lead me to the rest of them, okay? Is the leader here?"

She shook her head. "The main tribe boss isn't, but the ones who command the cult are. Tony and—"

"He's dead. I shot him outside. Who's the other?"

"I'm not sure of her name, but I can take you to her."

"Great. After you've done that, I want you to take this girl and get to the police, understand?"

The redhead nodded.

"You won't have to tell them of your involvement. You could say you were held here against your will."

"Fine, but let's make it quick. I don't want to be caught with you and have my life put in danger . . . Oh, Dad," she said, sobbing anew.

Storm ignored her as she worked on releasing the blonde "What's your name?"

"Jade. Please, don't hurt me. I'm only fourteen."

"Nobody will hurt you, promise. I'm going to get you out of here. Are there others like you?"

"Being held hostage?" Jade nodded, blinking away the tears. "Yes, they have a room filled with cages where they keep girls and boys . . ."

"Jesus. Why hasn't anyone done something about this? Nobody can steal a load of children and build a fucking temple in the woods without *someone* knowing about it!"

"People are scared. They have power, money."

"Yeah, and some of the authority are in their back pockets, no doubt," Storm said to herself.

"I don't know about that," Jade confessed.

"And what's your name?" Storm asked the redhead.

"Jasmine."

"Think you could give me a hand over here? There are so many keys . . ."

"It's the one with a red tab on it—it fits all locks," Jasmine confirmed.

Storm tried the allocated key on Jade's ankle restraints, which clicked loose. "Excellent.

Jasmine. Why don't you disrobe one of them for Jade, yeah?"

"Yeah, sure." She set about her task.

Storm eyed her. *Not that upset, considering she's lost her father. Maybe she's in shock? Perhaps she hated him for what he made her do? Keep a close watch,* she thought as she undid Jade's shackles.

With Jade loose, Storm helped her into a sitting position and took the proffered robe from Jasmine. "Here, put this on," Storm said, placing the garment over the blonde's head. Jade slipped her arms in, which revealed to Storm just how thin the girl was. Her ribs protruded. "They starved you?"

Jade looked down at herself, quickly pulling the robe over her body. "Do you mind! Pervert," she snapped.

"Sorry, I didn't mean—I was concerned, that's all."

"I . . . I didn't mean to yell at you. Forgive me?"

Storm nodded, helping her off the slab. "Can you walk?"

Jade shook her head. "No, I feel too weak."

"How long have you been here?"

"A week or so. They gave us enough to keep going. They snatched me from school, like most of the others. M-my parents must be so worried."

"Filthy bastards are going to pay with their lives. Jasmine, can you give me a hand with her? She needs our support to get out of here."

Without protest, Jasmine threw one of Jade's arms over her shoulder and helped support her weight.

Storm unjammed her gun, slung it over her back and fastened two machetes around her waist. "Do you know of a way around the water in the tunnel?" she asked Jasmine, putting Jade's other arm over her shoulder.

"You didn't see the bypass corridor?" Jasmine had true surprise in her voice. "I didn't think anyone would be able to miss it . . ."

"No, I didn't. I waded through the water to get here." She wanted to slap the redhead for making it sound as though Storm was thick for not seeing it, but suppressed her anger. "Get us there, quick."

"What then?"

"Lead us to the outside. Once there, you can help Jade out of the woods."

"And what about you?"

"I'm going back in."

"You're crazy! Come with us."

"I only wish I could. Before you take Jade to safety, I'll need you to tell me how to get to the rest of them in here."

"Okay, I can do that, but I thought you wanted me to take you?"

"No, I thought about it and it's too risky." Then something occurred to Storm. "How come the gunfire didn't bring more of them running?"

"Because there's multiple layers and depth to this place—you'll get lost. Here where we're standing is nowhere near the centre of operations."

Storm didn't like the sounds of that.

Once outside, Jade complained of needing to get off her feet, and so Storm and Jasmine lowered her to the floor and propped her against a tree.

Dawn was breaking.

As Storm obtained directions off Jasmine, she gathered up all the spare ammunition she could find on Tony and his fallen men.

"Will you pair be okay getting out of the woods?" Storm asked, handing Jasmine a canteen filled with water she'd found by the campfire.

Jasmine took it and gave it to Jade. "Yes."

"Get help out here."

Jasmine nodded as Jade panted from taking a long gulp of water. "Is there any food?"

"I think I saw some by the cave. Jasmine, do you mind? I need to get going."

"No, it's fine."

Storm nodded and walked to the entrance of the tunnel. She turned, said her goodbyes, told the girls to get moving as soon as possible and entered. Before venturing down the correct path, she stood in the shadows and watched Jasmine to see if the girl was only pretending to be on her side.

When she witnessed Jasmine feed Jade and move her into a more comfortable sitting position, Storm was sold.

She must have hated *her dad. God knows what he did to rope her into this mess . . . And what's the deal with the mother?* she wondered, turning to leave.

The main part to the tunnel was much brighter this time around, thanks to the rising sun. However, the farther she went, the darker it got, forcing her to rely on the flashlight.

"She said to take the right at the first fork, and to look for a bypass tunnel hidden within that path . . ." Storm muttered, branching off the main passage. She flashed her light on other sides of the wall until she found the hidden entrance. "Ah-ha! Got ya, you bastard."

She took it, which led to another fork in the path. Storm went left and immediately felt herself descending lower and lower until her ears popped. Soon she came upon lit torches on either side of her, lighting the way.

Storm put her flashlight away. "Well done, Jasmine," she uttered, creeping along the route. Up ahead, she heard voices, followed by laughter. She took the gun off her back and made sure it was ready to fire. "Time to pay the fiddler!"

As she crept farther down the tunnel, the talking became louder—it sounded to her like a group of males. Four, possibly five. She steadied the gun as she closed in on the mouth of the tunnel, noticing it opened into a room.

Shadows danced on the walls.

The smell of smoke and coffee was strong.

A guard post?

A figure moved across her path: a man holding what appeared to be a cooking pan. He had a gun holstered at his hip. When he stopped and turned, she thought she'd been rumbled, but he looked back at whoever was talking, laughed and ambled out of view.

Storm moved again, until she was able to peer around the corner and spy four men sat around a small wooden table. They were playing cards. A stack of cash littered the playing field. An oil lamp stood in the middle, lighting up their faces with an eerie yellow glow. Also, she spotted a near-empty bottle of whiskey and four full glasses.

"Are you sure you won't join us for a drink, pussy?" one of the men at the table asked. He was a hulking brute of muscles with a shaved head. His biceps rippled. He made the other men look like matchstick figures.

You're first, she thought as the others around the table laughed.

Storm looked at the man with the pan. He'd filled it with water and set it on a grill that covered a fire. He had his flank to her.

Maybe take him *first?*

She raised the gun but stopped herself from shooting. She gave the room one final examination.

I don't see another tunnel. Jasmine said there was another passageway . . .

"Who the fuck are *you*?!" the man who'd set the pan to boil asked.

The laughter around the table stopped.

Storm snapped out of her thoughts and put a bullet in the man's chest, which propelled him backwards and onto the fire, instantly igniting him. He didn't scream, suggesting the bullet had done the job.

Over the roar of flames and crackling body, Storm spoke up. "Don't you fuckers move!"

She cocked the rifle. "Where's the leader of this batshit crazy horror show, freaks?"

"You're dead," the bald man whispered.

"Keep your fucking hands where I can see them," she told the man to the right of The Hulk, who appeared to be making a move for something under the table. "I'm going to ask you once more, or I'll start shooting. Where. Is. Your. Boss?"

The Hulk grinned.

Storm fired.

Her slug tore through the face of the guy with twitchy hands. His body folded into his chair with heavy force, causing the seat's legs to snap off. He crashed to the floor in a heap.

She reloaded. "Well, sing up, ladies?"

The Hulk made to charge her but stopped when she turned the gun on him.

"Don't make me kill you, big boy. I just want your leader."

He pressed his lips together, so she was forced to kill another one of his goons.

"You're running out of men. One more and it's your turn . . ."

"Maybe we should tell her?" The Hulk's remaining man said.

"Keep your fucking trap shut, Ben."

"You promise not to kill us, miss?" Ben asked.

"If you're honest with me and start speaking right now, then I promise to spare you."

"Don't say a word, motherfucker," The Hulk raged. "I'll rip your fucking spine out."

Storm lined Ben up in her sights. "Start. Talking."

"Wait! Please!"

Movement behind Storm distracted her. She turned on her heel but was clobbered in the temple before she could complete her one-eighty manoeuvre.

The blow shoved her sideways, and she almost collapsed onto the burning body but managed to avoid it. As wooziness crept in, Storm saw Jasmine standing over her. She held a baseball bat in one hand and Jade's severed head in the other.

Somewhere from within the room, Storm heard laughing.

"You b-bitch," she managed, trying to raise the rifle to shoot, but it was snatched off her.

"Lights out, cunt!" The Hulk said, smashing Storm in her face with a robust fist.

Chapter 18
Now

When Jim failed to answer Jonesy's questions, the main thug ordered his men to scoop him off the floor and escort him and Laura into the living room, where they tossed them onto the sofa. Jonesy and his boys then stood around them, circling like vultures.

"So, Jim, are you going to co-operate with me? I'm giving you a solid fucking chance here, sunshine. Others don't get such a good deal."

"I don't know what the hell you're talking about! I've already told you."

"Well, Liz says different, and I've known her a lot fucking longer than you. She was scared, crying. Is that what you like? Does terrifying women get you hard?"

"Look, okay, I admit I went to see her, but I didn't threaten her. You *have* to believe me!"

"Care to enlighten me?"

Jim sighed. "Must we do this with my wife here? I don't want her having any part in this. Please."

Jonesy got closer to him, blew cigarette smoke in his face and smiled. "Yes, we fucking must, dickhead. Now, start spilling your guts or I'm going to spill *hers*. Understand?"

The muscles in Jim's jaw tensed. "If you insist." Jim told Jonesy about Owen, Sam and the strange incidents at Twin Jesters. "It's all being covered up, and Liz is in on it."

"Ha-ha!" Spurs bellowed. "You're trying to fucking tell us that there's *cannibals* running amok in South Wales?"

Berserko and Knucklehead howled with laughter.

Jonesy choked on his smoke but regained his composure. *A fuckin' nutter.* "You're going to have to try better than that, Jim. We're not a bunch of fucking retards who read the shit in your papers, pal. Got it?"

"I'm telling you the truth. If we don't stop Liz, then she'll flee back to Twin Jesters. She knows her cover's blown. You—"

"Spurs, shut him up, will ya?" Jonesy said, tiring of Jim's game.

A robust first slammed into the side of Jim's face, snapping his mouth closed.

"There's going to be much more than that, Jim, if you don't start telling me what I want—"

"You want to hear I threatened her? That I planned to go back there and do the *cunt* in?!"

"*Jim*!" Laura blurted.

"Well, I did, but I didn't tell Liz. I was hoping to surprise her. She killed my friend and countless others. She needs stopping. There, are you fucking happy? Now, let my wife go, bastards!"

Jonesy grinned. "That does make me happy, actually, and it didn't take that much to extract it from you."

"Why's it so important? I assume you'll give me a good kicking anyway. That's why you're here, right? Beat the piss out of me and warn me away?"

Jonesy gave a slight nod.

"Well, you best be prepared to do me in, because I'll be gunning for the bitch after this."

Jonesy blew more smoke in Jim's face. "I'll probably do that, but first, I'm going to get my boys to soften you up whilst I have some fun with Mrs Jim. How does that sound, sailor?" He slapped Jim's cheek and pulled away from him.

"You . . . you . . ." Jim went to stand but Spurs pushed him back down. "Pretty tough with your fucking goons around you, ain't ya?"

Jonesy grabbed Laura by her arm and yanked her to her feet.

She yelped. "Get your hands off me!"

"Mmm, you got curves in all the right places, babe," Jonesy said, eyeing her from head to toe.

"Drill her one for me, boss," Knucklehead chirped.

"And me, if you can manage it for a third time," Berserko added.

"I'll be having a piece of Liz, so I'm good," Spurs said with a smile.

Jonesy laughed. "Enough spunk in my gun to impregnate Asia, fellas."

They all laughed.

Laura started slapping Jonesy in the face, chest and arms. "You filthy pigs!"

Jim jumped from his seat. "Get the fuck— *oof*!" He doubled over after being punched in the guts by Spurs. His knees buckled and knocked together. He sat back down. Tears filled his eyes.

"Want more, puddin'?" Spurs belly laughed.

Jonesy dragged Laura away, her booted feet trying to find purchase in the carpet.

"*Jim*!" she cried, and then Jonesy wrapped her mouth with one of his fat hands. "*Mmmm*!" She thrashed her arms, body bucking, tears spilling down her cheeks. In her struggle, her jumper rode up her torso, revealing the undersides of her pert braless tits.

Spurs wolf whistled as Jonesy disappeared from view with his prize.

* * *

"It's all about the cash, isn't it?" Jim said to the spur-wearing oaf. "You two-bit punks probably couldn't give a fuck about Liz."

"I'd start worrying less about our business and more about what Jonesy's doing to your good wife upstairs . . ."

The other two goons smirked. The rotund one said, "Tell him, Spurs!" The other slurred a "Hell yeah!"

"You mother—" Jim stopped talking as bedsprings above him creaked and a headboard smacked the wall in a lethargic way. His mouth sagged. "You motherfuckers," he whispered, his head lowering. "Look, just do what you want with me and let her go. I'm begging you."

"It doesn't work like that, arsehole," Spurs confessed. "When we come knocking for retribution for a client, we take *everything* there is to take, friend. Right, Berserko?"

The rotund one nodded.

"Knucklehead?"

The one with slurred speech likewise agreed.

"We won't be leaving here until you're both destroyed." Spurs chuckled, his goons joining in.

"*Please!*"

"I guess you should have told the truth from the start—things may have played out differently for you," Berserko said.

"Yeah, maybe!" Knucklehead chirped, still laughing.

"Aye, *maybe* . . ." Spurs added. "We don't like our people feeling scared."

"Whatever she's paying you, I'll triple it."

The noise of the headboard bashing the wall increased.

Jim tried blocking it out, along with Laura's muffled sobs and yelps. Now and then, he heard flesh slap flesh.

Fucking pig!

"*Triple*, hey?"

"Like, three times the amount?" Knucklehead questioned.

Berserko tutted.

"I'm not sure, Jim" Spurs said. "We're loyal to our—"

"Four times the amount," Jim cut in. "I have over half a million in this house. You can have it all! Every fucking penny."

Spurs stepped back, rubbed his whiskers and looked at his friends. "Well, this makes things interesting."

"We should consult Jonesy," Berserko suggested.

Spurs gave his man a hard stare. "Do you think I'm fucking stupid?"

Berserko shrank away. "No, course not."

"Get him down here so we can talk it through," Jim pleaded.

"You know we could just kill you and take the money?"

"Do that and you won't get a fucking bean! I won't tell you anything, that's a promise. No matter how much you make me scream."

The look in Spurs' eyes told Jim the big bad biker knew he wasn't messing about; that no matter how much pressure he applied, Jim wouldn't back down.

The drumming headboard came to a close.

Jonesy grunted and yelled, "You sexy piece of arse."

Berserko and Knucklehead looked at each other and giggled.

Jim gritted his teeth. "Get Jonesy down here now or I'm taking my offer off the table. You can just fucking kill us."

Spurs looked taken aback. "You're fucking crazy!" He laughed, punching Jim in the shoulder, deadening it. "Watch him, boys. I think he may have found his balls, and we wouldn't want him bailing on us."

"You—"

Spurs walked off before Jim could finish.

Fucking charming, Jim thought, looking at the other pair who stared back at him. Berserko cricked his head until his neck popped, and Knucklehead cracked his knuckles. *I'm sure they'd kill me for a joint. Hell, they'd do it for fun!*

"Jonesy!" Spurs yelled out in the hallway. "Boss!"

"Y—*yeah*?" came a muffled response. "Wha' ya want, Spurs?"

"Jim has a counteroffer for you . . ."

"Is that so?"

"Half a million fat ones!"

"He thinks he can buy us off?"

"He has more than that in mind, boss. I think maybe you should come down."

"Okay, okay, give me two minutes."

As Jim listened to the conversation unfold, his eyes never left the heavies guarding him. And then the living room light glinted off the smooth surface of the marble ashtray Laura used to use for her cigarillos, catching his attention.

Turning his head, Jim noticed Spurs was still in the passageway.

If I'm quick, I could disable these bozos and give Spurs what I have left in the tank . . . His gaze fell on the ashtray again. If he reached his hand out, his fingers would be mere inches from it. *I could dive for it. Maybe punch that fat fuck in the balls first. By the time the second one knows what's happened, I'll have dashed his brains all over the carpet.*

Jim was about to bounce off his knees and throw his plan into action when Spurs re-entered the room.

"Everything okay in here?" Spurs asked.

His boys grunted.

"What about you, Jim? Okay down there?" Spurs laughed. "Hey, while you're there . . ." he continued, lowering the zip on his trousers.

The other men gaffed.

"Go on, son—stick it down his throat!" Knucklehead joked.

"Do you think I'm a fucking faggot?" Spurs snapped, pulling the zip back up. "I just wanted to see the look on his face."

They doubled over, whooping and slapping Spurs on the back.

Jim again thought about making a move, but didn't, and was glad of it because Jonesy then walked into the living room.

"What's all this horseshit, Spurs?!" he demanded, punching his open hand. Everyone shut up, straightened and looked at Jonesy. "Well? Have you all finished playing with each other like a bunch of girls at a sleepover? *Huh*?"

"Sorry, boss," Spurs and the other pair said in unison.

Jonesy cleared his throat. "Your wife's a great fuck." Laura's sobbing droned above. "Sadly, she won't be joining us for this little powwow, as she's unable to walk. Bled pretty bad." He smiled and sniggered. "You might need to consider changing the bed if you live through this ordeal, amigo." He lit a cigarette.

"I'll pay you half a million if you let me and my wife go."

Jonesy raised an eyebrow. "You think we're fucking mercs? Muscle for hire?"

"I had the opinion you guys would slit your mother's throat for a fistful of notes . . . But I could be wrong, of course."

Jonesy laughed. "And what do you have in mind?"

"I want your help in taking Liz and her family down. I have reason to—"

"Ah, not this cannibal shit again!" Berserko said.

Spurs cocked his arm back as if to punch Jim.

"*Wait*! I can prove it. Go to hers tonight, after she locks up, and look for yourselves. I'm sure she gets up to some nasty fucking activities after closing. I'm also guessing she's hired you guys to get her to Twin Jesters? I'm not wrong, am I?"

"Berserko, Knucklehead: get over there and have a sniff, okay? And make sure you give it plenty of time."

"Fine, boss," Knucklehead said. He and Berserko left.

"You better hope they find *something*, or I'm going to be really upset, newspaper man."

Jim lowered his head. "Can I see my wife?"

"Spurs, go and get the cunt. I need to ring Liz."

"Okay, boss," Spurs said, leaving the room.

Jim remained quiet as Jonesy dug a mobile out of his pocket. "Liz? Jonesy. Listen, the boys and I are a little held up with our friend. We're going to be a bit late getting to you. Huh? Another couple of hours, yeah," Jonesy said, laughing. "Let's just say we're having fun kicking this fuck's head in and shagging his wife silly. No, we'll be there. Just get ready to roll. Yep, see you soon." Jonesy hung up and pocketed his phone.

"Now what?" Jim asked as the sobbing, naked Laura was shoved into the room. She huddled up to him.

"We wait, pencil-dick. Relax."

* * *

When Knucklehead and Berserko turned up at the pub, it was past midnight and the lights were off on the ground floor. With their bikes parked down a smog-filled alley next to the boozer, they dismounted and strolled to the front.

"Man, why are we here spying on Liz? This doesn't feel right," Knucklehead protested.

"I feel ya, brother, but we do what the boss wants." Berserko, who'd kicked around with Jonesy and Spurs a lot longer than Knucklehead, would do anything to appease them. "And if it means doing sneaky shit, then that's what we have to do. Besides, we don't owe this here fuckhead Liz anything."

"True. But I like the woman. She's a fine piece of arse, dude."

"Stop thinking with your dick, brother—this is business, that's all."

Knucklehead nodded. "Look," he said, pointing. "There's a light on in that upper window."

"How do you suppose we get up there?"

"Maybe coming around the front was a mistake. Isn't there a hatch behind to enter the cellar?"

"Should be. Think she might have left it open?"

Knucklehead nodded. "It's not like we're going to find anything—"

"Might catch her skipping around the place in her undies! You'd like that."

Both men sniggered as they made their way to the rear of the pub. There, they found a steel hatch in the floor for beer deliveries. Knucklehead bent down, grabbed one of the handles and pulled. It cracked open with a groan.

Berserko winced. "*Shh!*"

"Sorry, I forgot to bring the WD-40."

"Ha-fucking-ha! Just keep it down."

Knucklehead pulled the door up as quick as he could to make as little noise as possible. Both men descended into the darkened room below.

"Where's the light switch?" Knucklehead asked.

"No, keep them off, man—we have this." Berserko pulled his lighter out of his pocket. "That'll be enough," he said, striking the Zippo.

"I still think this is fucking madness."

"Stop your bellyaching, man. You'll get paid either way."

"Yeah, I know. Still . . ."

"*Shh!* And keep your peepers open."

"For vampires? Or as in werewolves?" Knucklehead laughed.

Both men shifted through the cellar until they came to a set of steps that led to another door.

"This'll take us to the bar," Berserko said.

"Nice one, Holmes!" Knucklehead tried the door, found it unlocked, and pushed it outwards. It didn't so much as creak.

The men clambered through the opening and found themselves positioned behind the bar. A half-light lit some of the room, throwing their shadows. A muffled voice came from somewhere inside the building.

They shuffled towards another door, which led them into the passageway. A staircase presented itself. The lighting here was better, so Berserko killed his Zippo. Without speaking, he indicated they go upstairs.

Knucklehead nodded and led the way.

The carpeted stairs didn't call out a warning when stepped on, but it didn't stop Knucklehead from pulling his Kukri knife. Even though he knew there was no real danger—that it was just a woman living alone—it was better to be safe than sorry. And, with the business they were in, it paid to be cautious.

When they reached the top, Berserko leaned close to Knucklehead's ear and whispered, "Watch your step and keep as silent as possible. If Liz catches us, let me do the talking, okay?"

Knucklehead nodded. He was more than happy for Berserko to be the mouthpiece.

"Follow me. I'm sure there's a third floor, where the family quarters are."

Once they'd reached the end of the hall and entered the next room, they halted in the doorway. In the corner of the room, a TV played a blank screen, and the sound of chewing assaulted their ears.

"What the *fuck*?" Knucklehead muttered, craning his head around the door's jamb.

There was blood everywhere. Not fresh, but dried engrained blood—in the carpet, up the walls, on the ceiling and sparse furniture...

"Is that a *cot*?" Berserko asked, pointing.

"I didn't know she had a baby," Knucklehead admitted.

"No, I—" Berserko stopped talking when a face appeared over the back of the sofa. It was disfigured, and horrid. Blood drizzled down its chin. There was a flap of flesh clinched between its teeth.

"Jesus Christ!" Knucklehead blurted.

"Is there someone down there?" a female asked from above.

The thing looking at them growled softly.

Then another face peeped around the arm of the couch. Like the first, it was disfigured. Blood covered its face. Both creatures had long blonde hair.

"Are they *children*?" Berserko gulped.

"Nine-Ball? Billiard-Ball? Are you okay down there?" Floorboards creaked. "Girls?"

"I think we've found what we're looking for, man," Knucklehead said. "Let's get out of here. Now."

The faces disappeared.

Knucklehead pulled on Berserko's vest, dragging him onto the landing.

Snarls followed them out the room.

"Girls, what's going on?"

"Intrudersss!" a snake-like voice hissed.

"Get them, girls. Attack! I'll bring the gun."

"Fuck." Knucklehead turned and fled when the blemished girls bounded out of the room and jumped on Berserko, who tried firing a shot.

"Urgh-argh! *Help*!" Berserko wailed.

Knucklehead stopped in his tracks and looked back.

The girls were ripping through the man's clothes and shredding the skin about his chest. Then they bit into his cheeks, ripped his lips off and devoured his tongue. Blood squirted up the walls and flooded the carpet.

Berserko's knees folded, and he collapsed to the floor.

When the young girls started ripping his organs out through his arse and yanked open his stomach, Knucklehead fled downstairs, screaming like a girl as he went. Five steps from the bottom, his legs tangled, tripping him. He tumbled the rest of the way, smashing a few of the banister's spindles.

"Ugh, *fuck*!" he cried, scrabbling to his feet to hobble away.

"Argh!" someone screamed from behind.

Knucklehead looked over his shoulder. The twins were on the top step, hunched, their nightwear soaked. One held Berserko's detached cock; the other had his heart.

They were both chewing.

Bloody saliva oozed from their mottled gobs. Their lips pulled back, exposing ruby-red teeth.

Behind them, Liz appeared. "What the hell are *you* doing here?"

"I—we—"

"You came to check up on me? You took Jim's word over mine? Is that it? Well, now you know. Kill him, girls!"

Nine-Ball and Billiard-Ball bounded down the steps, their arms outstretched, their talons wiggling in search of fresh meat to rip from bones.

"*Shit!*" Knucklehead turned and ran for the window in front of him. He ditched his knife and pumped his arms and legs, and then threw his weight against the glass, which exploded into slivers.

Knucklehead screamed as he dropped through the air along with particles of glass and whimpered when he hit the concrete. He got to his feet quickly, his knees aching, and scurried down the alley to his bike.

He dug the keys to his hog out of his pocket and was close to crying when he heard the doors to the pub open.

Pools of light were cast across the floor.

Snarling sounds erupted around him.

"Kill him!" Liz demanded. "Before he gets away. *Quick.*"

"Fuck, fuck, fuck!" Knucklehead blubbered, jumping onto his bike and slotting the key into the ignition. When he turned it, his Harley kicked to life.

One of the twins flew at him, mouth wide, teeth exposed, about to snap down on him. He punched her in the face as hard as he could. A knuckle cracked, but he shrugged the pain off and straightened his motorbike.

As he pulled away, the other girl jumped on his back and sank her teeth into his neck, ripping open a chunk of flesh.

"Ugh! *Bitch!*" He pumped his elbow backwards, driving it into her guts, winding the girl and sending her sprawling onto the floor.

Knucklehead glanced in his wing mirror and saw Liz rushing at him. The girls were getting up off the floor. He dipped the clutch and got his bike moving, kicking up smoke as he powered away.

He heard Liz shouting and yelling but couldn't make out what she was saying.

Blood poured down his neck, and dizziness set in.

Got to get back to the boys. They'll patch me up . . .

His bike wobbled and weaved as he rode, but Knucklehead managed to keep going with relative safety.

Chapter 19
Now

“**W**here are they, Jonesy? It’s been hours.”

“Keep calm, Spurs. What, you *really* think they’ve run into a pack of blood-crazed cannibals?” The leader laughed, blowing smoke from his nostrils.

“If they have, you won’t be seeing them again!” Jim interjected, putting his arm around the still-sobbing Laura.

“Fuck off, douchebag. Did we ask for your opinion?” Jonesy raged.

Jim sat silent.

“I don’t like this, man, and if Liz does find them snooping around, she’s going to be pissed with us! All bets will be off.”

“Quiet, Spurs, will ya? You really that hungry for her pussy? She means nothing to us, and there’s more money to be made off Jim. Fuck her.”

“Man, she’s our people!” Spurs said.

"*Our* people?" Jonesy scoffed. "She couldn't give two fucks for the likes of you and I, man. Don't forget that. You think she likes you just because she gave you the come-on and a stiff prick?" Jonesy laughed.

Spurs' jaw tensed. Never before had he wanted to smack his boss. He had a lot of time and respect for Liz—not that any of the crew knew it, especially Jonesy. "It's not like that, so get off my back." His fists clenched. He didn't know if he could take Jonesy in a fistfight, but he'd give it all he was worth all day long.

"What, you want to thump me? Break my teeth? Smash my face in, Spurs? You look like you do. What's the matter? You got it hot for the bitch?"

Spurs stepped forward with every intention of putting a dent in Jonesy's jaw when a crash and rapid pounding sounds pulled him back from the edge of anger.

"Saved by the bell, Spurs?" Jonesy grinned. "We'll talk about this later, dude."

The look on his boss' face told Spurs he was in serious trouble. He'd be facing a beating for sure, possibly exile from the gang. Jonesy wasn't one for messing about. Spurs had seen first-hand what Jonesy was capable of doing to members who displeased him.

"Fine." Spurs gritted his teeth.

The pounding at his back became incessant.

"Shut the fuck up!" Spurs turned and screamed at the door.

"Let me in, guys!"

When Jonesy opened up, Knucklehead collapsed into the hallway. Blood poured out of him. His face was ashen, his lips taking on a purple hue.

"It's true . . ." he muttered.

Jonesy knelt by his side.

Knucklehead's teeth chattered. He grabbed hold of Jonesy's vest. "They k-killed Berserko. Tore him apart in front of my eyes. Two girls. They picked his fucking bones clean!" He shook his head, struggling to breathe.

"See," Jim said, making his way into the hallway.

"Who the fuck told you—" Jonesy started, but was pulled back by Knucklehead.

"Get the fuck out of here, man. Liz is going to come for you. Possibly here, who—who knows." Knucklehead coughed up blood, choked on it, and lay still. A whisper of a breath escaped him.

"He's fucking dead!" Spurs pounded a wall with his fist.

"Berserko, too. That cunt killed them." Jonesy got to his feet. "Now what do you think of your precious bitch, huh?"

"Now she dies," Spurs admitted.

"I'm going to help, even though you bastards raped my wife and assaulted me," Jim piped in.

"Why would you want to do that?" Jonesy asked.

"They killed my friend. I owe it to him."

"Right, okay. Look, if we get over to the pub now, we might be able to—"

"No," Jim said. "We need to let her get to Twin Jesters, to her family, so we can kill the fucking lot of them."

Spurs and Jonesy both nodded.

"I have a shotgun here, which I want to get before we leave."

"Fine, but don't think about using it on us," Jonesy said.

"I have bigger fish to fry, pal."

"Spurs, get all the weapons you can off Knucklehead's body and bike."

"Got it, boss."

"Can you ride, Jim?" Jonesy asked.

"I rode in my youth. Doubt I've forgotten."

"Good, then you can take Knucklehead's," Jonesy said. "Meet us out front when you're ready."

Jim nodded.

* * *

After Spurs and Jonesy left, Jim went to Laura, held her, sobbed and told her the score.

"You *want* to help those raping fucks?! After what they've *done*? Look at me, at your face! They've smashed—"

"It's got them out of the house and away from you. Plus, when they've helped me to do what I want, I'll put bullets in both their heads," he whispered. "Now, get up, dressed and go to your car. Drive to the hospital and get yourself checked. I'll be back before you know it."

"I don't know what in God's creation is going on"—she winced, getting to her feet—"but I want the *full* story when I see you next."

"You got it." He kissed her on the forehead and rushed into the other room where he kept his old shotgun and a few boxes of ammunition. By the time he returned to the living room,

Laura was climbing the stairs. "Will you be okay?" he called.

"Yes, just go and do what you have to, and as quickly as possible, so you can get your arse back to me."

"Of course." He blew her a kiss as he headed out the door. Before jumping on the bike, he threw the gun over his shoulders and put the ammunition in one of the hog's saddlebags.

"You're sure you know how to control that?" Jonesy asked.

Jim nodded. "I might have a bit of trouble seeing, but I'm fine."

"Yeah, I kind of feel sorry about beating you black and blue now, man," Spurs admitted.

Jim detected sincerity in the man's voice. *Since that argument between him and Jonesy, he's become a different person,* he thought. *Like Jekyll and Hyde.*

When Jonesy and Spurs pulled off, Jim followed.

* * *

Betty put the phone down and looked at the drones, Igor, and the soldiers at his back, one of whom—Hawks—was on the radio calling the back-up and bombing off.

"No, a total annihilation of the area is not needed, sir. We have the situation under control. The threat has been neutralized. Over."

"Come home, private. Your mission is complete. Over."

"Yes, sir!" Hawks looked up from his radio. "That's it—the heat's off us, Betty. But now we need to get the family to safety, before the clean-up troops move in."

"Why would they?" Betty questioned.

"They'll want to do a full investigation. Also, they might be worried we've missed something," he said, indicating his sister.

"Will the bunker hold us all, Mama?" Igor asked.

Betty shook her head. "No. I think you need to lead a party up into the hills and stay there for some time. The drones know how to hunt and survive—you'll all be fine."

"What about you, Betty?" Hawks asked.

"I'll take the rest into the bunker. There're enough supplies down there to last several years. Once things have blown over, I'll come out and start rebuilding."

"But a lot of the town has been destroyed, thanks to the tanks and grenades."

"I'm sure they'll get the place back on its feet at some point."

"This cursed place?" Hawks' sister said. "You'll be lucky. The army have been looking for an excuse to shut Twin Jesters down for years. This will be the official death of the town."

Betty sighed. "Those fucking clowns brought this on. All of it. You were right, Igor: I shouldn't have trusted them. All they want to do is cause mischief and see everyone and everything die! They have no loyalty."

"Have they gone back to their world, Mama?" Igor asked.

"You mean to say the stories are *true*?"

Betty looked at Hawks. "Yes, all of it." Then she went on to tell everyone how she used black magic to do it. "I thought they would help me gain control over Twin Jesters and the south. My family went with them, blindly following them . . ."

"*You* brought all this on?" Hawks asked. "Had you not heard of the jesters and their manipulative ways?!"

"I thought I could harness—"

"Oh, man," his sister said. "If they remain, they could—"

"I've banished them. They're not coming back."

"Ever?"

Betty shook her head. "*Never.*"

"You've rid the town of its curse?" Hawks wanted to know.

"Definitely. I did a blood sacrifice. It worked, trust me."

"Mama, I think I go now," Igor said. "We need to get to safety."

"Yes, boy, you do that." Betty watched as her son turned and addressed the family. When he was finished, she called, "Igor, come and give your mama a hug."

When mother and son separated, Igor gathered the family he'd collected from various hidey-holes in Twin Jesters and the surrounding woods and led them out the back door and into the hills.

Betty shed a tear, for she didn't know how long it would be until they would be reunited. She didn't like the thought of her local family being parted. She turned to the window, opened the curtain, and looked out onto the ruins that were once part of her magnificent town. Her empire.

Hydra would be devastated. What have I done? We had it all. I had to push for more. No matter what happens here, the legacy of my family, the Fucks, will live on! We are everywhere. Worldwide. We are unstop—

Something the size of a small rock came sailing out of the darkness, towards the window. She gasped, throwing herself to her stomach as the object smashed through the glass and rolled along the floor.

"*Grenade!*" Hawks yelled, diving on it.

Betty gasped, covering her head with her arms.

The blast was muffled.

Someone screamed.

Betty looked up and saw Hawks' guts dripping from the walls and ceiling.

What was left of her family—ten in total—moved forward and growled.

"Enemy approach—" Hawks' sister took a bullet to the head, as did a few of her tribe.

"Get down!" Betty ordered.

A score of gunfire erupted outside. The walls were peppered, along with the furniture and décor. China and other trinkets exploded into minute particles. And then there was silence.

"Give it up in there!" someone yelled from outside.

"Fuck you!" Betty replied.

"Nice," another replied.

"Show yourself, and I promise not to hurt the girls and baby," the first person said.

The girls? Baby? Liz! Oh, God . . . Betty went to get up, but one of her tribe members pulled her back down.

"No, not safe."

"What's it to be, bitch?" the person outside shouted. "Do I ice them? No problem . . ."

Betty couldn't move.

A gunshot rang out.

Someone screamed, "My baby!"

"Oh, fuck . . ." Betty muttered.

"Poke your head out, or I'll go through them all!"

Betty heard men laughing. "Hold your fire. Let's talk about this . . ."

"One . . ."

"You killed my fucking baby!" Liz screamed again.

"Two . . ."

Betty turned to the male cannibal who'd dragged her down and said, "Go into the forest and fetch Igor!"

"Three—"

"Don't kill them!" Betty stuck her hands up, and then peered over the windowsill. Two men she'd never seen before stood outside, dressed like bikers. "Who are you, and why are you doing this?"

"This is retribution, whore!" the bigger of the men said. "These bitches here"—he indicated Liz, Nine-Ball and Billiard-Ball— "killed our friends." He had a handgun pointed at Liz's head.

"Ha! They thought they were being so fucking sneaky, coming here by using the darkness as cover. But no, we followed them from the pub," the smaller man said. "Savage little fucks, ain't they?"

"Yeah, got 'em good!" the bigger man said, thumping Liz in the forehead with his gun.

Liz looked up at her captor. She was saying something. Nine-Ball and Billiard-Ball seemed too scared to move.

Probably worried that fucking psycho will put a bullet in their mother's head, Betty thought. Behind her, the male cannibal had almost crawled to the kitchen door in his escape to fetch Igor. *That's good. Go get help. These fucks are going to be sorry!*

The shorter male stepped forward. "I don't want to kill you. I just want to turn you over to the authorities and make a shit-ton of money off you freaks." He laughed, pointing his shotgun at Betty. "Now, are you coming out, or do I waste these bitches and come in and get you? If I do, I *will* kill you. Fuck the money."

Liz's hand moved to the biker's crotch, a smile pulling across her face.

Fearful the man walking towards her would turn around and catch Liz, Betty stood tall, the cannibals behind her gasping. "It's okay," she whispered. "Get ready to attack."

"Anyone else in there with ya?"

"No, the blast killed them all but me. You've destroyed my family, *bastard*!"

"Well, we'll see about that, won't we?"

We will, won't we! Betty thought, finding it hard to keep the grin from her face.

A blast rang out, wiping the smile away and startling those around her. Betty turned on her heel to see a badly beaten man standing at the back of the room with a smoking shotgun.

*   *   *

"Thought you could get the fucking drop on us, huh?" Jim asked, baring his teeth. He fired another shot at a cannibal moving towards him, blowing a hole in its chest and sending it out the window into the street. He cocked the gun and walked towards the woman who'd been conversing with Jonesy. "Your days are fucking numbered. Yours and your incestuous clan's. You've terrified these parts for long enough."

The woman didn't raise her hands. "You can lower the gun—your friends out front plan to take me in."

"They might, but I sure as fuck don't."

Her eyes narrowed. "You wouldn't have the balls, dickhead."

He grinned. "Come on in, Jonesy, Spurs—she's all ours."

When Jonesy got to the window, he stretched his arm out until the muzzle of his gun pressed between the leader's tits. "Bet you didn't think your day would pan out like this when you woke this morning?" He grinned.

Jim turned on him, firing his shotgun.

The shell removed half of Jonesy's face. "*Ugh!*" he called out, his body collapsing to the floor, disappearing into the darkness.

"What the fuck?!" Spurs said.

Jim saw the leader move in his peripheral, and so he slammed her in the jaw with the butt of his gun, knocking her to the floor.

"You fucking killed—*argh*!" Spurs screamed.

When Jim looked out the window, he saw Liz rip through the big man's trousers with her teeth. As she devoured chunks of his thigh, her daughters pounced on Spurs and tore at his body before he had a chance to hit the floor.

"Now what are you going to do?!" the leader asked. Blood spilled out of her mouth. Her tribe rose to their feet all around. "Do you have enough bullets in that gun of yours?"

Jim walked backwards, towards the kitchen door, plucking fresh shells out of his pocket and stuffing them into the shotgun's belly. When the pipe was full, he cocked it and fired, killing a cannibal, then another.

"Kill him!" the head female cannibal demanded, catching a shell to the face, which killed her outright.

"Come and fucking get it!" Jim yelled, pumping round after round into the advancing tribe until there was none left.

Blood dripped off the end of his nose and chin and gelled his hair. His breathing came in ragged rips.

"You can't win, Jim," a voice called from outside.

"Just fucking watch me, Liz!" he said, ramming the last of his ammo into the gun.

"I have family in the woods. I could get them if I wanted to . . ."

"Bring them! I'll kill them too!" The door at his back creaked. Jim turned, snapping the shotgun's cocking mechanism. "*Laura*! What—I told you to get out—"

"I'm sorry, Jim." She punched something sharp into his guts and twisted it.

The gun slipped from his hands. When he looked down, he saw a knife jutting from his belly. Blood pumped out of him. "W-why?"

"You're trying to destroy my . . . people, Jim, and I *can't* have that."

"Im-impossible!"

Laura shook her head. "Come on, babe. I eat most of my meat raw, my excursions at night, my impeccable sense of smell . . . And that doesn't include the thoughts and urges I have daily. As soon as you told me about these folk, I *knew* I was one of them, even if I don't yet know how we're all related. I feel it in my bones, but I can't explain it." She sighed through her nostrils. "I love you, Jim, but this is where I belong, with these people."

Blood poured out of Jim's mouth. He gritted his teeth, pulled his lips back, and wrapped both hands around her brittle throat. "I'll k-kill you, bitch!" He spat blood in her face, then squealed as she tore the blade down his body. Jim bucked.

"I'm sorry it had to end like this, babe," she said, pulling free of his grip, "but it's better off this way."

"*Bitch*!"

"Shh, Jim. Go to sleep."

The last thing Jim saw before he closed his eyes was Laura smiling down at him.

Chapter 20
Then

Her eyelids fluttered a few times before opening.

Storm gasped and gagged as a scream lodged in her throat.

She was suspended upside-down by her ankles, her hands roped behind her back.

"Mmm-*hmm*!" Her growl was muffled.

"Sleep well, princess?" a man asked.

Storm thrashed this way and that, trying to catch sight of the speaker.

The Hulk stepped out of the shadows. "Didn't hit you *too* hard, did I?" His laugh was coarse, jagged. It stung her pride further. "I'd be happy to patch up your sore spots."

Storm had to stomach-crunch to look him in the eye, and the grin she found on his face was infuriating. She wanted to uppercut it off him or wrap a baseball bat around his skull.

And then she spotted a golf club in his hand. Her eyes narrowed. He swung the iron like a pro, and the air it generated blew through her hair. The breeze caused her arms to gooseflesh.

"Think I could smash your teeth out in one?"

If I get out of this, I'm going to stick that thing up his arse! she thought. *Turn him into a fucking lollipop.*

"Bet I could," he continued. "I used to play."

I'll be playing snooker with your balls by suppertime, fuckwit. Storm glared at him.

"You want to rip my throat out, don't you? Kill me and piss on my bones, no doubt. You had your chance, sugar tits." He lowered the club and placed its head in her cleavage. The coldness startled her. "Ha!" he bellowed, letting her know he'd caught the surprise in her eyes.

"*Mmm-mmm*!" she screamed beneath her gag. Storm's nostrils flared, and the veins in her neck protruded.

"Settle down, cute arse—you're going purple in the face." With his free hand, he reached out and grabbed one of her tits. His fingers tweaked the nipple. "I'm getting first go, that's for fucking sure. I don't want sloppy seconds."

Storm's stomach lurched. *They want to fuck me* . . . She screwed her eyes up as tight as she could and swallowed the rising sick that burned at the back of her throat. *How in the hell did I let myself get caught?* She bucked and struggled against her restraints, reminding herself of a fish on a line. *Or a virgin's first time.*

"I'm going to make it hurt. You'll be bleeding, crying and begging for your miserable life to end, bitch." The Hulk traced the club from her tits to her pussy, where it lingered and brushed her thin strip of pubic hair.

How many *plan to rape me*?

She was determined not to whimper, so she steeled herself. *This isn't something new. They've done this sort of thing before.*

"You're going to feel as though you're being fucked by a freight train," he continued, thrusting his hips.

Go ahead, needle-dick! You can take my body, but you won't take my strength, mind and soul.

"What do you think about that, huh? There are a lot of horny dicks in this place," he said with a cackle. "And we're all going to have at your snatch, whore."

The thought jarred her, but she didn't show it. All Storm could think about was killing this sack of shit and escaping.

"The bitch awake then, eh?"

Storm's head snapped in the direction of the voice, and Jasmine came into view.

"You really are one dumb fuck, ain't ya?"

"Ha! She's trusting, is what she is, Jazz."

"A Samaritan. Is that what you are, dumb-dumb?" Jasmine laughed, encouraging the Hulk to do the same.

"When's Joe getting here?" Hulk asked.

"He's on his way."

"That bastard isn't fucking her before—"

"Hold your load, Jacob," she said. "Who said *anything* about *anyone* getting their dick wet? You know who she is, right?"

Jacob nodded.

"Good. Because Hydra is one fucked-off woman right now, and she's coming here with Joe to deal with this piece of shit."

"God*damn* it! I thought she was going to be thrown in the playpen with the rest of the strays?"

"She *does* have a great set of tits," Jasmine confessed, ignoring his question. "I wouldn't mind sucking on 'em." She looked at Jacob and they shared a smile. "Cunt killed my dad."

"I know, babe. So why don't we have a play with her before Joe and Hydra get here?"

Jasmine bit her lip and rolled her eyes skyward. "I don't know . . . We still have Ben to deal with."

"I'd forgotten about that chicken-shit bastard! Where is he?"

"I've tied him up in the canteen. Fancy dragging his arse in here? This pig can watch him die."

"Yeah, I'm game. Maybe then we can play with her, Jasmine?"

"Maybe."

Jacob smiled, lowered his club and walked toward the exit. "I'll be back in a while."

After he'd left the room, Jasmine circled Storm. "You're in deep, *deep* shit, Storm. You know that, right? And I guess you know *who's* coming for you?" Jasmine stopped in front of Storm and looked down at her. "*Right*?"

Storm nodded, then started speaking, but her words were unintelligible.

"I don't know what the fuck you're saying." Jasmine got down on her haunches and lowered Storm's gag.

"And I'm the stupid one?" Storm said, using her weight to swing herself towards Jasmine. She locked her teeth onto the youngster's throat and bit. Jasmine had little time to react as Storm chewed through a vein and caught a squirt of hot blood to the back of her throat.

When Jasmine pulled free, a strip of flesh came away, and she collapsed against a wall. "You—you *bitch*!" she sobbed, which turned to wet, sloppy gargles as her mouth filled with blood and spurted from the wound.

Jasmine slumped, her hands pressed to her neck. Her eyes rolled and she flopped to one side. A dark pool gathered beneath her.

"Fuck you, Judas." Storm spat a piece of flesh from her mouth, then worked at freeing her hands. "These knots couldn't keep a two-year-old in place." With her arms loose, Storm crunched up until she was able to reach the knot at her feet. After slackening that one, she lowered herself back into position. Her tummy cramped, and the blood rushed back to her head as she hung upside down like a bat.

"I need to get down before I upchuck."

She again doubled herself and yanked the last of the knot free, then yelped as she fell to the floor.

"*Ouch*! Bollocks!" Storm rubbed her shoulder. "Bloody funny bone." She giggled, got to her feet and stood over Jasmine, deciding to strip the girl of her tacky robe.

"Better to be sticky than to give these fuckers a free show," she uttered, slipping into the bloody garment. Once done, she noticed the girl had a machete sheathed at her hip. "Think I'll take that, too." After helping herself to everything Jasmine had to offer, Storm turned to leave, but heard someone grunt as they walked toward her. "Shit."

"This son of a bitch is heavy!" she heard Jacob complain. This was followed by a muffled cry.

Must be Ben. I'll have to kill him, too. I can't risk another one foxing me . . .

Storm took up her stance by the entrance and waited for the unsuspecting Jacob.

"I hope you ain't been having fun with her behind my back, Jasmine." Jacob laughed. "You hear me?"

Storm's heartbeat quickened. Sweat stung her eyes.

His footfalls came to an abrupt halt.

"Jasmine? You okay?" Something hard hit the floor. Someone cried. "Shut the fuck up or I'll cave your head in, Ben! Jasmine?"

Storm's grip on the machete handle intensified.

Do I answer, pretending to be her? No, that would be a bad move.

"If you don't answer me this instant, I'm coming in swinging!"

Storm clutched her breath, then let it out. "One . . ." she whispered.

"What's it to be?"

"Two . . ."

"*Jasmine*?"

"Three." Storm walked out of the room with the gown's hood up, covering her bowed head.

"Ah, there you . . . Whose blood is that?" he asked.

"Hers," she whispered, pointing into the room, hoping he wouldn't detect her.

"Fuck! What happened?"

"She got free. I had to kill her."

"Let me see." He marched past Storm and poked his head into the room. "We could still play with—*hey*!"

He turned to face Storm, who'd removed her hood.

She winked at him. "Boo!" She plunged the machete into the big man's stomach and ripped it downwards, spilling his innards over the floor.

Jacob gargled, collapsed to his knees and keeled over.

Storm took the Bowie from his hip and helped herself to the golf club lying next to Ben. "Don't mind if I do," she said, yanking the tape off Ben's mouth. "I'm going to ask you a series of questions, and if I like the answers, I'll set you free. If not, I'll smash your fucking face in and let these sick fucks eat you whole. Are we on the same page?"

"Yes! I'll—"

"Shut the hell up!" Storm swung the club. He whimpered. A dark spot spread across the crotch area of his robe. "Lovely."

"I'll tell you anything."

"How many are left?"

"I'm not sure. More than fifty?"

"*What*?!"

"Fifty. Most of them are sleeping in the chambers below. There are babies here, too. Many."

"Okay, where?"

"I'd have to show you—this place is intricate."

She could believe that. "Okay. Is there any dynamite or petrol here? I want to blow this place to the fucking moon and back, with you bastards inside!"

"N-no, I'm not like the—"

Storm swung the club, catching Ben in the jaw but not hard enough to break it.

"Ugh! Bitch!"

"I told you to put a fucking sock in it. And I don't want to hear the 'I'm not like the others' bullshit. That little fuck Jasmine sold me that lie and look what happened. Fool me once . . ."

"I'm telling—"

She hit him again. "Tell me what I want to know, and I'll consider sparing you."

"There's a weapons dump with all kinds of stuff—you might find what you're looking for there."

"Can you lead me to it?"

He didn't answer, so she put the club's head near his balls and shoved at the soft, meaty part.

"Yes!"

"Great. Because you're no good to me otherwise, Ben. Now, get up—come on—and lead the way."

"There's probably going to be guards along the way."

"No problem. You can help me dispatch them."

"B-but . . ."

"What? I thought you weren't like the rest of them?"

"Still, I can't go killing—I'm not like *that*, either."

"Well, I suggest you find your balls or I'll kill *you*. What's it to be?"

He sighed. "Fine. Follow me."

"And if you try warning anyone, same applies: I'll kill you."

He nodded, then moved off.

Ben led her down a series of dark, narrow corridors and through dimly lit chambers that homed a variety of torture devices and other trinkets. Everything, including the walls, had the society's mark etched onto it.

When they came across guards, Ben was true to his word and helped dispatch and lure them to their death. He was mortified when Storm killed women and two young girls.

"They're just as bad, Ben. Just because they're women . . ."

"I had no idea *what* I was getting myself mixed up in here. You have to believe me. A lot of the others feel the same. We were brainwashed."

"Spare it. Anyone in this cave deserves to die, no matter what."

"And I suppose that goes for me too?"

"The court is out on that one. You just concentrate on doing as I say and help me out of here. If you do, then you *may* be one of the lucky ones."

"I've proven that, haven't I?" he said, holding the flats of his hands up in the pale light. They were coated with the blood of the multiple guards.

"Proves nothing, pal." She placed the head of the club under his chin. "You sneaky fucks would say anything to get out of trouble."

He sighed. "Come on, this way."

They kept walking for another twenty minutes before Ben brought them to a sudden stop.

A glow came from a room in front of them, along with voices.

"This place is generally heavily guarded."

"What the fuck are you trying to pull here?" Storm asked, grabbing Ben by his robe and shoving him against a wall. "Are you walking me into a trap?"

"Would I have alerted you to the fact?"

He's got a point. "How many are there likely to be?"

"Three, maybe four."

"Guns?"

Ben nodded.

Fuck. I knew this plan sounded too easy. Now what?

Go in there and kick some arse, that's what!

"I'm going to give you a chance here, Ben, and if you fuck up, I'll kill you. Pull it off, I'll let you live. Got it?"

Ben nodded. There was hope in his eyes. "Anything. Name it."

"I want you to go in there and find out how many there are. Also, bring me a weapon."

"A gun? Knife?"

"The former would be good, yes. If not, whatever you can get your hands on."

He nodded, took a deep, shaky breath and started his way down the corridor.

"And if you try any funny business, like alert them or anything else, then—"

"I know, I'll be dead. You can trust me, honestly."

"That's what the last one said . . ." she muttered under her breath, watching Ben fade into the distance. When he vanished, she counted, "One Mississippi . . . Two Mississippi . . ."

Voices echoed up the corridor, cutting Storm off. She pricked her ears, trying to listen to what was being said.

What if he comes out and shoots me? He might, if he thinks he's got a good enough chance . . . No, I'm his only way out of here.

A loud noise startled her.

A rat scurried over her feet, squeaking as it went.

Storm crouched and squinted.

Harsh, bellowing laughter bounded up the tunnel. Her heart missed several beats. *He's playing them, that's all.*

She decided to creep closer.

This could be a bad—

A figure moved towards her, freezing her in place.

"Ben?" she whispered.

"Yes. Keep it down. I think one of them is watching me from the door. Move up the tunnel."

Storm did as instructed, and when she rounded the corner, she pressed her back to the wall and waited for Ben.

"What's going on?" she asked.

"When I picked up a rifle, one of them wanted to know what I wanted it for, so I told them I had rats in my room. I don't think they believed me, and Lillian, one of the guards, followed me to the door."

"Ben?" a woman called from the darkness. "Where are you really going with that gun?"

"Lillian," Ben whispered. "Here." He shoved a handgun in Storm's hand. "I managed to sneak—"

"You honestly think I didn't see you slip that Walther up your sleeve? What's going on? Do I need to raise the alarm?" A gun cocked. "Am I stupid, lad? If I have to come and get ya, I'll get ya!" Lillian sniggered. "The only damn reason I'm not screaming blue murder is because I like you, Ben—*ugh!*"

Storm leapt from the shadows and snapped the fat woman's neck in one swift move. After Lillian crashed to the floor, Storm stepped over her body and looked at the pistol Ben had given her. It had a silencer attached to it.

"You thought of this?"

"I took a guess at you wanting to make as little noise as possible."

She smirked. "How many more?"

"Four, I think."

"*Think?*"

"I'm not sure if there was someone in the outer storage room."

"Okay. Are the others in the same room?"

"Yes. Pretty much grouped together. Glenn and Dale were playing pool—"

"You have a fucking *pool* table down here?"

Ben lowered his head. "A dart board and jukebox too."

"Un-*fucking*-believable."

"But—"

"Shut up and move. Now, when we enter the weapons dump, I want you to play the fuck along, got it?"

"Of course."

She believed him. "Okay, get going." Storm thrust the pistol's muzzle into the small of Ben's back.

"*Ow*! Is there any need for that?"

"Move!" she demanded, shoving him with the gun.

"Ugh! Okay, okay."

When they got to the entrance of the weapons cache, Storm pushed Ben through the opening. He sprawled along the floor, dropping his rifle.

A chorus of laughter erupted from within the room.

"Enjoy your trip, Einstein?" a man asked.

"Yeah, send us a postcard next time," another male added.

Storm rushed into the room and put a bullet through the eye of a man getting up out of a chair. "*Ugh*!" was all he had time to say before he was thrown backwards, toppling over his seat and crashing to the floor.

"*Fuck*!" the guy who'd been sitting next to him said, going for the AK-47 beside his seat. Storm put two bullets in his chest and one in his temple.

"Look out!" Ben screamed, getting to his feet and shoving Storm off-kilter. She crashed to the floor and rolled behind the sofa when a machine gun opened up. It lit the room with its muzzle flashes. Over the noise, Storm heard the gun's brass casings chime along the floor as bullets thumped into Ben, turning him into a colander.

Storm covered her ears as Ben was propelled through the entrance. *Shit!* she thought. And when the machine gun's rattle ceased, an alarm somewhere in the cave started blaring. *Double shit!*

She broke cover and saw the gunwoman trying to reload. But she wasn't fast enough—Storm put a slug between her eyes. "Bitch."

"Don't shoot! I'm unarmed!" a man blubbered from within the room.

"Show yourself!" Storm demanded.

"You promise not to kill me?"

"Yes. Now, show yourself."

The man, who couldn't have been more than seventeen, stepped into the room from an opening adjacent to where she stood. Storm raised her gun.

"Wait!"

She emptied the rest of the gun's clip into his face and threw the empty weapon to one side. She searched the roomful of treasures and found the activation switch that controlled the alarm system. She turned it off, killing the horrendous sound bellowing around the room and cave.

God knows how many heard that fucking thing, she thought, picking up an AK-47 and a tank of petrol. Behind the fuel, she found a box of grenades and some sticks of dynamite. *I don't think I have time to go rescuing people . . .*

"What the hell did they need all this stuff for? World War 3?!" She slung the AK over her shoulder and grabbed as many explosives as possible. When she was finished, she kicked over three other cans of fuel and walked out of the room. Storm ambled back to Lillian's body, pulled pins out of three grenades and lobbed them down the corridor.

She laughed as they rolled into the arsenal, but she didn't hang around to celebrate, running as fast as she could in the direction Ben had brought her.

Before getting clear of the next passageway, an almighty blast erupted from behind, taking Storm off her feet and carrying her through the air. The cave rumbled. Black dust descended, covering her in soot. Coughing and spluttering, she got to her feet and wiped the grime from her eyes.

"*Jesus!*" The stench of burning fuel assaulted her nostrils.

A deafening cracking sound ripped through the cave, and Storm heard people screaming and crying all around.

Chunks of rock fell from the ceiling. The ground trembled.

"Shit, what have I done?"

The rock underfoot split apart, sending her legs in opposite directions. Storm jumped to her left and jogged up the corridor. She chanced a look behind and saw the walls and ceiling collapsing further. More dust billowed into the air, cutting off her vision.

Keep moving! Don't look.

When she found her way back to the temple/sacrifice room, she doused it in petrol and lobbed a grenade in along with a couple of sticks of dynamite.

The room blew.

More screams and cries.

Fire licked its way out of the room and followed Storm's path.

The heat within the cave was becoming unbearable. Sweat dribbled down her forehead and underarms. Smoke engulfed her.

"I need to get the hell out. Now."

When she came across others in the corridors, she went unnoticed thanks to the destruction and the clothes she was wearing. Also, sight was impaired due to the smoke and dust.

People were in a blind panic as they tried to get out.

Storm saw women holding monstrous babies, and hoped they'd burn up.

She kept moving.

None of these fuckers are making it out of here!

After thirty minutes of what felt like going round in circles, Storm made it to the main entrance.

She almost cried with relief.

The sun had started to rise.

"We have to get out of here! The whole place is collapsing!" a man said from behind, pushing Storm towards the exit.

"*Hey*!" was all she had time to say as she was scooped up and carted off. She noticed there were a few others behind the bloke manhandling her.

When they were outside, Storm was set free, and when the man who'd grabbed her turned to look at the cave, along with the others, she opened fire. The bullets whizzed out of the AK's barrel likes wasps from a disturbed hive.

With all targets down, she stopped shooting and staved in the heads of those still wriggling with the butt of the assault rifle.

"Please! Don't shoot!"

A teenaged girl crawled out of the dwelling behind her, flames lapping at her feet.

Storm pumped her and the young boy who ran out behind her full of lead.

He was on fire, and wouldn't have lasted anyway, she argued with herself. *I would have mowed him down regardless.* She smiled.

Confident there were no others coming out, Storm lowered the gun. "And that's the end of that."

"I wouldn't be so sure if I were you, you fucking *bitch*!"

Storm raised the gun and turned on her heel. Five people in front of her, three of whom she already knew: Paula and her two overgrown freaks she called sons. The man and woman wearing robes were new to her.

More cult freaks!

"I think it's time I put an end to you, Paula."

"What do I have to do to kill you, Storm?"

"Try harder, that's what."

Paula smiled. "Do you have enough bullets left to kill us all?"

"Shall we find out?"

"Now wait a minute!" the man said, getting between Paula and Storm. "I don't want to—"

"Shut the fuck up, Joe. I'm the leader, *not* you."

"Joe?" Storm scrutinised his facial features and let the name bounce around inside her head. "You were the town's mayor, weren't you?!"

"Still am," he uttered.

"Incredible. And I'm guessing you're the money backer and cult fucking leader?"

He couldn't look at her.

"Well?" She cocked the gun and aimed it at him.

He nodded.

Another burst of gunfire tore the early morning apart. Joe propelled backwards and somersaulted through bushes and low-hanging branches.

"You—you *whore*! Do you know what you—"

"Pipe the fuck down, or you're next," Storm threatened, turning the gun on Paula. "And I wouldn't want that. I want you to fucking suffer."

"I'm sorry, Hydra, but I want no further part in this!" the woman in the robe said, starting to remove the cult gown. "Tony's already dead, along with a score of others. It's over. All of it."

"Who are you?" Storm wanted to know.

"Lucy. Hydra—*Paula's* sister."

"Well, isn't this cosy?"

One of Paula's sons growled and took a step towards Storm.

"Get back, big boy, or I'll put a hole through your chest." She bared her teeth.

"You harm him, and I'll gut you like a fish, Storm." Paula sounded calm, but she was visibly shaking.

"Not nice, is it, when someone *fucks* with your family?" Storm smiled and fired, her bullet smacking into a tree and covering the huge cannibal in splinters.

He snarled.

"Fuck this." Lucy turned and started walking away.

"Get your arse back here, Lucy," Storm demanded, pointing the gun at the woman's back.

Tempest and Typhoon threw themselves at the unsuspecting Storm, who managed to fire the AK's remaining bullets, which struck Lucy in the head.

"Get her, boys!" Paula commanded.

Storm tried to wrestle the brutes off her, but they were much too strong and soon had her pinned to the leaf-scattered floor.

"Y-you *bastards*!" she screamed, red-faced, the veins in her neck protruding.

She felt hands all over her, as if there were more than two on her.

The robe was torn from her body. The weight on her chest was so excruciating, Storm could hardly breathe.

"Get . . . get off!" she wheezed, and then felt a hard dick thrust inside her. She yelped as fluid trickled down her thighs. "You sick *fucks*!" She tried rolling her shoulder to dislodge her arms and hands, but she was kept there.

One of the boys was growling and grunting in an inhuman way, which scared her more than anything.

When he was done, they got off her, but Storm was too weak to stand. The fight had been drained from her. She flipped onto her stomach and crawled for the gun. Before she could get there, weight crashed down onto her once more, and again a cock was jammed inside her.

"*No!*" Her fingers brushed against the butt of the Kalashnikov before the other brother stepped on her hand. He stood looking down on her and smiling as his sibling sodomised her.

Her world slanted.

Black spots danced before her.

"*Ugh*!" she groaned, saliva drizzling out of her mouth.

Storm fought to stay awake, for she feared they would kill her for sure if she blacked out.

And then the weight on her back disappeared.

"Drag her over to the trees, boys," she heard Paula command. "We can tie her up and leave her to die. Nobody's going to find her."

"Can we soften her up first, Mama?" Typhoon asked.

"Yeah, please?" Tempest begged.

"Make sure you do a proper job this time, boys. No more fuck ups. Look how much destruction she's caused! Lots of clan and family members are dead, and our breeding factory has been demolished. Fucking bitch. Still, *we're* in good shape."

"We still have Twin Jesters and the family—" Tempest started.

"Shut up!" Paula snapped at her son. "We don't want to give her any information."

"She'll soon be dead, Mother," Typhoon stated, then laid into Storm with fists and kicks, spurring his brother into action.

* * *

By the time the boys were finished, they were breathless, and Storm was nothing more than a bloody mass.

"Tie her up tight," Hydra said, watching her sons rope the unconscious but muttering Storm to a large oak tree. In her hand she held a can of fuel, which she used to douse Storm. "Get back, boys."

They did as they were told and watched as their mother picked up a gun and fired at the floor. A spark was created, a small fire started.

"Let's get out of here," Hydra said as the flames snaked towards the hapless Storm.

When they were clear of the immediate area, they heard Storm screaming.

Hydra could only smile.

Chapter 21
Then

*I*t's been close to fifteen years since the boys and I set fire to Storm, and a lot's happened. Here's where I'd like to bring my history up to date. Immediately after burning the bitch, I took the boys back to Twin Jesters, where I mapped out a fresh plan. And, thanks to Luke's money, it was pretty easy.

It took three years to rebuild the cave, and twice as long to regain the numbers lost. It was a dark day, but we moved forward, and no mistakes have been made since.

Naturally, my boys and daughter have grown, and have helped build the family further by breeding. Things are moving along well. Skull would be proud.

I'm now the grandmother to twenty-plus children, who have been shipped out of Twin Jesters to various locations. The older children who survived the cave fires have been sent out to work close by and all around. Some of them own homes, and soon we'll have complete control over the town and surrounding areas.

Our legacy will live on forever.

We are not for being defeated. Not now—we are much too strong. Luke's money, as I said, combined with the board members' (which was all left to me), has helped me secure power in parliament, the army, and various other places of high power.

I'm everywhere, and when I am gone, there will be others to take my place, to keep this home, our HQ, going.

* * *

Hydra looked up from her ramblings at her sons, who were sat before the TV. They were drinking glassfuls of blood and stuffing fresh flesh into their mouths from their latest kills.

Such good, obedient boys.

Hydra glanced around, feeling a ping of sadness. The house had been full a few years ago, but Daniel, Michael and Jason, along with Cerberus, had been homed elsewhere.

She was about to start writing again when there was a knock at the door. *Who could it be at* this *hour?*

Hydra looked over at her boys, who snapped their heads in her direction. They'd got much bigger over the years, outgrowing Skull in height and weight.

"Settle down, boys. I'll get it," she said.

To safeguard herself, Hydra picked up a large pair of scissors from off the table.

There was another knock, and, like the first, it didn't sound urgent.

Not many visitors come this way. And if they do, they get eaten! she thought.

Hydra walked down the hallway towards the door. "Yes? Who is it?"

No answer.

Another knock.

Hydra shuffled closer. It was possible the person hadn't heard her. She clutched the scissors tighter. Behind her, she heard her boys gather at the living room door.

Hydra stopped and looked back at them. "Stay there, out of sight."

She couldn't understand *why* she was so spooked. *A bit late for a caller . . .*

Through the window in the door, Hydra could see night had fallen.

A third knock came, followed by a fourth.

"Who's there?" Hydra was now standing behind the door, her free hand resting on the security chain.

"Gas company, ma'am," a man confirmed.

"At *this* time?!"

"There's been a leak on the street. This is an emergency." His tone was assertive; not pushy, but business-like.

"Just a moment—I'm not decent." Hydra walked back into the living room and parted the curtains to a sliver. Parked directly out front was a van marked with the British Gas logo.

She laughed, her shoulders hitching. Hydra let go of the curtain. Sighing, she went back to the hallway and told her sons that everything was okay.

"Tidy up a bit—we have company," she said, disappearing out of the room.

Hydra slipped the chain off the door and threw the deadbolts back. After depressing the handle, she pulled the wood out of the frame and opened up. "Sorry," she said, smiling and then holding her hands to her chest.

Her smile turned to a frown.

The fat, jowly man before her, whose uniform was ill-fitting and arguing with his wrists and ankles, sported a bright red face. Beads of sweat glistened along his forehead. In his hand he held a toolkit.

He gulped. His mouth opened, then closed before he uttered a word.

"Is something wrong?"

"*Ugh*!" he groaned, getting on tiptoes. Blood trailed out of his mouth and dribbled down his chin. "*Argh*!" The tip of a knife punched through his chest, and he was shoved towards Hydra.

The gasman tripped over the stoop and fell like a collapsing building.

Hydra was too slow in dodging the dying man—he crashed down on top of her. From where she lay, she could see the knife's haft protruding from his back. Her eyes then flitted to the massive figure standing in the doorway.

"Who—are—*you*?!" Hydra wheezed; the wind stolen from her.

The gigantic man, who bent down to gain access to the house, stepped into the light. The door closed behind him with a crashing thud.

Her attacker filled the hallway, his shoulders inches from scraping the walls on either side.

His face was heavily disfigured, much like her sons'. When he smiled down at her, Hydra noticed his teeth were broken and misshapen, his lips non-existent.

"Fuck!"

"Mother?!" her boys yelled in unison. They stood in the doorway to the living room, their mouths covered in gore.

The killer growled. "Snack." His guts growled with anticipation.

"*No*! You leave them alone. Who are you?!" Hydra screamed, trying to dislodge the gasman.

Man Mountain stepped over Hydra and her new playmate, stopping a few feet from Typhoon and Tempest. He looked over his shoulder at Hydra. "Mammy will deal with you, *bitch*!" He sniggered, his enormous stature dwarfing Hydra's sons, who jumped at him like attack dogs.

"*Nooo*!" Hydra grunted and growled as she fought with the carcass, almost wrestling it off her at one point.

"We meet again, *Paula*!"

"What—who's there?!" Hydra stopped struggling and looked around the body, down the hallway. A much smaller figure stepped out of the gloom. "No-no, it *can't* be! It's been fifteen years . . ."

"Fifteen years, three months, six days, three hours, four minutes and"—Storm looked at her watch—"thirty-three seconds, to be precise, and it looks like your boys are losing the fight against *Skull*. Yep, that's right. Skull. My *son*. One of your lads' son—*your* grandchild, fuck-face. And I'm sure I don't need to tell you who I named him after? Best therapy ever."

"W-what—"

Storm laughed, stepping into the light cast by the bulb in the hallway ceiling.

"Thought I'd play you at your own fucking game, Paula, or Hydra, or whatever stupid fucking name you go by."

"Sweet *Jesus*!" Hydra gasped when she saw Storm's face. Half of it was missing; the hair that side too, along with the ear and most of her lips.

"Pretty, aren't I? The perils of escaping a fire too late, I suppose."

"But—but we heard you screaming. I saw the flames reach you!"

"*Argh*! Mama!" Typhoon screamed.

"Bastard!" Tempest yelled.

"Call him off, please! Please! I'm begging you. You can kill me, or whatever, but spare them."

Storm got down on her haunches, putting her face close to Hydra's. "You must be fucking kidding, right?"

"Killing them, or me, won't do you any good. You know that, right? My clan's worldwide, and we practically run Twin Jesters and South Wales. You can't beat us. The society, if not my family, will run you down."

"The society? You mean that fucking bunch that's been backing you?"

Hydra nodded. Behind her, screaming and loud crashes continued.

"Yeah, I aim to shut them down completely over the next few days, Paula. In the time I've been away, raising my son in the woods, out of sight, I've been planning. I know where all the head people live and work, and without the money people, the rest will crumble. You have powerful friends, and it's a shame they're not here to see you die."

"Y-you *cunt*! If I get up, I'll kill you!"

"That's not going to happen."

* * *

Storm reached to the gasman's back and pulled out the knife, which retracted with a sucky slurp much like a penis did after energetic sex. "Any last words?"

"*Boys*!" Paula cried. "*Help*!"

"Oh, and before I kill you, I just want you to know you have a granddaughter, too: Eight-Ball. How cool is that, right? She's Skull's twin. Fair play to your boys—they got me with the double-baby money shot!" Storm winked, got on her knees, and repeatedly stabbed Paula in the face until there was nothing left of it. "My children and I won't stop until we've killed every last one of you sons of bitches!" Storm spat in the woman's face.

She got up, taking the knife with her, and walked into the living room to find Skull beating one of the boys into oblivion. The other was slumped against the smashed dining room table, his throat torn out.

Storm smiled. "I think he's had enough, Skull."

Skull stopped hammering his fists against his victim's face and got up.

"Hmm, maybe he hasn't quite yet," she said, seeing he was still breathing. Skull went back to finish the job, but Storm stopped him. "Allow me."

"*Ugh!*" the boy choked on his blood. More of it trickled out of his mouth and nostrils. "Please . . ." he begged.

"I'll make it quick, but only if you tell me where the rest of your family's hiding. You have a sister and brothers, no? I've been watching you."

He narrowed his eyes and shook his head. "F-fuck *you*."

"Fine." She took the knife and placed the serrated edge against the cannibal's lumpy throat and violently drew it sideways, opening it up and draining him within seconds.

"What now, Mammy?"

"Back to the woods. With this bitch dead, there's going to be hell to pay, Skull, and we don't want to give them an easy target. When things die down, we'll begin hunting again, making this place our *first* port of call . . ."

* * *

It didn't take long for Paula's and her sons' bodies to be discovered, leading to a massive manhunt a few days later. Storm and Skull had left behind plenty of clues, but because they were both off the radar, there was nobody to track the DNA and evidence to.

Over time, her family grew.

Skull mated with Eight-Ball, and Storm found she was lucky in the fact that some of her children's children came out normal-looking, free of genetic problems.

These babies, the pure ones, were kept from the violence until they were old enough to understand. But Skull, Eight-Ball and the other oddities would be sent out in time to infiltrate Paula's family.

Ten years after killing Paula, Storm died of natural causes, leaving her children to pick up where she'd left off. And, to this day, they breed and walk among the Man-Eating Fucks, scheming their revenge; planning to rid the world of them…

END

About Your Author

David Owain Hughes is a word-slinger of horror and crime fiction, who grew up on trashy b-movies from the age of five which helped rapidly instil in him a vivid imagination. He's had multiple short stories published in various online magazines and anthologies, along with articles, reviews and interviews. He's written for *This Is Horror*, *Blood Magazine*, and *Horror Geeks Magazine*.

Hughes is the author of six horror novels, four short story collections and a plethora of novellas. Although he predominately writes within the bracket of horror and its multiple sub-genres, he's recently branched out into crime fiction and is slowly carving out a superb series of crime/noir thrillers under the umbrella title of *South Wales*.

https://www.facebook.com/DOHughesAuthor/?ref=hl

http://www.amazon.co.uk/David-Owain-Hughes/e/B00L708P2M/ref=sr_ntt_srch_lnk_3?qid=1458241417&sr=1-3

http://david-owain-hughes.wix.com/horrorwriter

https://www.goodreads.com/author/show/4877205.David_Owain_Hughes

https://twitter.com/DOHUGHES32

<u>Other HellBound Books Titles</u>
<u>Available at: www.hellboundbookspublishing.com</u>

Man Eating F*cks

A dark, incredibly entertaining excursion into the delightfully twisted imagination of David Owain Hughes....

An average teenage girl and her father find themselves caught up in a brutal nightmare at their local recreational centre, when an age-old enemy comes stumbling out of the woods to crash a heavy-metal gig; a gig that has all the promises of being killer. This is one blood-soaked gig you won't want to miss!

Praise for Man-Eating F*cks from Ty Schwamberger (author of The Fields, Deep Dark Woods & The Death of a Horror Writer.) *"Man Eating F*cks is old school horror, but with a new, blood-soaked twist! David Owain Hughes effectively creates enjoyable and lethal characters in this tale that is sure to keep you up at night. This is the type of tale that you need to read with a light on…I'm serious. You better put your seatbelt on 'cause you're in for one helluva ride. Look out, Hughes might very well be headed to the major leagues after this twisted tale! Highly recommended!"*

Man Eating F*ckers

The eagerly awaited sequel to Hughes' critically acclaimed *Man Eating Fks...***

Two years on from her nightmarish descent into the woods, Storm is piecing her life back together, but trouble is forming...

A new threat is rising - one that promises to grip, shake and spin Storm's world out of control. But that's not all, as a 'friend' and sympathizer also poses a risk from the shadows, combined with a face from the past...

With the cannibals lurking in the background, waiting for an opportunity to deal white-hot vengeance, can father and daughter survive?

**** Features a bonus, previously unpublished short story by David Owain Hughes****

Puckered

Percy is kinky.
Percy is perverted.
Percy is a loner.
Percy is sneaky…

…But most of all, Percy wants to be left alone.

Whether it be a nagging mother or something from his past, it feels like he is always trying to escape something. Will he be able to find his own peace, or will the real world catch up to him?

There will be blood.
There will be s**t.
There will be unusual sexual kinks.
But most of all, there will be murder…

Psychological Breakdown
By
David Owain Hughes

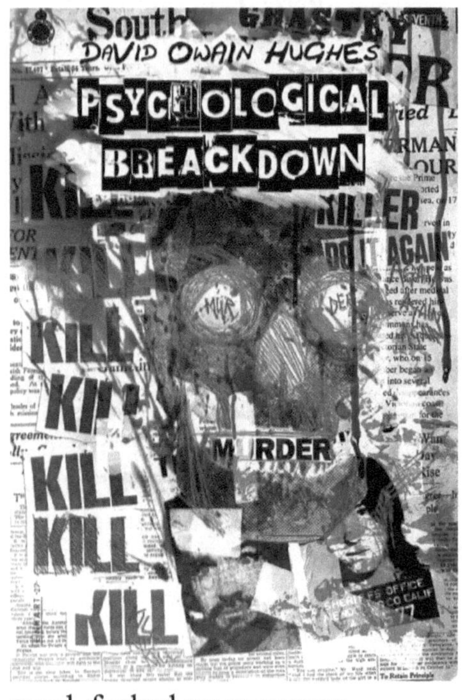

Within this tome lies eighteen tales of mind-bending terror, as Hughes delves into the human psyche and dishes out stories of what becomes of the broken minded, spirited and downright irked.

Part these blood-drenched pages at your own peril, for you will find diseased minds geared towards revenge and bloody chaos, with a few twists, turns and surprises thrown in for good, fucked-up measures.

Keep the lights on!

Cold Cocked

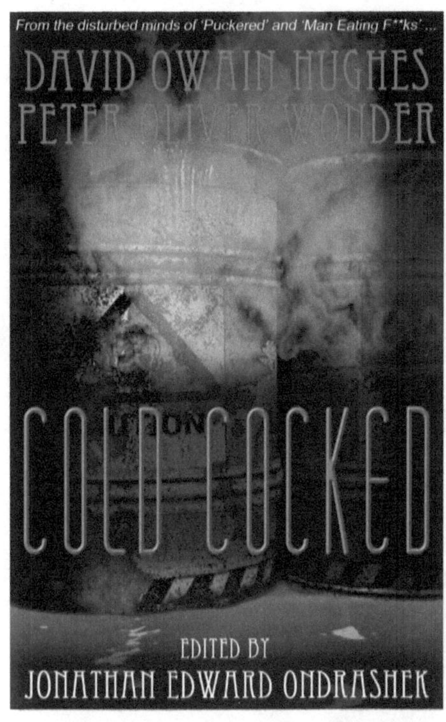

Another exemplary bizarro novella from the great and incredibly disturbed minds behind 'Puckered'!

Betty is sexy.
Betty is scarred.
Betty is an outsider.
Betty is a genius…

…But most of all, Betty wants recognition.

Whether it be a controlling mother or ghosts from her past, it feels like she is always trying to please someone. Will she be able to find her own peace, or will the real world catch up to her?

There will be blood.
There will be j**z.
There will be unusual sexual releases.

But most of all, there will be murder…

Follow Him

True love doesn't die - it devours. Just outside the sleepy town of Dreury, a mysterious cult known as The Shared Heart has planted its stakes. Its followers are numerous. More join every day. Those who are lost and suffering seem to be drawn to it; a home for the broken. When Jacob finds himself in need of such a home, he abandons his dead name and gives himself over to the will of The Great Collector. However, love refuses to let Jacob go so easily; his ex-fiancé, Nina, kidnaps him in the hopes that he can be deprogrammed. As she attempts to return Jacob to the life they once had, a terrible fear creeps in: what if there isn't enough of her Jacob left? When The Great Collector learns of his missing follower, the true nature of The Shared Heart is unleashed. Nina discovers what Jacob already knows: that hidden behind the warm songs and soaring bonfires is a terrifying and ancient secret; one that lives and breathes and hungers. And it's coming for them.

Satanic Panic

An incredible homage to 1980's horror!

Satanic Panic, a mass hysteria created in the nineteen eighties, has returned to a small college town in the Midwest.

Ritualistic murders and the presence of the occult have bled below the surface of the town in the form of icy accidents and other coincidences.

And when three lifelong friends find themselves on the radar of a killer—and leader of a satanic cult—they must fight for what's good without being seduced by the evil that possesses their campus.

The Toilet Zone
RESTROOM READING AT ITS MOST FRIGHTENING!

Compiled and edited by the grand master of 80's schlock horror, Bret McCormick, each one of this collection of 32 terrifying tales is just the perfect length for a visit to the smallest room....

At the very boundaries of human imagination dwells one single, solitary place of solitude, of peace and quiet, a place in which your regular human being spends, on average, 10 to 15 minutes - at least once every single day of their lives.

Now, consider a typical, everyday reading speed of 200 to 250 words per minute - that means your average visitor has the time to read between 2,500 to 4,000 words, which makes each and every one of these 32 tales of terror - from some of the best contemporary independent authors - within this anthology of horror the perfect, meticulously calculated length. Dare you take a walk to the small room from where inky shadows creep out to smother the light and solitude's siren call beckons you?

Dare you take a quiet, lonely walk into… The Toilet Zone

Invasive Species

A monster has come to Maldus, Arkansas, and the residents of the small mountain town are too busy to notice. With the monster comes something even more terrifying and threatening than gnashing teeth or razor-sharp claws.

The monster has brought change.

The residents of the small mountain town are too busy to notice at first. Busy with things such as addiction, racism, work, or land deals. Unnoticed, the change the monster brings in its insidious wake spreads like wildfire.

Unnoticed, the town of Maldus falls prey to an Invasive Species.

David Owain Hughes

**A HellBound Books LLC
Publication**

http://www.hellboundbookspublishing.com

Printed in the United States of America

354